Soul of the Sword
By Michael Slamon

Prologue

In the remains of a crumbled military fort, one room stayed lit among the dark. Within the room sat two men. One was a human with thick plated armor and various scars tracing his face. The other was an elf in regal armor, thinner than the human's but traced with elegant filigree and runes.

"Must we continue this way? Skittering through the shadows?" asked the elf.

"The war between the gods has taken its toll but there are many who still serve them," replied the human. "Until deemed otherwise, we cannot afford to alert them to our mission."

"I understand that but the more time we waste with petty skirmishes the more our people will suffer."

The human swirled his chalice around, sprinkling wine along the floor. The strong wind howled through the keep, chilling the stale air. Moonlight shone through cracks in the stone and reflected off their armor.

"I know what it's like to have one's home left at the brink of destruction. I know what it's like to see everything you care about go up in flames." The man let the chalice fall from his fingers. "Dur'Zaan's plan is sound. When we find more members for our new Order, we will save everyone from this war."

The elf tried to find the words but instead only nodded. He had come to trust the human over the years. No bond is stronger than those formed in the flames of war and they have seen more than their fair share of death.

"Come, my friend. Let's ensure the others have done their duty." The two stood up and wretched their blades from the mangled corpse by the fire. They left the room and traveled down the shattered hallway, trailing blood along their path.

Hooded figures were executing a handful of soldiers with differing tabards. One was bright white with a golden sun, while the other was a simple black with no design, representing the endless void. Overseeing these executions were three dwarves clad in dark grey armor. There was no look of joy or hate as the soldiers were cut down. They merely did what they had to do.

The main entrance was collapsed and charred where the siege was focused. Standing among the rubble was a rather large orc with his scarred chest laid bare. His large bloodied axe rested against a nearby pillar, still dripping. He was collecting trinkets from the fallen soldiers and filling a large chest. He nodded at the pair as they walked past and entered the courtyard.

A pale woman with a spear etched with runes was overseeing the supplies, ensuring proper inventory. She kept her men working at top efficiency to guarantee their mission was a complete success. Her soldiers were reclaiming their arrows from the field of corpses while others were gathering stored food.

"There are seven of us but there are still a few who remain to be found." The man cleaned his blade using a black banner.

"We will need a larger staging area to host this army we plan on creating," said the elf. "We can't linger in caves and hope to topple a kingdom."

"This is true. We will use what transpired here to our advantage." He balled up the banner and threw it on top of a pile of bodies.

"How?"

The man smiled. "The gods are divided and so too are our people. We will offer the choice of unity or death. Some will refuse but eventually all will agree." Rain began to fall, washing the blood off of their armors. "It's almost time now."

"Time for what?" wondered the elf.

He stared at the blood on his gauntlet, watching the rain wash away what remained. His mind shifted to distant memories of a time in his life now lost, forever. The thoughts didn't harm him though, they merely hardened his resolve and reassured him of his mission.

"To make good on my promise."

Chapter 1: A Promise to Keep

The once peaceful Belvarri Plains were now drowning in smoke and flames. Set ablaze by the united bandit clans, the land became nothing more than ash and smoke. All could hear the roaring war horns of the bandits and their opposition among the King's army.

"The Crimson Raids will never end!" echoed the bandit leaders, famous words that would burn their way into history.

General Belmont, though thin in stature, exhumed the might of giants. His tabard bore the gryphon crest of Kalboria and his shining armor proved impervious to the bandits' attacks. His men fearlessly followed him on their horses, running the bandits down in the fields.

"Drive them to coast, men! They can't threaten the villagers with their backs to the open water." Belmont skewered three of the criminals in one attack.

With endless determination, he and his army barely broke a sweat in putting the bandits down. The clan leaders, however, would not simply lay down and die. It was here they would make their final stand with blood and fire. The open fields were set ablaze and they would use this to their advantage.

The bandits wasted no time in raiding the farms for supplies. While the soldiers were busy navigating the flames and fighting in the fields, the criminals ransacked and hunkered in the settlements. The larger villages were targeted first and used as fortified encampments to offer resistance. The farmers that fought back were easily killed and those who tried to surrender were used as hostages. These weren't fighters, just innocent people making a living and keeping to themselves.

The war horns of Kalboria echoed over the hills as Belmont made quick work of the outlying camps and established his own. He wasted no time in delivering justice to the lawless brutes, meeting their savagery in kind. The main force of the bandits took to the central farms to muster their remaining might. The coastal villages were targeted for their ports to build ships for their escape.

A small cluster of houses remained untouched but not for long. An elf with raggedy silver hair was gathering his neighbors in preparation for their escape. Aside from his leather gloves and shoulder pads, his apparel was sweat stained commoner clothing.

The only thing of note on his person was the extravagant sword on his back. The blade itself held a bright sheen that reflected the sun's fiery glow. Strange runes covered the base of the curved blade and led into a guard in the shape of a black and gold dragon wing. The runes continued down the hilt and ended at the pommel made of a deep blue stone. Though roughly cut, it shone beautifully.

"Maxwell. Benjamin. Start moving everyone to the woods. I'll be with you shortly." The elf turned his attention to the sound of screams coming from the nearby houses. Smoke was growing closer and so were the bandits. The sounds of war were nearly deafening as the battle reached their home.

The elf's neighbors gathered their tools for weapons and started evacuating their land. Small sacks of food were all that they could carry with little risk. Families had to leave everything else behind to the bandits. Their home, their trinkets, their land, all left for plunder.

The elf ran towards his house but an arrow pinned itself into the door. He stopped in his tracks. His pointed ears twitched and perked up to the sound of menacing laughter. He could hear a bow string being drawn back. Without hesitation, he unsheathed his blade and swatted the second arrow out of the air.

A small party of bandits came through the field of crops. They wore all types of armor, presumably pillaged over the years. Men and women of all races made up their ranks. With the bandits, there was no racial hierarchy and women were more than welcome to take up weapons. If you had the heart to kill, they would take you as their own.

"Looks like we found ourselves a fighter." One of the bandits said, wiping blood from his axe.

"It's about damn time. I was getting tired of killing weaklings," said another, laughing. "I was beginning to think Belmont's knights were the only fun."

"With the knights you faired a better chance." The elf shifted his feet into a battle-ready stance, blade out in front with his feet firmly planted in the ground.

The bandits couldn't help but to laugh. A one-eyed man with a thick black beard of braids stepped forward. "Tough talk for an old elf." His voice was gruff but carried itself like the call of a dragon. He motioned for two of his men to approach him. "Let's see how tough you are with your guts on the ground."

The two bandits charged the elf. The silver hair merely hid the man's agile nature. He dashed forward and slid down to his knees, between the bandits as they raised their axes. One quick slash left one with their innards spilling to the dirt. He quickly got to his feet and thrusted his blade through the other's throat. Without a second thought, the elf pushed his advance and charged the bandits.

The next bandit came at him with a shield and mace. The elf sidestepped the bandit and sliced off his shield arm before piercing his heart. Another came from behind with a dagger but a quick hard kick to his face sent him reeling back with a broken nose. Two more bandits charged, the first leaping through the air for a plunging attack. The elf rolled just behind where the man landed. He reversed his blade and thrusted it backwards. Blood trickled down the length of the blade.

The elf slashed through the air, slinging the blood into the second bandit's eyes, effectively blinding her. He went to finish her off but an arrow pierced his upper thigh, forcing him to the ground. The one-eyed bandit tossed the woman aside and kicked the elf backwards, his bloodied sword sent just beyond his reach. One bandit rushed over to pin the elf, not realizing he had already removed the arrow from his leg. Before he knew what happened, the bandit was squirming in the mud with the arrow in his throat.

The leader slammed his boot down on the elf's chest. He pointed his crude iron sword downward and began prodding his chest with the point. The elf gritted his teeth as his blood began to stain though his shirt. He reached for the bandit's leg but the full weight of the man crushed the air out of him.

"Well, you are certainly one hell of a fighter. If we had a handful of men like you, the chieftains would've dealt with Belmont's army a long time ago." The bandit stared down at his opponent, almost in admiration. He was hesitant in killing someone who could be of use.

"Instead, you'll all die here in these fields like worthless rabid dogs." The elf spit at the bandit.

The man laughed. "Why fight us and fall? Belmont, the King, they don't care for you. They're more than willing to let you die here. Like us, you are just collateral damage to them."

"I don't care for the King's politics. I don't care for the knights' duties," the elf struggled, coughing out the words. "But everyone should be willing to fight against the evil of this world and beyond. Evil like you."

The bandit's look of admiration quickly shifted to fury. He stomped his boot down on the elf's ribs, forcing him to cry out in pain. "Evil? We are free. The rulers of these lands seek to conquer us but we fight with tooth and nail and—"

"You pillage and conquer everyone else. You are not heroes rebelling against tyranny. You are rabid dogs, picking at the scraps." The old elf held a piercing gaze locked on the one good eye of the man above him.

The man's face turned red. Such defiance in death wasn't something he never witnessed but to have his motives so brazenly brought to question sent him over. The bandit raised his sword high, primal fury overtaking him.

"Do it, coward!"

The bandit began to yell but before he could sink his blade, a young voice interrupted him. He smiled at the sudden realization that he wasn't alone. The elf tried to shame him but now he would repay him in kind.

"No! Get away from him!" The elf looked back in horror, ignoring the heavy boot stifling his breath. A young elf boy with scruffy golden hair and bright green eyes stood a few feet back with a knife in hand.

"Run, boy!" The old elf grabbed the bandit leader's leg. "Get out of here."

An arrow soared through the air, toward the boy. He tried to spin away from its path but wasn't quick enough. The arrow head carved its way across the boy's cheek before pinning itself to the porch. The boy clutched his cheek, blood dripping between his fingers. As a bandit approached, the boy unleashed his own primal fury.

The man had little time to react and paid the price for underestimating his opponent. The young elf launched himself at the man. He pulled his head back by his hair and began stabbing repeatedly into his neck like a wild beast. The bandit collapsed but the boy kept stabbing, filled with too much rage to realize he was already dead.

More bandits appeared but the one-eyed man kept them from interfering. He looked down at the older elf. "It seems it runs in your blood. Such ferocity and defiance in the face of death. It is admirable." He sunk his blade down into elf's ribs, causing him to writhe in pain. "But foolish nonetheless."

"Father!"

"You're next, child." The bandit leader stepped off the old elf and pulled the curved sword from the nearby patch of grass. "Such an exquisite blade for a simple farmer. Something about him is beyond such a meager life. Fitting that his weapon kills his son." He charged the boy, sword raised.

The young elf met him head on and leapt for the man's chest. The bandit caught him by the collar and tossed him to the side. His face scraped along the hard dirt and dry grass. As the man approached him, he launched his dagger at his face. The bandit quickly dodged out of the way.

"Nice try, kid. But it's the end of the road." Suddenly, a volley of arrows killed the bandits in the field. The others began shouting as a group of knights charged from behind. Belmont had finally breached the defenses.

The one-eyed man was too distracted to realize the elf boy who leapt for his back. Suddenly, a sharp burning pain overtook his right shoulder. He looked over to see the young elf's hand glowing a fiery orange. He dropped the curved sword to reach for the boy but was too slow. He kicked off of the man's back, sending him forward and building some distance.

The knights ran the bandit party down from horseback. Heads rolled among the crops while spears impaled most. The final gasps of air were for naught. The bandits were overwhelmed and slaughtered.

The elf reached for his father's weapon but it was too large to wield properly. Instead, he lowered the sword, one hand on the hilt and the other on the blade. Screaming wildly, he charged the one-eyed man and speared the blade through his heart as he turned around. The last thing the man saw with his good eye was a pair of fiery green ones staring back at him in disgust and pain.

The boy rushed over to his father who was barely clinging to life. Blood trickled down the corner of his mouth and stained the dirt under him. "I thought I told you to run."

"I wasn't going to leave you." Tears ran down the boy's face, breaking up the partially dried blood on his face.

"Hmph. Looks like I'll have to leave you now though," the man said with a struggled breath.

"No. You can't die. I need you," his son pleaded.

"Look around, son. You don't need anyone to take care of you. You stood up to those bandits on your own and won." Blood flowed more freely now from his wound.

"But not without your help."

The father reached up and caressed his son's scraped cheek. "I need you to stay strong. There will come a time when people need someone to guide them, to protect them," he said, searching for the right words to ease his son. "Take my sword and be that person who can protect them. Promise me."

The boy's tears slowed down but he still struggled to speak. Everything he had was taken from him in one brief moment. His mind was racing and his heart beat thrummed in his ears, muffling everything around him.

"Promise me, Valdryn."

Chapter 2: Meant for More

The words echoed in the boy's mind as he stared at his reflection in the mirror. His hair was kept short and after joining Belmont. He wanted to be like the other knights but Belmont wouldn't allow him to join the war effort. Still, he trained with a wooden sword and shield, wanting to be on the frontline and killing as many bandits as he could.

Belmont could sense the raw potential but he wasn't looking forward to sending more boys to die, especially one so young. Belmont and his army had decimated the bandits in a few short months, fracturing the united clans. A few of the chieftains still remained but most we're either dead or captured. He left the bodies of the bandits to rot in their camps as a reminder of what happens to those who defy the law of civilization.

The knights made quick work of the bandits in the skirmishes across the plains. They couldn't build up fortifications fast enough and they were spread too thin to offer much of a battle. Some of the camp were even found deserted, with only the mangled corpse of the chieftain remaining. Belmont chalked it up to the underlings not wanting to die but not looking to end up in chains either.

Valdryn was allowed to spar with a few knights to help cope with his loss. The knights often underestimated him but for a young boy, he was filled with such fury. He attacked like a crazed animal but the strength behind each swing and the speed in his movements was something noteworthy. He was in the middle of learning how to wield a knife properly when a man in plain clothing arrived.

"Valdryn. Belmont wants to see you." The messenger left as quickly as he arrived.

"You did good today, kid," saluted the knight. "A few more years and you'll be feared among all bandits, surely."

He sheathed his knife and saluted the knight. "Thank you, sir."

Belmont had found this village damaged and abandoned. In a few short weeks, he had it rebuilt and repurposed into a small fort-like base of operations. The homes and other buildings offered ample living space and hosted many soldiers.

To ensure the camp was never crowded, those who weren't resting or on guard duty, were out on patrol. They would often bring back rescued hostages, runaway bandits or even scouts. Belmont would have these criminals in interrogation for hours, looking for any and all information.

Valdryn walked the path leading to the large building at the center. He had been here before, only a year prior. Though it has changed from the war, he could still recognize the buildings. From the shops where his father would trade produce to the garden where he would sneak away from with his mother's favorite flower, all of it turned face in a time of war.

The young elf observed a pair of guards escorting a man in chains out from the center building. The right side of his face was swollen and bruised. His warpaint faded and his beard was caked in blood. He dragged his feet, muttering incoherently to himself.

"You deserved worse," Valdryn muttered to himself.

A handful of guards were on duty around building. Valdryn always took it upon himself to salute them whenever he would enter or leave. Valdryn followed the trail of blood droplets that led to Belmont's office in the back. One of the guards was mopping up the blood, shaking his head. Whether he didn't appreciate the task or was uneasy after the interrogation, Valdryn could not say. The young elf stepped foot into the office, saluting the commander.

"At ease, soldier," Belmont held back a chuckle. He was wiping his hand of the caked blood. Bloodied utensils were resting in the nearby basin. "Don't mind the mess. We do what me must, do we not?"

"We all get what we deserve, sir," the young elf said, sternly.

Belmont nodded in agreement as he tossed the stained rags in to a bucket as his feet. He looked around at his new office. Portraits and name plaques decorated the walls. Some were of whole families and others of couples, young and old alike. Valdryn focused on a particular one labeled "Dha'Najeed".

The commander took notice. "You know them, don't you?"

Valdryn nodded. "Saleera, the girl, is…was my best friend." His eyes narrowed as he clenched his jaw. "This was one of the first villages to fall to the chieftains. One of the knights told me they made it out since they weren't many bodies but…" his voice trailed off.

"Their name, they were from the eastern lands?" wondered Belmont.

He nodded, letting a single tear roll down his cheek.

"It's okay to feel sad and—"

"I'm not sad, sir," he interrupted. "I'm angry. Frustrated. I want to see the bandits burn."

"Then you'll be happy to hear we're nearing the end of this war," he said, proudly. "Only four chieftains remain and we have one of them cornered. He also happens to be the most respected among them. Once he's gone, the others will step in line."

Valdryn looked at Belmont in disbelief. All he could remember is the large bearded man and his underlings laughing at his father as he was dying. He looked down at the scar in his palm. He remembered the pleasure of driving his father's blade through the man who killed him.

"That's why you called for me?" Valdryn asked.

"I believe you deserve to know," replied Belmont. "And I'll be leading a small group of fighters to personally capture him."

"Can I join you?" Valdryn asked, with hope in his eyes.

"You know you can't. The battlefield is no place for a child," he said. "But you will have your words with him before he dies. I promise you that."

Valdryn couldn't help feeling overwhelmed. He could feel his blood boiling with a ringing in his ear muffling the sounds inside the room. He stared at the blood and the utensils that drained it from the savage. He took deep breaths and brought his focus to the noise outside the windows. The soldiers were training, making final perpetrations before the battle. The rallying cry they shouted put Valdryn's mind at ease.

A storm of flaming arrows lit up the night sky. They burned away at the crude woodwork of the hastily crafted gates. Karstahd, known among the bandits as the Sea's Hammer, fashioned a small base using various ship parts to reinforce his position. There were large ships in the final stages of being built but Karstahd ran out of time.

The bandits had the high ground but Belmont's force was overwhelming in both training and equipment. As opposed to forcing their way through the main gate, Belmont's forces held their position. Eager for a fight, the bandits rushed their positions but found no success. The clashes were ended quickly, the knights were bloodied but they stood tall among the corpses of their enemies. The arrows loosed from the wall ricocheted off of the knight's plate armor and shields.

"Kill the bastards!" shouted the soldiers.

"Crown's dogs!" the bandits hurled back.

While the battle raged on in the field, ballista bolts crashed through the makeshift huts in the back of the fort and kept the savages close to the main gate for cover. Belmont and his select few were given a specific path to follow from the scouts to avoid becoming collateral damage. Belmont walked past a handful of dying bandits, injured by the siege equipment. His men moved to finish them off but he motioned for them to remain focused on the mission.

"Stay your blades," he ordered in a hushed voice. "Leave them to their fate."

The screams of agony partnered by the devasting crashing of the siege equipment would mask Belmont's approach. A few stragglers stumbled among the wreckage, standing between Belmont and his goal. He held three fingers out and swiped them at the bandits. The soldiers quickly moved behind them and slit their throats.

"Leave them where they fall," Belmont ordered. "Any who find them won't think twice about what happened.

Belmont led his team inside the large tower but were met with opposition. Half-starved, they moved sluggishly but fought to the bitter end. Belmont and the others smashed through their defenses with ease, carving a path between them.

"Where's the unrelenting fury you animals are known for?" mocked Belmont. "Killing unarmed innocents is easy. You're not used to a force that can fight back, are you?"

More approached him but met the same fate as their friends. One dropped to his knees, begging for mercy. Belmont replied with a boot to his face. Teeth went flying and blood leaked from a broken nose. Before he could find the strength to move, the commander removed his head.

"Mercy is given to those who deserve it," Belmont spat.

His fellow soldiers rushed ahead of him and cut down the remaining bandits. Some threw their weapons down, hoping for shackles rather than the blade. One fought back with fists but the soldier blocked with his sword, slicing fingers on impact. Before they could celebrate, burning debris began to fall around them. A fire had begun to grow above and started to devour the tower. The orange glow quickly spread downward like a start crashing to the world.

"The tower was supposed to remain untouched by our archers," said Belmont. He thought for a moment on the possibilities until he came to a logical conclusion. "Everyone out now!"

Belmont and the others made a break for the door but the roof caved in and blocked their path. The room began to swell with smoke as more fire crept its way down. Some of the men tried to clear the path but the heat was too much.

"What do we do now?" panicked one of the soldiers.

"Keep your head and find a way out. Karstahd is hiding somewhere, and that's our way through." The commander learned early in his career a level head is required to survive. Even the smallest doubt can have disastrous consequences.

The men looked around everywhere. Some looked for hidden switches while one picked up an axe and tried hacking at the wall. Another tried to climb the stairs to jump through a hole in the wall but the fire had grown too fierce. Belmont underestimated Karstahd and his willingness to drag everyone down with him.

Belmont and his soldiers were choking from the smoke, their eyes nearly blinded in the chaos. He barely noticed the blood on the ground. In one area particular spot, it hadn't pooled as it should. He could make out the edges of a hatch door. "Over here," he shouted.

The others joined him and hastily moved the bodies, revealing a hatch under the bloodstained rug. With a quick heave, the hatch flew open and they found their escape. None too soon either, as the flaming rubble collapsed above them.

"Where are we, sir?"

"Smuggler's tunnels," said Belmont.

"How long has Karstahd been here then?"

"These tunnels have been here for a long time." Belmont grabbed a torch from the wall and led the others to the main chambers. Luminescent plants reflected a vibrant blue light off the surface of the water. "Valdryn was more helpful then he realized."

Broken storage crates littered the first room. A few chunks of moldy bread littered the bottoms of the crates. Belmont studied the situation, allowing everyone to catch their breath. He focused on the ceiling when he noticed it began to quiet down.

"The fort is ours," he said. "The rest is up to us."

He led his men through the tunnel, peering around corners to avoid any ambushes. They came to an open chamber with an exit on the far side large enough for a sailboat come through. No archers were around and there was a small room in the center with a faded tapestry serving as a door. A stone walkway bridged the room and the storage platform with four guards on either side.

"Two take left. Two take right. I'll lure them out."

The soldiers nodded and slowly approached from the shadows. Belmont approached, clutching his side. He took haggard breaths and dragged his feet. Stepping with a limp and dangling his shield arm, he posed no threat.

"So, the dogs sniffed us out," mocked one of the guards.

"This one doesn't seem to offer much bite," mocked another.

Belmont pointed his blade at the guards, seemingly fatigued. "By the King's decree, I sentence you to do death. Surrender now and it will be quick."

The guards burst into laughter, mocking the injured man before them. Like wolves to a meal, they circled their prey. The other guards approached slowly, banging their weapons on the floor. The cavern echoed with laughter and clanging noises, intermingling into a deafening mockery.

Belmont closed his eyes and smiled. His tapped his sword on his shield three times and in an instant, his soldiers leapt from the shadows. One of the bandits had his throat torn open before he could even react. Another found two blades protruding from his chest, the wound wider than his eyes.

"There's more of them!" shouted the guard by the central room.

Belmont led the charge as more bandits emerged, looking for a fight. They got more than they bargained for when he thrusted his blade into the gut of the first man out. He used his shield to shove him off the blade and into the water. The sound of gurgling was drowned out as his body crashed into the cold depths.

There were far more guards than anticipated but the soldiers did not falter. They kept close together in a makeshift phalanx, pushing the bandits back. A lanky man, heavily tattooed and scarred, appeared from the room.

"For Karstahd!" the man shouted as he brandished two short blades. He charged the soldiers amidst the chaos and leapt for Belmont, tackling him to the ground.

"Hold formation," Belmont ordered. His shield had slid away, leaving him at a disadvantage. He kicked the bandit off of him but wasn't quick enough to reclaim his shield.

His opponent screamed incoherently, entering a blood frenzy. Slashing wildly, carving at the air, Belmont was kept on his defense. Blocking each swing with own weapon was taking its toll. It was hard enough keeping track of the blades but the force behind each swing sent vibrations up his arms.

The man missed one of his swings and Belmont pressed the advantage. Rather than trying to block however, the man merely danced around the blade. He quickly dropped into a leg sweep, knocking Belmont to the ground and leaving his blade just out of reach. Before he could reach for his weapon, the lanky man pounced on top of him, ready to drive his blades down.

Belmont quickly grabbed for the man's wrists, struggling to keep the blades away. Such strength without the muscles was a frightening sight. Some of the more devout members were known to imbibe otherworldly potions but Belmont had never seen it firsthand. The strange bandit continued shouting random foreign words but Belmont could only focus on his men as Karstahd appeared.

Before he could say anything, the chieftain's mighty hammer cracked the skull of one of the soldiers. His body fell to the floor with blood leaking from the helmet. He shattered the knee of another soldier before he could retaliate. The young man's screams were stifled by the weight of the hammer.

"Is this the best Belmont can muster?" wondered the lanky man. "Mere children playing at war."

Belmont was losing his grip and the man knew it. He looked into his widening, crazed eyes and remembered all the men and women who died under his command, trying to put a stop to the bandit threat. If he died here, it'd be all for nothing.

A quick flash of red over took Belmont and the lanky man began to scream. Blood covered both of their faces as Belmont bit half of his nose off and spit it across the floor. Belmont grabbed his blade and shoved it through the man's throat and his screams were turned to choking spurts.

"Now that, is the best Belmont can offer," shouted Karstahd. "A beast among men."

The other two remaining soldiers retreated back to Belmont, bloody and broken but still alive. There was no way out but that didn't bother them. They were ready for one final charge when suddenly they heard shouting above them.

"Go. Both of you," muttered Belmont. His men looked at him, unsure. "They need to know we're down here. I'll buy you time."

Belmont stepped between them and the bandits. The soldiers backed away, albeit reluctantly. He was outnumbered but he could still feel the anger coursing through his system, fueling him. When he heard the soldiers above shouting for him, he attacked. They were caught off guard with his speed. Slicing away, Belmont sent limbs through the air.

"Now this is a fight," laughed Karstahd.

"It will be your last," said Belmont, as he decapitated another bandit. One panicked and tried to use his shield but rather than using his blade, Belmont used his full weight to send him into the water below.

He gutted another, and hefted the blade up his body. The gaping wound poured blood all over the floor. Belmont's unrivaled speed and combination of martial prowess and primal ferocity made quick work of the bandit's numbers, forcing Karstahd to step in.

The chieftain was a hulking mass of muscle, bringing his hammer down in full swings with ease. Belmont ducked and rolled away from his attacks, knowing full well the kind of damage that would be inflicted. The hammer struck the ground with such force that it left small impact craters with each strike. The commander could even feel the shockwaves of each hit.

"Don't cower now, Commander," cheered the brute. "You came for a fight, so fight."

As Karstahd missed his next strike, Belmont charged in. The chieftain used the haft of his hammer to block the strike but Belmont was pushing the advantage. Karstahd wasn't as much of a threat when forced to be defensive.

What was left of the chieftain's men stepped in to help but he ordered them back. This was between them and no one else. It seemed as though Belmont would win when the echoes of soldiers charging came from the tunnel. He was distracted, if only for a moment, but that's all Karstahd needed. Using his hammer's pommel, he cracked Belmont in the side of his head. A single bead of blood dripped from a small cut.

A handful of soldiers stormed the cavern. Karstahd's men formed a small shield wall between them and the duel. Valdryn had snuck in among the soldiers and saw Belmont was in danger. As the soldiers fought, Valdryn ran past and went in for the kill. He leapt onto Karstahd, catching him off guard but only for a moment.

He headbutted Valdryn and threw him down but recognized something about him and laughed. He noticed Belmont getting back on his feet. He grabbed the young boy and used him as a shield to keep the commander at bay.

"Not a step more, Belmont and your mage might get to live to see tomorrow."

"My mage?" replied Belmont. "You must be mistaken, dog."

Karstahd laughed, "My scouts told me of a young elf that killed my second a few months ago."

Belmont thought back on the day he met Valdryn but shook away the doubt. "Let's settle this. Just the two of us. And everyone else gets to walk out of here."

"I think not, Belmont," he spat. "You have more mages waiting outside?"

Valdryn could hardly hear the two men going back and forth. His mind drifted back to the day he lost everything. All he could focus on was the hopelessness and fear that overtook him when the bandits descended upon his home. The rage when the bandits struck down his father. The fire he summoned to burn the bearded man.

He felt that same fire once more, but stronger now, primal and pure. His hands glowed a bright orange and melted through the haft of the hammer, breaking Karstahd's weapon in half.

Before the chieftain could react, Valdryn spun with his knife. The heated blade singed and cut through Karstahd's knee. The elf managed to summon an otherworldly strength and picked up half of the hammer which in turn mirrored the same orange glow. One quick strike was all it took.

Everyone heard the sickening break as the hammer impacted Karstahd's skull, caving in half of his head and leaving behind scorched flesh. His body fell over and sunk to the bottom of the cavern. The Sea's Hammer and his legacy was ended by a small child and that would be the only thing people remember about him.

The men were celebrating back at their camp. One less chieftain was a victory for everyone. The ones who surrendered to Belmont's men gave up everything they knew about the remaining chieftains and the strategists were already making plans. One of Belmont's lieutenants paraded Karstahd's hammer around, rallying the troops into joyful cheers.

"You should have told me, Valdryn," Belmont took a seat beside him and offered him a fresh mug.

"I didn't know how. The first time I used it was at home, when the bandits came." Valdryn looked deep into his mug.

"I know. That's why you're leaving for the capital tomorrow."

Valdryn's focus was broken. "But, Sir, I'm—"

Belmont put his hand on his shoulder. "It's not a punishment. You are clearly meant for more than hunting bandits. Your talents will go to waste here."

"But what good can I do from the capital.?" He asked.

"You won't be there for long. I have some contacts there that will help you. There are plenty of guilds and academies that could use someone like you." He had already made his mind up. He wasn't going let this child's life be decided on a battlefield, not like this. "You'll get to make a true life for yourself."

Valdryn smiled. What better way to honor his father than by being the best he could be? He looked at the soldiers he trained with, his friends, enjoying the feast. "What about the other bandits?"

Belmont laughed. "Go and savor this victory with your brothers. You let me handle the end of the raids."

The young elf smiled and joined the soldiers in their revelry. They hoisted him up on their shoulders, hailing him as a hero. "All hail Valdryn, the conquering hero! The Bandit's Bane! Champion of the Plains!" He wasn't sure about how his father would feel, hearing him being heralded as a conqueror. But for a brief moment he was a hero and that was enough for him.

<u>Chapter 3: The Hunt Begins</u>

Twenty years had passed since Valdryn lost his home. His hair was now shoulder length with the tips of his ears barely peeking through. His face was covered in a thick golden-brown stubble, now a spitting image of his father in his younger years. The arrow that nearly took his life left a scar along his right cheek.

He stared out over the cliffs, watching the naval ships drop off more workers from the mainland. The old hopes and dreams of rebuilding the Isle and its populace were slowly becoming a reality. It was time to return to its former glory.

The fresh sea breeze and faint noise of the waves rolling over the rocks below were calming. He often found himself up here after training sessions reflecting on his journey. The faint noises of sparring soldiers eroded at his concentration. He couldn't help but think back to that day.

"I promise, father," he muttered under his breath.

"Master?" interrupted a young man, his short brown curls moving with the wind.

"It's nothing, Jonas," he sighed. "Just speaking to myself."

Valdryn and Jonas were practicing with their spells in the training grounds just outside the shrine to Ruvast, the fallen God of Magic. The shrine was covered in offerings left by thankful devotees. He had given his life many centuries ago to stop the Devouring Abyss and its corrupted gods from breaching the mortal plain.

The shrine was more of a temple at this point after the additions over the years. A tall statue stood on the cliffside, facing towards the eastern half of the nearby mainland of Kalboria. Even from this far away, the mountains scarred by the war of the gods could be seen.

"Let's get back to training, Jonas." Valdryn took a deep breath, pushing the memories down once more.

Jonas nodded and turned his focus to the target dummies. Flame spells were one of the more basic paths but could be dangerous in the hands of a master, something Jonas was far from. He conjured flames that flickered in his palm and launched them through the air, albeit without any power behind them. The flames impacted and sizzled into smoke, hardly heating the target.

Valdryn couldn't help but to laugh as Jonas's frustration grew. It reminded him of the simpler years at the Academy. Magic was an easy concept for most to learn but the potential for greatness varied with each individual. Valdryn mastered advanced levels of spell casting but even he had much to learn about the more complex practices. Unlike most battlemages, however, Valdryn preferred utility over combat magic.

"Focus, Jonas. You must control your emotions, otherwise—"

"They'll control me," Jonas mocked in a defeated voice.

"Otherwise, you'll look like a fool in a fight." Valdryn pointed three fingers at the target. It shimmered like the night sky before the invisible barrier dissipated.

"That's not fair!" Jonas exclaimed. "How am I supposed to get past your barrier magic?"

"It was a novice level spell at best, apprentice," Valdryn replied. "If you had tempered your confidence with knowledge and understanding, you would've sensed it."

A human woman in her late thirties strolled up behind the master and his apprentice. She had long, curly brown hair that ended just past her shoulders. Her pearly white robes were laced with lavender hued filigree. She had a smug expression though that was nothing new.

"To what do we owe the pleasure, Master Sandra?" Valdryn bowed.

Sandra returned the bow. "Just making sure our local Blademaster and his apprentice were ready for the mission. The sun will be setting soon." The tension in the air grew thick, its weight bearing down on the trio.

"We're ready. Jonas is just brushing up on his spells." Valdryn glanced at Jonas. His apprentice turned red and bowed.

"Apologies, Master. My mind is often too focused on my lessons," said Jonas.

"Well, he won't learn anything from you then," Sandra laughed. "You're unmatched with a sword but even you struggle with some of the basic spells."

"I'd hardly call conjuring storms 'basic'", replied Valdryn. "Besides, there's nothing wrong with honing your sword arm."

Sandra smiled. "I'll take a master of the arcane over a warrior any day. You of all people should know that soldiers have their uses but it's the mages that win the battle," she sneered. "Either way, Tariv is waiting for you at the armory"

"We'll head there now. Thank you, Sandra." The two bowed and Sandra departed. Jonas started to follow but a strong grip on his shoulder held him in place.

"One final lesson before we prepare," he said. His eyes stared at Sandra as she departed, his gaze never breaking.

"Master?" asked Jonas, sheepishly. Valdryn rarely had such a stern look on his face but it always meant someone or something got under his skin.

"Sandra is the perfect example of being too talented for one's own good." He looked down at his apprentice, a hint of worry betraying his stoic visage.

Jonas furrowed his brows. "What do you mean?"

"She's one of the best mages I've ever seen, but her pompous attitude holds her back." Valdryn unsheathed his blade and showed it to his apprentice. "We are more than one aspect of our life. It doesn't matter how sharp the blade is without a hilt to hold it, a body to wield it properly, and a mind to hone the necessary techniques."

The boy nodded in understanding but his mind was hung up on something else. "I don't mean to pry, Master, but what did she mean about soldiers and mages?"

Valdryn smiled and sighed. He returned his blade to its scabbard. "When I was just a boy, I killed the chieftain, Karstahd, with my magic. He let his strength and victory over Belmont go to his head which allowed an angry child to kill him with nothing more than a little bit of fire and his bare hands."

Jonas was caught off guard. Not knowing what to say, he just stared blankly. He had seen just what his master was capable of in a fight but they rarely ever talked about his past. All he ever knew was that bandits attacked his home. He always received strange looks from the masters but he figured it was just elder envy.

"Pride is useless, no matter the skill. It will leave you blind and it will lower your guard," he continued, placing one hand on his apprentice's shoulder. "Don't let pride be your downfall. Even when you are named a master, always train your mind and body."

"I understand, Master," Jonas nodded.

"Good." Valdryn smiled. "That means I'm doing something right."

Valdryn entered the armory and was greeted by Tariv, a half orc battlemage. They didn't bow to one another as standard mages would. They clanked their bracers together, magic energies sparking across the metal. "Perfect timing, Valdryn. The lieutenant just took some of the city guards to their positions." He was standing at a table with a map of the city sprawled out on top. One building was circled in red with one line following a road that came to a three-way fork.

Jonas couldn't help but laugh at the similarities between them. Following the same ideologies regarding magic, Tariv relied on his mighty hammer more than one would assume. The weapon was standard steel but near double in size to the average counterpart, a perfect marriage of lethality and simplicity.

"Excellent. If everything goes according to plan, we should be able to take the cultists without incident," Valdryn studied the map, memorizing the different paths a runaway could take. The blue lines marked the path the guards will hold to funnel any escapees ensuring they never lost track for long.

"It'll be like the good days." Tariv stroked his chin, tracing the scar that ran along his lower jaw.

Valdryn laughed to himself. "You'll never let me live that down, will you?"

"Not as long as I live, brother," Tariv smirked.

"Live what down?" Jonas asked.

"It's nothing, Jonas," Valdryn motioned for him to pay no mind. He approached the armor stands with thick dark leather. He inspected the gear to ensure they were properly prepared for the long night ahead.

"Nothing? Ha, if you won't tell him, I will." Tariv pulled up two chair and handed one to Jonas. It was hard to deny the man's eagerness to tell the story. Jonas wasn't about to pass up another chance to learn of his master's past either.

"If you insist," Valdryn rolled his eyes. "You're probably a better storyteller than you are a fighter anyway."

Tariv laughed and waved Valdryn away, paying the comment no mind. "Come, Jonas. I'll tell you of a time when your master, the illustrious Blademaster, nearly let a Vorlin rip my head off."

"A Vorlin?" Jonas asked, confused.

"You know, a giant lizard with razor sharp claws longer than your sword." He tried to motion with his hands the size of the beast. Jonas merely shook his head. Tariv looked disappointed and let out a deep sigh. "What has he been teaching you?"

"Vorlins are known for being territorial but this pack was abnormally aggressive," the half-orc explained. "The academy instructors considered it a perfect opportunity for the recruits to get real world experience with combat magic."

Valdryn stepped out of the armory for a moment to watch the sun set. His favorite memories often revolved around watching the sky change colors as the sun went down. He could still hear Tariv boast about his grand slaying of the brood mother but his focus was drawn to a different memory of that day. A moment that Tariv wasn't there for.

The younger vorlins fled as the battlemages burned their nests. The bigger ones remained and defended their home to the very end. Where the mages searched for a nest, they instead found a hive. The instructor moved with the bulk of the students, hunting down the vorlins that ran away, while Tariv and Valdryn stayed behind with the rest to deal with the larger ones.

Valdryn tried to finish off one of the injured reptiles but another vorlin charged from behind and leapt on top of him, forcing him to the ground. Suddenly, under their weight, the ground gave way and they fell into a damp cave. The only illumination came from the beam of sunlight shining through the hole above.

The sound of the fighting above prevented him from hearing the predator stalking around him. The beast jumped from the darkness, slashing at

Valdryn. It raked against his chest but didn't pierce deep enough through his armor to hit flesh. Doubt and fear began to cut away at his defenses. The beast attacked once more, this time colliding with Valdryn's sword arm. His blade fell from his grip and clanged along the floor and into the darkness.

His heavy breathing echoed through the cave. Unarmed and separated from the others, Valdryn's hope was all but faded as his heart raced and his breathing quickened. Suddenly he could sense another presence with him. Something told him to close his eyes and focus. The voice was familiar. It called him back to a happier moment in his life.

He closed his eyes to the darkness around him and blocked out the predator. The beast also seemed to sense the new presence as it grew less aggressive and more defensive, studying Valdryn. The young battlemage could see his father once more, standing next to a younger version of himself. It was their first hunting trip together. His father made everything an important lesson to learn. Valdryn remembered how frustrated he would grow as he missed the prey with every arrow. His father's words brought him back to the danger around him.

You mustn't lash out at what you cannot see. Let your prey come to you and strike when it least expects it.

Valdryn felt the presence fade, and the creature rearing up for another attack. With a deep breath, he held his arms out. The beast leapt with claws extended. Instead of tasting flesh, it was met with a flash of heat and fire. Valdryn erected a small fire barrier that exploded on impact. The cavern began to go up in flames but the beast wasn't ready to give up yet and charged once more.

Valdryn slid under the beast and towards his sword. The vorlin quickly turned and charged for one last attack. In one quick motion, Valdryn grabbed his blade and slashed upward as he stood up. The vorlin's headless body crashed into the wall, it's blood combusting as it hit the fire.

Valdryn looked up when he heard voices calling down to him.

"Valdryn!"

"Valdryn." Tariv called out to him.

The past seemed to fade away once more as he reentered the armory. His memories helped center himself before every mission. Relearning old lessons were important as well for someone with his status. He couldn't afford to slip and dull with all eyes on him.

"Everything good?" Tariv asked, almost concerned.

"Just thinking about that day, when you almost let an overgrown lizard get the better of you." Valdryn laughed.

Tariv huffed and looked over to Jonas. "Must've been dropped on his head when he was younger."

The laughter was cut short when Sandra walked in with two hooded figures, each wielding twin axes. "Was Tariv telling one of his jokes again?" She had a natural talent for freezing a room.

"We were just passing the time while we waited for you, Sandra," said Valdryn, never really showing his disdain. Though they hid their rivalry for the sake of professionalism, it didn't take long for everyone to notice.

Sandra smirked back. "Are we ready to proceed then?"

"The plan is sound. We'll take them all out tonight." Tariv crossed his arms in confidence.

"What is the plan, exactly?" As an apprentice, Jonas wasn't usually privy to planning stages of their missions.

"We've been studying cultists for a while now and we know a few of them have been meeting at one of the vacant houses, here." Valdryn pointed down on the map. "We'll flush them out and let one of them get away. We can follow them back to the rest"

"So why all the guards?" Jonas asked.

"They'll be making sure the cultists don't have reinforcements waiting for us," said Tariv. "And they can help force the runaway down a specific path."

Sandra nodded in approval. She looked out at the final passing rays of sunlight, "It's time."

Tariv pointed to Valdryn. "Shall we begin the hunt, brother?"

Valdryn flexed his scarred hand, getting used to the leather gauntlet. He could feel the material tighten around the mark. A quick flash of the one-eyed bandit came to him. His mocking laughter filled Valdryn's mind. "Let the hunt begin."

Chapter 4: According to Plan

With the sun setting over the capital, the torches were lit by the night guards. Ruvo's nightlife was mostly quiet tonight. A small gathering was taking place where the residential district meets the market district. There wasn't a curfew but the guards blocked off the construction zones and the docks.

A few clusters of empty houses were scattered throughout the city. Some were bought by wealthy merchants to use for larger stores while the rest were simply waiting for a buyer to come along. The battlemages hid among the shadows, surrounding a particular section. The leather armor was a stark contrast to the usual plate or mail that Valdryn had grown accustomed to. It was far from a battlemage's vibrant traditional armor but tonight was about speed and stealth.

They had surrounded a two-story building triple the average length of the surrounding houses. The outside appeared fairly clean with only a few spots of mildew on the lower half. Layers of dust were visible from outside the window. Three thick boards were nailed to the front door, barring entry.

"Are we sure this is the place?" A battlemage unknown to Valdryn asked. "It seems abandoned."

"That window suggests otherwise." Jonas replied

"Which one? They're all dusty."

"Not the one on the far right." Jonas nodded at the window. "Must be the lookout."

"Good observation, Jonas," Valdryn said. "This is the place."

"How do we get in without being spotted?" Sandra asked Valdryn.

He paused for a moment, studying his surroundings. He thought back to the blueprints of the housing closest to the harbor. "This building was originally meant for the harbormaster and his workers but was purchased by some merchant who we now know gave a false name. There were two entrances on the other side of the building, the cellar and the balcony."

"Not the best ways in," said Sandra. "But I suppose neither is the front door." Valdryn couldn't decide if her concern was for safety or her own sense or perfection.

"I will take Tariv and Jonas around the back and go through the cellar," he said. "You and two others will make your way to the roof and use the balcony. You should be able to use the neighboring buildings to reach it."

Sandra nodded and scanned the rooftops until she found a path she liked. She pointed to two of the battlemages and followed the shadows to her destination.

"What about us?" One of the remaining battlemages asked.

"You two will stay here and wait for us to flush them out." Tariv rested his hammer on his shoulder. "Their only escape is to run through the city, away from the docks, and lose us in the streets and alley ways. You'll let one slip by but kill the others."

"Let's see if we can beat Sandra into the building, shall we?" Valdryn crept low and found his own path around to the cellar entrance. Jonas and Tariv followed closely, not wanting to risk being spotted by the lookout.

Before they turned the corner, they heard a man clearing his throat. Valdryn motioned for them to stay still. He peered around the corner to find two men sitting at a small table next to the cellar, a deck of cards between them.

"I've got you now," one of the men said.

The other one simply laughed when he revealed his cards.

"Impossible! You're a damn cheat," he sighed. "Another round?"

Valdryn held up two fingers but he waited before attacking. He kept one hand on his belt and braced himself against the wall.

"Why not? They're taking longer than usual tonight. I wonder why."

"Hell, if I know. It's our job to not know a damn thing until they tell us," he shrugged.

The two men began to laugh as they shuffled the cards. The night wind howling above muffled some of the noise. Valdryn pulled two knives from his belt. He muttered something under his breath. He sprung from the corner and launched his knives at the guards. They found their marks in the throats of the two men, silencing their laughter.

"What were you waiting for, Master?"

"I had to be sure they were cultists. Drunkards can be found throughout the city at night. It's better to be certain than to have innocent blood on your hands."

Tariv knelt down by the cellar doors, paying no mind to the corpses. He pressed his ear against the door to listen in for anything. All seemed quiet until a noise from above broke his concentration.

"You boys took your sweet time." Sandra was leaning over the balcony while her companions worked on unlocking the door. She flashed her famous condescending grin.

"Are you ready to get your hands bloody this time?" Tariv mocked.

"You underestimate my magic, Tariv. Good luck swinging that hammer in the tight corners. Try not to bring the house down on us." She disappeared into the house and shortly after, the shouting began.

Valdryn nodded at Tariv. He brought the full weight of his hammer down on the doors. Wood splintered everywhere as chunks of door ricocheted down the stairs. Valdryn ran down first, followed by Jonas then Tariv.

A handful of cultists were waiting, weapons in hand. Valdryn's quick swing of his blade tore through the first man's chest. Jonas ran to his Master's side and blocked a sluggish swing of another cultist.

"Down!" shouted Tariv.

Valdryn instinctively ducked. From the corner of his eye his saw a hammer's head crash through the cultists in front of him. He could hear the sound of bones breaking. Jonas rolled to the side but was quickly surrounded. Valdryn charged forward, slashing in every direction. Blood sprayed the cellar walls, turning the basement into a slaughterhouse.

Jonas slid out of one cultist's reach as he bashed another with his pommel. He thrusted his blade through the man's gut and quickly spun him around to face the others, shielding him from the oncoming daggers. With one quick slash from behind, the two cult members were decapitated.

"Good work, Jonas." Valdryn wiped the blood from his blade on a cultist's robes.

He nodded at his master. "I try."

Valdryn laughed and shook his head. "Onward and upward then."

Jonas charged up the stairs towards the sounds of shouting and metal against metal. Sandra had cleared the second floor and made her way down to the first. Singed wood and shards of ice fell from above. The frenzy was nearing its end as only a handful of cultists remained.

Valdryn scanned the room, looking for a way to ensure his plan worked. "Tariv, make an exit for us."

"With pleasure." Tariv looked for the best path and found it quickly. He charged forward. Two cultists found themselves flying, stuck on Tariv's hammer before they suddenly crashed through the window. The surviving cultists followed after them and tried to escape. The two battlemages standing guard leapt from the shadows and cut some of them down. Valdryn jumped through the window to see the cultists fall. A breath of relief came when he noticed one of them running under the archway. Everything was still going according to plan.

The escapee wasn't subtle in his getaway, leading the battlemages right to the others. The cultist had cut himself on broken glass of the window just moments ago. The small trail of blood allowed for Valdryn to track him with precision to a warehouse just on the outer edge of the construction district. The guards played their role perfectly and herded the man down the path of least resistance.

No one had come in or out since their runaway arrived. The guards that joined them in the pursuit now formed barricades to contain the rest of the mission. Valdryn and Jonas took to the roof of the warehouse while the others closed in on the doors. Sandra took the rear entrance so Tariv took the front. They could overhear the cultists arguing amongst themselves.

"You damned fool! You could've led them straight here." The voice was distinctly female, middle-aged.

"I had nowhere else to go. There's only a handful. We can take them." The runaway had a scratchy voice. Valdryn noted him as being slightly older than the woman.

"Did you not see who they sent after us? Barathel spared no expense to purge us from this city. They didn't come for prisoners." The woman pointed towards a handful of her brothers and sister. "You. Keep watch at the doors while I think."

"What are we going to do?" asked the runaway.

"We?" The woman paused but never turned to face the man. "*I* will find us a way out of here. As for you, you have far outlived your usefulness. The master has no need of a worm like you." A dagger suddenly slid out from the woman's sleeve. The man staggered backwards but couldn't muster a single word, his heart pounding through his chest.

Before the woman could punish the man, Tariv smashed through the front door with his warhammer, signaling Sandra to breach the warehouse from her side. Her hands swirled with electricity as she extended her reach towards the cultists. One of the cultists erected a barrier of fire while the others drew their swords and daggers. Another cultist was conjuring a poisonous cloud but two crossbow bolts shattered the windows and pierced his chest.

"That's our cue, Jonas." He placed his hand on the skylight. A quick pulse from his hand had shattered the glass and the pair descended upon the cultists.

Valdryn landed on the one casting the barrier, his blade piercing through the shoulder and out of the ribcage. Jonas landed behind his master and thrusted his blade through the eye of another. With the barrier down, Sandra and her mages were able to attack. Lightning arced through a small portion and filled the building with the scent of charred flesh.

Valdryn and Jonas swung their blades in unison, the fruition of years of training. Jonas used wide arcing slashes to keep them at bay while he picked them off one by one. Valdryn parried the oncoming attacks with ease, felling the assailants in their foolish attempts. One tried to attack from behind but Jonas blocked the swing. Valdryn disarmed him at the wrist and Jonas delivered the killing blow.

The man they chased here charged Tariv with what remained of the cultists. With one swing, the hammer cracked three skulls. The sound of bone on steel would make most tremble with unease, but not Tariv. He inherited his combat frenzy from his orcish mother, an awe-inspiring warrior with a similar passion for wielding hammers.

The others tried to escape but were met with the city guards instead. The last thing they heard was the sound of crossbow bolts carrying them away to the darkness they supposedly longed for. The man they chased was pinned to the ground with a bolt in his knee.

"Nice swing, Tariv," said Valdryn "Come, Jonas. Time to get some answers."

Valdryn stood over the man, placing the tip of his sword under his chin. The man trembled but was wracked with pain in his leg. Valdryn's bright green eyes sapped the man's ability speak so the battlemage spoke first. "Remove your hood."

The man struggled to pull his hood back with his quaking hands. He looked to be in his late forties, maybe fifties. His calloused hands hinted long days of work as a craftsman. "What's your name?"

"My friends call me Gabe."

"We're not your friends," Tariv chimed in.

"I, uh, suppose not." He took a gulp of air and saliva, his nerves remaining on edge.

"You have one chance at staying your execution." Valdryn lowered his blade to Gabe's throat. "Who is your master and where is he hiding?"

###

Three figures garbed in tattered robes stalked the dark alley ways. One of them was bulky but barely taller than the average human's waistline. Another walked with pride but his white beard under his hood gave away his age. Their leader moved with determination and made no sound with her steps. She was a shadow of death in a city for the living. Something was clenched in her hand but hidden beneath her sleeve.

"So, what're we doing here exactly?"

The woman never turned around to make eye contact. "Should've been paying attention, dwarf."

"We're here to silence the initiates, one way or another." The old man unsheathed his sword slightly and smiled.

"Ahh, and here I thought this was a rescue mission," said the dwarf.

The pair laughed as they came to the end of the alley and into the open street. The woman remained focused on a watchtower. "The scout said Valdryn is leading the hunt. There is no rescue for them. Most of them are probably dead by now. We just need to ensure the survivors don't talk."

"Valdryn? We're as good as dead then too," worried the dwarf.

The old man turned to face him. "Calm down. We'll make sure none of the recruits talk and then we're gone."

"Like it'll be that easy," scoffed the dwarf. What happens if Valdryn chases after us?"

"He *will* chase us and that's when we'll have our chance," the woman interjected, from the top of the tower.

The dwarf and the old man looked puzzled. "What do you mean?"

The woman jumped behind them. She had a bloodied bow and a small quiver of arrows stamped with the crest of Ruvast. "There's something waiting for Valdryn in the forest when he chases after us. We'll do as the master commands and then we'll offer him a prize of far more value."

"Where did you get that bow?" the dwarf wondered, rubbing his temple.

"The watchtower," replied the old man, shaking his head. "You really should start paying attention."

"They're at the warehouse. They're further along than I expected," said the woman.

"We'll have to move fast then," replied the old man.

"Agreed. Take the dwarf and make sure the escape route is kept open. Our horses will be just outside." The woman traced her path to the warehouse using her palm. She made a mental note of the construction site and the guards in her way.

The old man and the dwarf left the woman and proceeded down the road. The woman made her way down to the warehouse. The guards were easy enough to sneak by. They were too distracted by the commotion at the warehouse to be staring at shadows.

Only a few were unavoidable, but that hardly mattered. The woman jumped off of a stack of crates and fired an arrow into the back of a guard's skull. As her feet touched the ground, she swung the bow around and broke another guard's nose. She dashed forward, sliding between the two surviving guards with her arms extend to either side. Blood dripped from her sleeves while the guards' throats suddenly opened.

The screams of an older man were on the wind. The woman found a vantage point where she could make out the battlemages. She spotted Sandra, master of the arcane and Tariv the Hammer who was interrogating the last of the recruits. Valdryn, Blademaster of the Isle, oversaw the mission with his apprentice.

"They clearly were not taking any chances here." She knocked her arrow and pulled back on the string. "So, neither can we."

Gabe's lips quivered when he tried to find the words. "I…uh…I can't say. They'll kill me."

Tariv shook his head and spun his hammer. He brought the full weight of his weapon down on Gabe's hand. Gabe screamed in pain as his fingers contorted into a mangled mess shattered bone and bruised flesh.

"Please! I can't say anything!"

Tariv raised his hammer once more. "Then I'll keep breaking your bones until you can."

"Wait! Please!"

Tariv tightened his grip but Valdryn's hand on his shoulder stopped the hammer from bearing down on the broken man. Tariv let out a deep breath and gathered himself once more. He turned away from Gabe, disgusted with him. He closed his eyes and breathed deep, attempting to subside the blood frenzy.

"Your master will want you dead regardless of you talking or not. Take a look around." Valdryn motioned towards the dead bodies. "You helped make this happen. Your only chance of survival is convincing *us* you're worth keeping around."

The man paused, looking at the bodies, blood everywhere. He could still smell the charred bodies from inside the warehouse. His mind was damaged, his body broken. "Okay. I'll talk. The master, he—"

A black arrow pinned the words in his throat, allowing only blood to leave his mouth. Sandra quickly put up a barrier to shield them from any more attacks but this proved to be an act of precision. He died in mere moments, the blood parting his lips.

"Where did that come from?" Shouted Tariv as he surveyed the rooftops.

"Give me a moment." Valdryn grabbed the arrow and closed his eyes. Few have knowledge of arcane tracking and even less have the ability to use it. He once heard that with enough practice and power, one could track a target across the sea. Valdryn had a small grasp on the subject but it was enough. He could see a red smoky trail moving fast and towards the main gate. He could barely make out three silhouettes before the vision faded. The arrow turned to dust and mingled with Gabe's blood.

"Get the horses. They're escaping through the main gate."

Chapter 5: Moonlit Run

Ruvo faded in the distance as Valdryn and the others made their way across the open fields and towards the Lunar Forest. The enchanted sap glowed with the vibrant moonlight, illuminating the paths among the trees. One could feel like they walked among the very stars if they weren't chasing a trio of murderers.

The escapees had already put enough distance between their pursuers to keep the marksmen from landing their arrows. Valdryn and Jonas had followed down the same path while Sandra and Tariv flanked to the left and right. Two of the riders had bows of their own but their accuracy was poor, only good enough to keep the battlemages on their guard. Jonas deflected the ones he could and dodged the rest. The arrows could be heard snapping and ricocheting in all directions.

Valdryn's eyes were closed with his left hand extended out. He was projecting a small aura that scorched any arrow that came close. His right hand was resting on the horse's head with the fingers evenly spaced. Small pulses gently emanated from the finger tips, calming the beast and enhancing its reflexes.

Sandra finally closed enough distance and ordered her pair of marksmen to fire. One bolt pierced a rider's back while the second landed just in front of his horse. The mount took off to the left and collided with the two other riders. The cultists were thrown from their saddles while their horses recovered and ran off.

One rider was dead though it was unclear if it was the bolt that killed him or the tree he crashed into. Another was dazed from the fall. His height clearly noted him as a dwarf. The leader was an elf woman with pale blue eyes and a burn scar taking over the right half of her face. It had healed years ago but it would forever haunt her reflection. She was clenching her side when the battlemages approached.

Tariv and two others approached from the left while Sandra and her marksman held the right. Valdryn and Jonas approached the woman, weapons raised. He scanned the surrounding area, looking for anyone lurking in the night. She appeared injured and her companions were no longer of any use to her. She was alone against the wolves.

Valdryn noted how close the temple was and how silent the woods had fallen despite the wildlife reports. The horses seemed uneasy and kept their distance from their masters and their enemy. The moonlit sap streaks reflected an eerie blue glow over the area but somehow made the clearing feel darker.

Valdryn looked to the woman's side, searching for something. No wound, not even a single drop of blood. She wasn't hit by a crossbow nor did she have a nasty tumble when the horses collided. Valdryn stopped moving and placed the flat end of his blade against Jonas's chest. He cocked his head to the side as his ear perked up. *Very clever.*

"Secure the dwarf and be ready for a fight," He muttered to Jonas. Jonas nodded his head and changed his course.

"Something wrong, Battlemage?" The woman said with a haggard breath. She stared at Valdryn and his apprentice, her eyes quickly exchanging looks between the two.

"You've committed several severe crimes, you and your little cult. I'm willing to show mercy if you surrender." He kept his distance, walking at a slow pace to keep the distance advantage.

"Surrender? Didn't know your eyesight was that bad. I'm not exactly in fighting condition at the moment." She let out a groan and even gritted her teeth. The silence was only broken from her heavy breathing.

Valdryn laughed. "I was talking to your companions."

"You already killed the old man and the dwarf isn't of use to anyone." Her mouth grew into a wicked curve.

Valdryn shook his head. "I mean the others."

The woman's smile faded when she saw Valdryn's stance change. "Kill them now!" she shouted. Valdryn took the knives from his belt and launched them into the trees. Three bodies clad in dark fur and leather armor crashed through the branches. Her reinforcements emerged but were met with the battlemages' wrath.

Sandra let the lightning flow through her, searing flesh and bark without mercy. The trees snapped and splintered with each lighting arc. The ashes of her enemies swirled in the air with the remains of the singed bark. The pain in their screams was undeniable but they quickly fell into silence.

Her marksmen proved to be equally skilled with an axe as they were with their crossbows. While their opponents attacked with a berserker rage, the marksmen moved with grace. With only a few swings, cultists fell left and right. Ash and blood fell all around them. The moonlit sap illuminated the twisted beauty of their dance.

Tariv unleashed all of his might, crippling all who came into his range. He enhanced the power of each swing with his magic, nearly tearing off limbs. His men made quick work of the ones collapsed on the ground. Armor caved in and bones snapped under the hammer's might. It was less of a battle and more of a slaughter any time Tariv was involved.

Jonas was dueling the dwarf who wielded spiked maces. The concussion he received prior to the ambush left him with a blurred vision. To compensate, he flailed his weapons wildly. While not the most practical fighting style, the maces did keep Jonas at bay while Valdryn battled the leader.

The woman closed the distance much quicker than anticipated and slashed at Valdryn with two jagged crescent sickles. With each slash they reflected the moonlight. They were made of a strange cyan crystal that seemed as durable as steel. Valdryn dodged most of her attacks so as to learn her movement. He would occasionally block to test her reactions though she would simply retaliate by following her routine. One slash from the left, another from the right, and finish with a crosscut. She used an unrelenting fury to win her fights. She relied on speed and catching her opponents off guard. Fighting head on was not in her expertise.

Valdryn moved with her blades as a stream would move along the rocks in its path. Each slash would come close but never made contact. Her frustration was building and so her attacks became a wild flurry. Valdryn stopped dodging and chose to hold his ground. He parried all of her attacks. Her rage induced attacks became taxing and drained her energy. Her heavy breathing and tiring posture gave her away.

The dwarf brought both of his maces down in a vertical slam. Jonas slashed at one arm, forcing the dwarf to drop his weapon. He followed up with a shoulder bash which knocked the dwarf to the ground. Jonas placed his boot on the dwarf's throat. He turned to see Tariv finishing off his assailants.

The full weight of his hammer was brought down on one man's head. The pop and cracking noise churned Jonas's stomach. The other remaining ambushers had surrendered to Sandra and her marksmen. They all looked to their leaders fighting in the center, mostly in awe for the sheer speed of each fighter.

The woman grew sluggish with each attack while Valdryn remained calm with each deflect. Their duel had gone on for too long and her footing had grown sloppy. The woman finally retreated back to her routine and gave Valdryn the opening he wanted.

When she went for the crosscut, he raised his sword and her blades hooked on. He flipped his blade, pulling the woman in, and bashed her face with an uppercut using the hilt. He followed with a downward slash at her leg, forcing her to her knees, and finished with a left hook which knocked her to the ground.

Blood dripped from her nose as she looked up at Valdryn. Her weapons had fallen away from her, leaving her defenseless. "Well played, Blademaster."

"Your men were making too much noise," he said, almost mockingly.

She looked at the survivors with disgust. "Between us, the boss has been lax lately in recruit selection." The woman spit in their direction.

Tariv walked over to join his friend, coated from head to toe with blood. It wasn't an unfamiliar look for him but was still hard to look at nonetheless. A grin of triumph ran from ear to ear, the blood frenzy finally subsided.

"Speaking of your boss," Valdryn said. "You're going to tell us everything you know." He pointed his sword at her, hinting at his dwindling patience.

The woman burst into laughter. "That's not gonna happen. You're gonna have to kill me."

"Maybe. But not here and not today." He nodded at Tariv. The woman went to stand but a quick strike from Tariv left her unconscious.

"Tariv. Sandra. Secure the prisoners and get them back to Ruvo." Valdryn sheathed his blade.

They nodded at the Blademaster and huddled the prisoners together. Sandra muddled an incantation and the air around them came to life. Ethereal shackles bound the prisoners' hands together. Tariv threw the unconscious woman on the back of his horse and they departed Jonas and his master.

"Follow me, Jonas. I want to see something." He led him in the opposite direction as the others.

Jonas fell in line with his master. "What is it, Master?"

The pair came to the end of the tree line. Before them, stood a clearing with a pathway leading up to the mountains. At the end was ancient temple with moss-covered ivory bricks. The nearby field was littered with siege machines from ages ago, overtaken by weeds. The area itself was like a museum dedicated to a long-forgotten conflict.

"Their ambush was too clustered. They were meant to stop us here so we would easily be transported to their hideout." Valdryn looked back at where the ambush took place.

"The Temple Arcanum? No one lives there but squatters and archaeologists." Jonas quoted his readings on the reports regarding the Isle. Though it felt more like a tourist guide, it offered some insight into the history.

"During my younger years at the Academy, I came to the Isle with a company of soldiers. We were tasked with dealing with a rise in bandit activity," said Valdryn. "In my hours dedicated to research, I came across the reports of a few paladins."

"Paladins? Like the Burning Sun?"

Valdryn nodded. "In their reports, they noted numerous secret passages and the cavernous labyrinth that lies beneath the temple. On the surface, we see only what the Isle allows us to see. Think of who or what could be hiding in its depths."

"I thought General Barathel already raided the Temple?" asked Jonas.

"He was going to but instead, he relied on diplomacy with the Temple Guardian, Galadus," sighed Valdryn. "I was just an aspiring battlemage then but I accompanied the diplomatic team. In hindsight, it was all too simple."

###

The interior of the Temple was mostly comprised of makeshift tents of various sizes. The bigger tents held vendor supplies while the smaller ones were used for private matters. Most of the bedrolls were out in the open with light shining through the holes above. The temple sheltered a colony of its own and it showed no signs of slowing in growth.

Galadus, a retired member of the Burning Sun, took up the title of Temple Guardian in hopes of restoring the Temple Arcanum to its former glory. The title was meant to be handed down from one Guardian to the next but after the temple was abandoned, tradition wasn't a priority.

A tall man with a freshly shaved head and simple robes was accompanied by twelve soldiers and led by the current Blademaster, Matthias. They made their way through the crowds of the entrance hall currently used for the markets. A small group of temple guards dressed in tattered robes and bits of leather armor awaited them near an illuminated tunnel. Their faces were hidden behind helmets with a cage-like design for the faceplate. It allowed for them to see but the underlying cloth kept their identities unknown.

"Galadus has been waiting for your arrival," one guard said in a stoic voice.

"Apologies for the delay," said the bald man. "The storm had slowed our progress."

The guard beckoned for them to follow. The tunnel was illuminated by a plethora of torches running down its entire length. Guards were evenly spaced down the tunnel, more than enough to scare off any trespassers.

Young Valdryn stayed near the front of the group with Matthias. Serving as a temporary guard, he had to be in uniform and use a standard issued sword. It felt unnatural for him to be away from his father's sword but he was still a worthy opponent even with a rusty knife. Mathias understood the young man's potential and so he wanted him to stay close to the diplomat.

"What do you think of this place, Valdryn?" Matthias asked.

"It's a lot livelier than I expected. And well-guarded too," he said, surprised.

Matthias nodded. "Galadus is doing everything he can to get this place up and running again."

"Do you know Galadus? Personally, I mean." Valdryn was interested in the armor of the guards. It was mostly just bits and pieces of old armor but they still managed to somehow look regal and fierce.

"Yes. We worked together on assignments in our younger years. He was always the perfect

representation of the Order of the Burning Sun."
Even after the effects of time and battle injuries,
Matthias radiated the aura of a champion.

"How so?" Valdryn wondered.

"Relentless in his pursuit for justice but
always willing to lend a helping hand in the most
mundane of activities." Matthias smiled at the
memories. "And he has one hell of a sword arm."
Some of the temple guards escorting them
chuckled. Suddenly, they didn't seem too
intimidating.

"I've never seen Galadus fight before." One
of the guards said. The mask may have hidden his
face but his voice gave him away as a young man,
maybe around Valdryn's age.

"Time has finally gotten the better of his
fighting skills, but his mind and heart are as sharp
as ever," said Matthias.

They reached an open room with a
makeshift cabin in the middle. Multiple armed
guards patrolled the area while some were
stationed on the walkways above. They reached
the entrance to the cabin before coming to a halt.

The lead of the escort turned around to face
the diplomat. "Some of you will have to wait
outside. I'm afraid there isn't enough room for all
of us."

"Valdryn, Boris, and George. You're with
me. The rest of you, wait out here."

The small group entered the cabin. It was
mostly empty save for a large table in the center

with a handful of seats. Galadus was at the far end, stoking the fireplace. A hooded man with a graying beard sat closest to Galadus. The temple guards and diplomatic escort spread out.

"Matthias!" Galadus shouted with arms wide open. "It's good to you my old friend."

"Likewise, Galadus. I just wish it was under better circumstances."

"True enough. Please have a seat." Galadus took the chair next to the hooded man on his right. Matthias and the diplomat sat on his left. "Now then, I believe introductions are in order." He put his hand on the hooded man's shoulder. "This is Balvas. He was a historian for the Burning Sun and is a close friend of mine."

Matthias nodded in Balvas's direction. He placed his hand on the diplomat's shoulder. "This is Erickson. My personal guard."

Valdryn and the others looked confused.

"Ahh, the false diplomat trick. I believe I told you of that one." Galadus smiled. He gestured for Matthias to take some food off of his small plate.

Matthias returned the smile and took a cherry tomato. "Indeed, you did, my friend."

"Did you run into any trouble?" Galadus took a small grape and a sip of water.

"We had a few altercations with bandits and the local wildlife. Nothing we couldn't handle." He pointed towards dried flecks of blood on his wrist guard. He did his best to look presentable but combat makes that difficult.

Galadus looked around the room at Matthias's guards. "With a handful of armed warriors and you at the lead, I'm sure those bandits must've been blind to make any attempt."

"If only that were true," Erickson said. He let out a deep sigh, grabbing for one of the mugs and filling it with water. He hoped for something stronger.

"What do you mean?" Balvas asked.

"When we checked their bodies, a few of them had special markings." The tone in his voice was less reminiscent. "Valdryn. Show them."

Valdryn nodded and approached the table. He reached into his pack and pulled out a bloody chunk of cloth. He sat it between Galadus and Matthias with a hint of hesitation and concern.

"Unravel it, Son." Galadus requested.

Son. That word always left him feeling uneasy. He regathered himself and unwound the cloth. A severed hand with a strange tattoo on the palm rested between the men. The tension in the room shifted as the fingers began to twitch.

"How is it still moving?" one of the temple guards asked.

"Dark magic," replied Balvas.

"Void based, to be exact," Matthias interjected. "The runes suggest a necromantic ritual. Someone has been using undead bandits as spies to monitor the island."

The group fell silent. This type of magic was vastly unknown, only mentioned in history books. They couldn't help but stare at the twitching digits on the necrotic arm. "Magic is a natural part of our world, taught to us by Ruvo. For this perverse magic to linger after his sacrifice is both worrisome and sickening," Erickson said, not even trying to hold back his anger.

"So, it's true then. Necromancy has come to our Isle." Galadus stroked his stubbled chin. He let out a long deep breath. "After all this world has lost to the Dark Ones, they still find willing servants to do their bidding."

"We have reasons to believe they live here or at the very least, used to."

"What makes you say that, Matthias?" Balvas wondered. His face was hidden beneath his hood but his inquisitive stare could be felt by all.

"Because of this place's history." Galadus knew what he was going to say. Matthias's silence confirmed his suspicions. "This was where Zilendras fell in battle after all."

###

"Who was Zilendras?" Jonas asked.

"One of the twelve Abyssal Knights," he said sternly. He stared at the moonlit sap running down the trees. The Isle was made of such beauty but knew little more than death, even after the war.

"Abyssal Knight?"

Valdryn sighed, not out of annoyance but from the weight of such a question. Each knight was a hero in their own right and only they could speak to the full account of who they were until the end. "Get the horses. It's a long way back to Ruvo. I'll tell you on the way."

Chapter 6: Bloodied Past

The Isle was overtaken, consumed by war. When Ruvo left to join the rest of the pantheon in the final confrontation, his isle was attacked by the servants of the dark and other opportunists. The pantheon was known for inspiring devotion and strength in their followers. The guards he left behind remained stalwart in their defense of their master's home, besting each attempt at an incursion. After the pantheon's sacrifice, the fourth Abyssal Knight raided his island. Cut off from his masters, Zilendras would ensure all would suffer while he still lived.

He came to the Isle aboard damaged ships flying friendly sails. Before the city guards knew the truth, Zilendras landed and slaughtered half of Ruvo in one night. His small army hosted mortal traitors and monstrous creatures from the void. He himself was once an elf of high regard but the darkness contorted his soul and shaped him into a beast.

Razor-sharp teeth lingered behind cracked and blackened lips. His skin was the color of ash and his black veins shown underneath like encroaching vines. His eyes were a smoky purple that gave way to no emotion. Most of his armor had been abandoned after being nearly destroyed but what remained was caked in blood and grime.

He cut his way through Ruvo with no mercy, just the intent of absolute destruction. The remaining survivors held their ground at the Spire of Arcanum. They were low on supplies and their barricades wouldn't hold forever. The militia that formed unfortunately had more heart than skill.

Zilendras and his army would have easily decimated them had it not been for the timely arrival of the Order of the Burning Sun. As devout paladins of the Goddess of Light, Allistara, they wielded a portion of the Light's power. With Knight-Commander Caius leading them, Zilendras didn't stand a chance.

Caius had taken the docks first while Zilendras was distracted with the Spire. His warships shattered through the boats in their way. The debris littered the water's surface as the masts sank below. Even an orc's blood frenzy paled in comparison to the righteous devotion of paladins. With little resistance, the paladins swiftly swept through the remains of the city. They drove a wedge between his army and forced Zilendras to retreat.

"Zilendras. You coward, come face me!" Caius shouted.

"Not today, Paladin. Your end will come soon enough." Zilendras summoned forth more beasts from the shadows. They were no match for the Order and the light but they were numerous and bought Zilendras enough time to escape.

Ruvast's devotees occupied the illustrious temple at the Isle's center. Zilendras turned the once beautifully etched halls into a crimson work of art. He stared at the corpse of one of the priests. Old age and a heart attack had claimed him before Zilendras could reach him. The Abyssal Knight slammed his fist into stone floor, each bash harder and faster than the last.

"No. No one gets to escape me," Zilendras said with a contorted, angry frown. "I will drag you all back from your eternal rest. You will all serve for such insolence!"

Zilendras smeared the blood from his knuckles on the face of the priest. The black blood seeped into the eyes and began turning the skin into a familiar ash color. He dragged the boy through the temple, past the corpses, and outside the entrance.

A black smoke rushed out from the temple and flooded the fields. Armed corpses of the fallen guards and bone monstrosities stepped forth. Though their bodies were poised for battle, their voices in unison screamed out, "Free us."

"Zilendras is nothing more than a coward and a defiler." Caius stood before his men, his back to the Temple and the fields of undead. "He and his men will suffer for their transgressions." He nodded towards his archers. A storm of fire arrows scorched the fields.

The disembodied screams that came from the fields haunted the wind, a never-ending echo of sorrow. A soldier approached, Caius. "What do we do now, Sir? Should we attack?"

"No. His power is waning and soon the creatures he summoned will dissipate, leaving only mortal men between us and him." He kept motioning for his archers to continue their bombardment.

"What if he keeps raising the dead against us?" asked the soldier, fear creeping in.

"He can't raise the dead from ash, soldier. He's lost and knows it. If we wait him out, they'll be too weak to pose any real threat.," he explained. "He'll have no satisfaction from drawing us into a trap now. I won't allow it."

The fields were ablaze but some of the creatures pressed on. The archers picked them off but the larger beasts rushed the siege equipment. The catapults and ballistae were reduced to scraps but the paladins quickly surrounded them. The light they wielded dissipated the dark magic like fire consumes paper.

Three months had passed. Three months of dead returning until there was nothing left to return. In the final week, the risen dead simply fell apart moments after their resurrection. The Knight-Commander had taken one-hundred of his men inside the temple. Just as Caius predicted, the only defenders left were mortal men and women who couldn't resist the promises of power. Now they were hardly strong enough to hold their weapons.

The Order had no mercy to offer, just swift retribution. One by one, the defenders would be cut down. The black blood of the traitors covered up the dried red stains of the innocent. As his men slaughtered their way through the temple, Caius walked among the bodies of the fallen. Dried hollow husks garbed in temple robes littered the halls, their faces frozen in anguish.

"He kept some alive to feed off of their souls," a paladin said in disgust.

"So many innocents were risen as abominations but that pales in comparison to having your soul ripped out and devoured in front of you." Caius tightened his grip on his sword. "Zilendras! Where are you hiding?"

A distant choking laughter echoed from deeper within the temple. The coarse voice reverberated through the halls. "Just follow the bodies of the men and women you failed, Paladin."

Caius hastened his steps, his men following close behind. The sound of metal boots stomping through the temple drowned out the laughter. The men could feel the fire in their hearts growing with each step. This is what they trained for. Destroying the darkness was their purpose.

The closer they got to Zilendras, the more they saw him for the monster he truly was. Bodies were hanging from the ceiling, seemingly drained of blood and soul. Some of his own followers joined the victims nailed to the wall. The fading stain of blood covered the end of the hall. The laughter grew louder with each grotesque scene.

Zilendras awaited his fate at the heart of the Temple. A giant hole sat at the center of the floor, an endless pit of darkness. He was surrounded by what remained of his forces. Their bodies were twisted and contorted into broken creatures from a nightmare. Their eyes were a solid black, seemingly hollow.

"This is what awaits you, Paladin. You and all your people will be reclaimed by the abyss. You will be nothing more than trembling husks when the Master returns." The creatures howled screeched, their bones creaking eerily.

Caius looked at the twisted men and women before him. It was hard to tell if it was disgust or fear that filled him. Perhaps both. His blade emitted a sharp golden glow. Among the dark, his light shone bright. "Why would you do this? Why would you serve this darkness so willingly?" he wondered.

"This world is broken beyond repair. This is merely a mercy killing of the weak and fearful. The strong will endure and build a new world," he shouted with a dry toothy grin. "You devote yourselves to gods who never cared. Their lies cover up the fact that they're no different than me."

Caius took up his sword with both arms. "You're nothing but a puppet, Zilendras. Something to be discarded after serving its purpose. Killing you will be a mercy you don't deserve."

Zilendras conjured his sword from a pool of shadow. "And that thought will harm you far more than you could ever harm me."

The twisted servants of the darkness leapt at the paladins. The lost souls screamed in agony with every moment, only fueling their rage filled attacks. Black blood spilled from their mouths but death would not come easy.

Caius charged for Zilendras, ignoring all others. Two knights, one serving the light and the other serving the dark, dueled in the home of a fallen god. Zilendras was weaker, thinner then when he arrived on the island. His hatred for life and obsession with the darkness held him together enough to be a formidable opponent for Caius. His skeletal figure moved with such grace that even the Knight-Commander was impressed, though he'd never admit it.

Their blades clashed and ricocheted off one another. Zilendras sliced at Caius and his armor, but could not find flesh. Zilendras himself removed his armor earlier with only a tattered robe to keep him covered. It became a battle of Caius's defense versus Zilendras's speed.

"Take heart, Caius. When this day is done. History will remember you as a hero, regardless of the outcome, albeit temporarily." His vortex of slashes packed more strength then one would assume.

Caius gritted his teeth. Their blades locked and he threw a quick left hook. A sharp tooth skittered across the floor. "And you will die here, faded and forgotten."

Zilendras replied with a bloody grin and sharp cackle. He lurched forward, wildly swinging his blade down on Caius's guard. The unrelenting assault reached for his throat but the light would defend him this day.

The paladin held strong against the attacks. He could sense something off in his opponent. It was as if Zilendras wanted this battle to end though it didn't matter to him who the victor was. He pushed the thought aside, ignoring any and all distractions. Caius saw an opportunity and took it.

He parried the last swing, knocking Zilendras off balance. A quick slash disarmed the Abyssal Knight, who was now clutching his chest. Black blood trickled down from the gash. Caius picked up the sword born from shadows and approached Zilendras as he dropped to one knee.

"Any last words, Zilendras?" Sweat dripped from his brow as he caught his breath between words.

He grinned. "Just a parting message. I will take great pleasure in watching your world burn. You can rest peacefully knowing you won't be around to see it." Blood dripped from his mouth and chest. He extended his arms and embraced the Paladin's swift justice.

Caius shoved the shadow-blade through Zilendras's chest, knocking him backwards into the pit. His laughter echoed upward, a final haunting of an anguished soul. Whether he simply fell out of earshot or the bottom of the pit was what silenced him, no one could say. The knight-commander looked down at the pit, sensing something not of the natural order.

"It's done then, Caius?" asked one of his knights.

The Knight-Commander never broke from staring at the pit. "For Zilendras, it is. But for us, I fear it'll never be finished."

Valdryn and Jonas had finally reached the open field between Ruvast and the Lunar Forest. They had taken their time, keeping their horses at a slow pace. Valdryn spotted a few creatures in the shadows, scavenging the remains of the bandits they left. The glow of the sap dimmed, as though it served its purpose and departed the pair.

"So, Caius killed an Abyssal Knight right here on the Isle?" Jonas asked.

"Well, some would argue that they're unkillable but yes. I believe Zilendras died in that pit." Valdryn pet his horse, calming its nerves.

"Who was he exactly?" Jonas wondered. "Before he became an Abyssal Knight."

"Well, he was once a renowned battlemage and councilor. As that story goes, he lost his family during the war. Sickness and famine overtook his home and blamed his king's complacency," explained Valdryn. "He betrayed his king and sought allies in the darkness to usurp him and save the rest of his people. He found power but was reborn in darkness and would forever remain out of reach from the spirit realm, never to see his family again."

Jonas looked back at the path from where they came. He expected something darker. Abyssal Knights were pure evil after all. He slaughtered innocents before his end, how could such a being seem so normal?

"That's sadder than I expected. I almost feel bad for him." Jonas furrowed his brow, not sure how to feel.

Valdryn smiled and nodded. "I felt the same way until I remembered something my father said."

"What was that?" Jonas asked.

"It's easy to act out of anger or regret or sadness, but it takes strength to acknowledge such feelings and act against them. You can cry and you can scream and you can even curse the gods, but the pain will only ever hold you back from true peace…"

"…let the pain go and peace will find its way back to your heart and soul."

Valdryn looked surprised. "You remembered?"

Jonas nodded. "Of course. It was the first thing you taught me after…after I lost my mother."

Valdryn looked up at the sky. It was speckled with stars, like a never-ending pool of lights. He could point out several constellations he learned as a child when he and his father would stare at the night sky. It was a passion of his mother's and his only remaining connection to her. Everything else was gone.

"You took me in when others would pass me by and leave me in the dirt. I will never forget the lessons you taught me." Jonas smiled though clearly holding back tears.

Valdryn smiled but never looked away from the stars. "And you certainly give me grey hairs much like a son would, Jonas."

The two laughed their way back to the city gates, with the stars watching over them. But Valdryn's mind remained on the temple. For the ignorant, the Isle is a place of beauty and magic but its history was stained in blood. Of the Abyssal Knights, Zilendras was one of the most feared and his remains rested somewhere below. If the darkness had been buried there, then it was only a matter of time before someone powerful enough came and unearthed it.

Chapter 7: Mercy for a Name

General Barathel had been in charge of the military presence on the Isle for the past thirty years. He is said to have no equal on the battlefield nor in stratagem. His family's honor and legacy garnered him much support and allowed him to rise as the youngest general in the history of the Kalboria military. Many years passed but eventually he was given command of the Isle.

The walls of his office in Ruvo were littered with trophies of his career. The left side held weapons of different designs he acquired during his expeditions into ancient ruins. The right side tells a story of his military career. Each suit of armor he wore as a representation of his rank was evenly spaced along the wall. A pulsing stone heart of a golem gave off a faint blue glow, illuminating his desk in the back.

Barathel and Valdryn were sitting at the large table in the center of the room. Valdryn's eyes kept finding their way to the relics on display. In the corner was a war drum gifted by the minotaur tribe on the other side of the Isle. The dented helm of a self-proclaimed bandit chieftain rested on the bookshelf. Barathel was going over the reports in front of him but Valdryn inherited his father's love for history.

"Excellent work last night," said the General.

"Thank you, Sir. It was far from a difficult assignment," Valdryn replied.

"If only I had a few men like you during the Crimson Raids." Barathel reached for his cup to take a deep sip. "It would've been over in mere days and many more villages would've been saved."

"You're too kind, Sir." Valdryn was cleaning his blade to occupy the moments of silence. The general often made remarks about his military career and other similar events. Talking of the Crimson Raids would fill his mind with too much sorrow, too much regret, so Valdryn just ignored the words the best he could.

Barathel looked up from his notes and eyed the blade. "May I see your weapon, Valdryn?"

Valdryn looked up, hesitant. "Of course, Sir."

He handed his weapon over to the General, albeit reluctantly. He traced the scar on his hand and tapped his foot quietly on the wooden floor. Visions of the villagers from his childhood flooded his mind.

"What an exquisite weapon. Light-weight, durable, and…" he paused for a moment as blood ran down his finger, "…and deceptively sharp it seems. The design is unlike anything I've seen outside a book. What's its origin?"

"It was my father's. He gave it to me before…" the words were caught in his throat, "…before he died."

"Was he a soldier then?" Barathel wondered.

"Part-time blacksmith and retired treasure hunter actually. He found it during his travels and repaired it over the years," he said, proud of his father's accomplishments. "He was unsure, but he believed it dates back to the time when the Gods were still among us."

"He might have been right," the general replied.

"How can you tell?" Valdryn asked, excited on behalf of his father.

"I recall reading about ancestral weapons when the Gods chose mortal guardians of among the different races. This type of blade was wielded by elite warriors known as the Balaven, not unlike our battlemages. Our ancestors crafted these weapons to wage war against demons but when the Gods arrived, they perfected the design." He handed the sword back to Valdryn. "It suits you."

"He always thought it would," said Valdryn, sadness in his heart. He looked at his reflection in the blade. He could recall all the times he was told how much he looked like his father.

"I'll finish going over the reports soon enough," said Barathel. In the meantime, go and check on our prisoners and see if any of them have talked yet." Valdryn bowed and made his way to the door. Before he could close it behind him, the General called out to him. "One last thing. Your father, what happened to him?"

Valdryn couldn't bring himself to turn around. He simply replied with his head hung low, "The Crimson Raids. He died saving everybody. Saving me."

"A glorious death then," shouted the General.

"A needless death," Valdryn muttered under his breath before shutting the door behind him

Ruvo didn't have torture chambers so prisoners were interrogated in their cells. If the crime was simple and no one was hurt, community service was the punishment. If the crime was more severe, death was almost a certainty. If you were spared the headsman, it was most likely because your mind was already broken behind bars. Its dungeon was never meant for permanent residence.

Tariv occupied one of the wings with last night's prisoners. Six cells on either side, each one filled with a dead cultist, save for one. He was in the back-right cell with the woman Valdryn bested in a duel.

"You will talk," Tariv barked.

The woman replied by spitting in his face. Tariv responded by breaking a rib. She merely laughed, "You'll have to do more than break a few bones."

"I intend to." Tariv left the cell when he heard someone enter the halls. This part of the castle was never occupied, save for a few guards when necessary. It was dimly lit, feeling more like a cavern than a castle. Though often walking with silence, Valdryn's footsteps let out an echo here.

"The General sent me to check on your progress," he said. "I hope it hasn't been too difficult for you."

Tariv motioned towards the cells. "With all their talk of 'supreme power' and 'darkness conquers all' you would think they could handle more than a few minutes of interrogation."

Valdryn walked past the cells towards Tariv. He inspected each one along the way. A few bled out, the lucky ones Valdryn thought. The others seemed to test Tariv's temper, and were left unrecognizable as a result.

"Well supreme power is no match for a half-orc with a short temper," said Valdryn, nearly gagging from the stench.

Tariv motioned for Valdryn to follow, not in much of joking mood. "I'll take that as a compliment."

When they reach the final cell, Valdryn analyzed the prisoner's injuries. She had shallow cuts running down her arms, almost in a pattern. Her left eye was bruised and her hair, stiff with sweat and blood kept the burned half of her face hidden.

"Ah I was wondering when the duelist would show his face again. Ready for another round? Or perhaps you've come to assist your hound?" Through all her injuries and shameful defeat in the forest, her wicked smiled never faltered.

Tariv stepped towards her but Valdryn held his arm out to impede his path. "My only interest is the name of your master. Are you going to talk or will my 'hound' need to bite harder next time?"

The woman laughed away the threat. "I've been waiting for him to do his worst so we can finally see who's enjoying this little dance of his more." She winked her bruised eye at Tariv. With both fists clenched, Tariv stormed out of the cell. His heavy footsteps reverberated through each cell.

"Have I upset your little—" Valdryn's hand held the words in her throat with his tightening grip. She was caught off guard, expecting a more chivalrous approach. She was wrong.

"Enough games. Listen well or I can assure you that your final moments will be far from enjoyable." Valdryn's voice had grown as cold and stiff as stone. His patience had worn thin and being reminded of his father didn't help. "We know your cult hides within the temple. I am tired of all this death but I will not hesitate to take your life if it means saving the people of the city. You can either join your friends in an unmarked grave or earn a stay of execution."

Valdryn released his grip and the woman broke into a coughing fit. She struggled to catch her breath but the foul stench in the air only made matters worse. She could still feel the Blademaster's grip.

Tariv returned with a leather sack. He emptied the contents on the cell floor, revealing rusted tools for torture. The metal clanking rang in everyone's ears but Valdryn and the woman never broke eye contact.

Tariv picked up a few rusty hooks and a warped hammer. The woman looked at the pair of battlemages before her. Tariv inflicted the physical pain but the fury and intensity in Valdryn's eyes struck a nerve she didn't even know she had.

She barely choked out her next words. "His name is Balvas."

###

Galadus stared at the severed hand on his table. He followed each finger as it slowly twitched, as if trying to grasp the weapon it held before it departed its owner. The flesh had already begun to decay and emit a foul stench. It didn't help that the air was still, enveloped by the scent.

"Necromancy has and always will be strictly forbidden, as decreed by the four great kingdoms ages ago. Any who break this or any other of the sacred laws will be punished most severely." Balvas was shaking from the rising anger. He took a moment to gather himself. "But how can we be certain this is cult activity and not an isolated incident.?"

"Only a cultist would risk practicing such dark magic on Ruvast's Isle," Matthias replied.

"Even rogue mages understand the weight of such magic."

"It would be foolish, childish even to risk grievous punishment for the sake of insulting a fallen god," said Balvas.

"And yet still I would not put it beneath them." Erickson shifted in his chair, feeling the tension growing.

"Enough." Galadus slammed his fist on the table. The severed hand clenched its fingers. "This bickering will get us nowhere. Let us look at what little we know. Bandit activity has increased on the Isle for the past few months. It was simple robberies until your superiors arrived, Matthias."

"What are you saying?"

"Ulterior motives, Blademaster," said Balvas. "Your superiors aided Belmont in putting an end to the Crimson Raids. These bandits are some of the survivors. It's all about revenge, plain and simple."

"Except for necromancy," a young Valdryn interjected.

The three older men turned to face the young man. Matthias shot him a chastising look while Galadus's attention was drawn back to the severed movement on the table. Only Balvas gave off an impression of anger towards the interruption.

"The boy makes a good point," Matthias said, breaking the silence.

"Wouldn't you be willing to go to certain extremes if it meant putting an end to those who destroyed your life?" asked Balvas.

"But necromancy, Balvas? How many bandit clans do you know to have access to that kind of power?" scoffed Mathias.

For once, Balvas did not have the answer. He stroked his beard in hopes the words would come to him, but they never did. The sudden noise of a blade being unsheathed broke everyone's concentration.

Galadus was standing over the severed hand with his dagger raised. "It matters not who the culprit is or what their motives are. It will end the same way regardless of circumstance." He slammed the rusty dagger down on the necrotic hand. The fingers twitched, as if it felt the pain. Galadus tossed the blade and hand into the fireplace. "Any who practice necromancy will be met with Allistara's justice."

The hand ceased to move as it became part of the kindling. Embers rose from charred flesh and bone. "Return to your city, Matthias." Balvas motioned for the guards to escort them out. "Inform your superiors that we will end this swiftly and personally."

Matthias nodded and left with his men close behind. Galadus never looked away from the flames to see his friend off. Once a paladin's fire was stoked, it would prove difficult to put out. He called Valdryn to him as they were escorted through the halls.

"I'm sorry, Sir. I talked out of turn." Valdryn's voice was low.

"Nonsense. Sometimes the youngbloods need to remind the old ones of what's at stake." Matthias bore a reassuring smile.

Valdryn nodded, feeling better about his error. "At least we're now going to be able to do something about these bandits."

Matthias laughed. "I'm afraid *we* won't be doing anything."

"Sir?"

"I've put in a recommendation to expedite your journey through the academy," said Matthias. "I foresee a great career in your future. Far greater than observing old guards play politics."

"I…I don't know what to say, Sir."

Matthias looked back at the way they came. Something itched at his mind. Thunder shook the walls of the temple as the storm began anew. "There's a darkness lurking here, Valdryn. If you ever return here, don't let it consume you."

Chapter 8: The Calm Before

Once Barathel learned of Balvas, he dispatched a small portion of his forces along with the aid of Ruvast's battlemages. His chief lieutenant, Verric Kanis, was given command. While he was far from good company, he got results and that's the only thing of worth to Barathel. It took three days to gather reinforcements but he was able to position several camps on the edge of the forest to establish a perimeter around the temple.

Valdryn had been tasked with assembling a small team that would join him in the temple. Jonas was an obvious first choice. He also wanted the two battlemages that accompanied Sandra during the previous night, twins named Ava and Bannon. They proved themselves to be both sharp in weapon and wit. He found their tent, not too far from his own.

"We're more known for combat, not diplomacy, Sir." Ava was sharpening her axes when he approached them.

Bannon was practicing with throwing knives, each one landed inside the innermost ring on the target. "We appreciate the offer nonetheless, Blademaster."

"You can leave the talking to me. You're there for if and when things turn sour," Valdryn explained. "We'll be surrounded and meet resistance every step of the way. I could use your help when the fighting inevitably starts."

The twins stared at Valdryn, contemplating his request. Ava held a finger out to Valdryn, while motioning for her brother to huddle up. "One second," she said.

While the twins were debating, Jonas leaned in over his master's shoulder. "Are you sure we need them? We're in a whole camp of fighters."

"And out of this whole camp of fighters, I know how the twins fight," he said. "We can trust these two for when push comes to shove."

Ava and Bannon quickly appeared in front of Valdryn. "We accept your offer," said Ava.

Valdryn reached out and shook their hands. "Excellent. Meet us at my tent in a few hours."

"Since we're gonna be surrounded, someone with a good shield-arm wouldn't hurt," Bannon explained. "Old Davon trained some of the soldiers with tower shields. Maybe he could spare some recruits."

"You make a good point. See, you're not too bad at talking," Valdryn joked.

Bannon laughed. "But I'm much better with my axes." He bore a toothy grin while flipping an axe.

"Of that, I have no doubt." Valdryn and Jonas left the twins to search for Davon.

Davon was running his men through a refresher course in a clearing a short walk from the camps. An ancient golem overtaken by moss and vines served as the target. Four soldiers were defending it against four attackers. The attackers struck the golem, cheering as the defenders cursed them in defeat.

Valdryn and Jonas stood at a distance, measuring the recruits up for themselves. Valdryn remembered seeing similar training at Belmont's camp when he was younger. It was a good way for soldiers to bond, improving effectiveness of the whole unit.

"It's a shame Tariv won't be joining us. He would be worth twenty good men," said Jonas. He was always fond of the battlemages but Tariv was like a barbarian of the legends.

"At least forty," Valdryn said. "Either way, Barathel needs him to continue working over the prisoner."

"You mean the one who refused to talk until *you* showed up?" Jonas said with a smile.

Valdryn smirked but knew better than to encourage him. "Now what team of defenders would you say would be the most effective?"

Jonas paused for a moment, studying the new set of defenders. "The first team was sloppy but their orc didn't let anything past him. The third team had the best coordination but they looked lost without Davon shouting orders." Jonas stroked his stubbled chin before concluding, "The fifth group worked well together without relying on Davon."

"My thoughts exactly," agreed Valdryn. His brief time with Matthias taught him the power in observation. It wouldn't be enough to simply rely on the academy's books and scrolls for the rest of his life.

The pair found their way to Davon's side. His shaved head and silver-lined mutton chops made him standout among the new bloods. A stray arrow left him blind in his left eye but nothing could ever dampen his warrior spirit.

"Ah, Valdryn, it has been sometime since we last spoke." Davon and Valdryn clasped each other on the forearm.

"Not long enough, old friend," smiled Valdryn, happy to see a familiar face.

"So, what brings you to my new training grounds?"

"I'm in need of a few fighters with good shield arms." Valdryn took a look at some of the guards standing by.

Davon gestured towards the current group of defenders. "They're my best." As the attackers moved closer, the defenders in the back broke from their position and circled around them. The attackers were immediately swarmed and defeated.

"I'll be the judge of that." Valdryn approached the defenders. He stuck his blade into the dirt. He turned to Jonas and raised his eyebrow. Jonas nodded and disappeared into the crowd of trainees. "Davon tells me you're the best. Prove him right."

"You…you want us to defend against you."
The defenders looked at the battlemage, confused.

Valdryn took one step forward. The
defenders immediately fell into position. Valdryn
sprinted towards the defenders. He launched
himself at a defender, kicking off his shield and
flipping backwards through the air. The defender
staggered back. Valdryn charged again.

Two of the defenders broke formation and
surrounded him. Going easy on them, he used his
magic to merely keep them off balance. Their
vision spun like a night of drinking but they were
surprisingly prepared and quickly regained their
footing.

"Davon must've caught you boys down in
your cups more than once," he mocked.

"Well boys, looks like we won again." A
defender declared.

"That was…easier than I thought," one of
the victors said, trying to hide their confusion.

Valdryn smiled and pointed towards the
golem. Jonas was sitting on top, waving down to
the defenders. "Yes, I would agree."

"But…but you said we were to defend
against you."

"Did I now? Never trust an enemy to be
honest with you." He turned around to face Davon,
whose face had turned red at the quick defeat of
his best.

"You got cocky you idiots." Davon marched
through the mud towards them. "An enemy will

always deceive you, even on the battlefield. A shield wall must hold its ground and remain alert, not abandon its post and attack."

Valdryn put his hand on Davon's shoulder. "I'll leave Jonas with you to decide who we'll bring with us. You make sure they know what fighting a true enemy is like."

Davon shook his head at the defeated soldiers. "You best believe I will." Davon approached his men. "Listen up you louts."

Jonas stood by his master while Davon patronized the recruits. "So, who are we choosing?"

"I trust your judgement."

Jonas seemed stunned. "But it's your team."

"And your years of being an apprentice are nearing their end. You will soon be given tasks of your own." Valdryn reached out and grabbed Jonas's arm. "You will need to be able to make decisions and face their consequences on your own. Consider this one of the last lessons I have to teach you."

"I… I won't fail you, Master." Jonas smiled.

Valdryn returned the smile. "I know you won't, Jonas. I've seen you go from a thief to a young man of honor. I couldn't be prouder of you." The pair shared a moment of silence. The howling wind drowned out Davon's rough words. "I need to find the infiltrators Verric suggested and see if they're up to the task." Jonas left to inspect each recruit individually while Valdryn departed the training grounds in search of his last recruits.

Valdryn found the men he was looking for, Marcus and Frederick, a few tents down from Verric's. They were conquering all new comers at a game of King's Dice. It can be confusing for most at first but play a few games and it becomes second nature. Each player has six dice with four different images. Each dice has one crown, two skulls, two swords, and one shield. The objective is to have the most crowns at the end of the round. The first to win three rounds wins the game, the prize pool, and the resentment of the losers.

A seat opened up when the losers stormed out of the tent after rolling three skulls three times in a row. Valdryn took the man's seat next to Marcus and across from Frederick. Marcus had a unique brand seared into his left arm. Three crossed spears, each with a skull placed on the tip burned into the forearm marked the ex-criminal for a lifetime of military service.

Frederick earned the nickname "Four-Fingered Fred" when he lost his left ring finger during the Crimson Raids. Anyone who called him that to his face though would often lose their savings and a few teeth during a night of King's Dice.

Marcus didn't look up from his dice to greet the new player. "The prize pool has gotten too big for pocket change. You better have—"

Frederick launched a chicken bone at Marcus. "You can look up from your dice for one second and greet our honored guest."

Marcus flicked the bone back across the table, knocking over a small tack of coins. "What's so special about—" Marcus chokes up when he realizes who took up the seat next to him. He awkwardly tried to clear his throat. "Forgive me, Blademaster. I didn't realize you would be joining us."

Valdryn extended his arm and shook the nervous man's hand. "At ease, soldier." He shot a glance at Frederick and nodded his head.

Frederick chuckled to himself as Marcus turned red. "So, Master Valdryn, what brings you to our little game? I hope no one has wasted your time with their complaints after we took their gold."

"Nothing of the sort," he assured him. "I'm here on recruitment business."

Marcus grabbed the pitcher from the center of the table and filled up a mug for Valdryn. "Recruitment for what?"

Valdryn took a sip from his mug. "I need a small team to accompany me into the temple. I've already got a handful of good fighters but I'll need some men who can stick to the shadows and watch our backs while we're in there."

Frederick tossed a grape in his mouth before washing it down with the last of his drink. "We'd have to check with the Commander before we can commit."

"It was his recommendation that led me here," Valdryn said.

Frederick and Marcus glanced at each other. It was one thing to scout out enemy territory, but a whole different story to willingly walk into the lion's den. Marcus rubbed the brand on his arm. Frederick stroked the silver streaks in his beard.

"I won't make you come with me but our chances of success are higher with you two." Valdryn studied the pair, watching their faces contort in thought.

"Tell you what, Battlemage." Frederick grabbed a cup of dice and slid it across the table. "One round. You win and we'll join you."

Valdryn reached for the cup. "You sure you want to leave it to luck?"

Frederick shook his cup and slammed it down on the table. "What you call luck, I call fate." He lifted the cup up. Three crowns, two shields, and a skull. He sat the crowns aside and rolled again. This time he revealed a skull and two crowns. "And it looks like fate doesn't want me in that temple tonight."

"Five crowns. Not bad." Valdryn motioned for Marcus to take his turn. "I knew someone like you once." Marcus rolled his dice but Valdryn kept his focus on Frederick. "His name was Samson, a new recruit during my lessons on the Isle. He believed that fate was looking out for him because he always seemed to walk away from every fight unscathed."

"Damn swords are killing my rolls." Marcus was getting flustered as luck, or fate, didn't seem to favor him as much as his comrade.

Frederick leaned forward on the table. "What happened to Samson?"

"He died in his sleep. He fell ill, probably from something he ate." Valdryn didn't really have an emotion regarding the situation.

Frederick raised his eyebrows as he struggled to find the words. Was the Blademaster threatening him? He shook the notion from his mind and cleared his throat but was still unsure how to respond.

"Ah four crowns for me," Marcus said, upset. "Your turn, Valdryn."

Valdryn flipped his cup with only one shake. The two potential recruits stared at him with a mixture of confusion and excitement. "Samson was unscathed because his fellow soldiers watched his back. When you're in the temple, put your faith in *me*, not fate, and we'll watch out for each other."

"You still need to beat my five crowns, Battlemage, before we join you," Frederick said.

Valdryn lifted his cup. Marcus's jaw practically hit the table. Frederick was left in a speechless half frown, half smirk. "Like I said, trust me when we're in the temple and we'll make it out of there in one piece."

The battlemage stood up from the table and took a single gold coin from the prize pool. "My tent is on the other end of the camp. We leave tonight." He left the two men and their winnings, their gaze focused on the six crowns that sealed their fate.

Verric's tent housed the war table where the siege commanders discussed how to proceed. To Verric's left stood Valdryn and Sandra who were in charge of the mages. To the right sat Siege-Engineer Gordok Ironveins, a dwarf with crimson war-braids and a pudgy face covered in mossy green warpaint.

"How are we on siege engines, Gordok?" Verric never seemed to blink during a conversation. His pale eyes never broke focus, not even for a second.

"With what we've put together on short notice, I'd say four maybe five ballistae and three catapults." The isle wasn't supplied with much to begin with so Gordok and his engineers had to repair some old abandoned equipment.

"That's it?" Sandra was always hard to impress.

"All due respect, ma'am, I'm the siege expert here and I say a few ballistae paired with our surprise is more than enough for a few cultists."

"Our surprise?" asked Valdryn.

"Aye, Sir. On Barathel's orders, we managed to repair one of the fire-core cannons," he said, proudly. "If five were enough to conquer the temple during the war, one should be enough to scare a few cultists into submission."

"How did you manage to reignite the core?" asked Sandra.

"Gordok couldn't fix the core but his modifications will allow you and your mages to overcharge it with arcane energy." Verric pointed to the war table with a layout of the surrounding area.

A charred stone represented the temple with four yellow flags evenly spaced in a half-circle around the stone. "The flags represent siege locations where our ballistae and archers will be positioned. Nothing enters or leaves without one of ours noticing."

Valdryn walked up to the table, eyeing a red flag lined up with the center of the charred stone. "I take it that's our cannon?"

"If things don't go our way, the cannon will guarantee a quick end to any problems," said Verric, with a cold tone.

"What about the rear?" inquired Gordok.

Sandra used a piece of charcoal to mark various spots around the back of the temple. "With the coast to its back and the mountains on its side, there's nowhere for them to run. They're trapped like rats."

"And Valdryn will be our rat catcher." Verric placed his hand on Valdryn's shoulder. "You and your team will go into the temple and confront Balvas. Do whatever it takes to bring him down."

Valdryn's bright green eyes made contact with Verric's pale ones. "What about civilians?"

Verric took in a deep breath, never breaking contact. "It is highly unlikely that not one of those civilians have aided the cult in some way. Those who are guilty will die."

"And those who are innocent?" Valdryn wasn't one to accept collateral damage, let alone be responsible for it.

"No one is innocent," Verric said sternly.

Silence fell on the tent. Valdryn and Verric never saw eye to eye and now he was expected to follow his orders, to the letter. Belmont told Valdryn about men like Verric, too eager for personal achievement. Verric doesn't care for life as long he found the glory he was chasing.

"Don't worry, Valdryn," Gordok played with the flags on the map. "We're here to put on a show. You're here to make sure it gets done. We shouldn't even have to activate the cannon."

Valdryn nodded in agreement. Something felt wrong about Verric and his plan. But Gordok was right. As long as he did his job, there would be no needless deaths tonight. As long as things go according to plan, only one person has to die.

Chapter 9: Temple of Ruvast

Valdryn and Jonas led the others once night came. Valdryn sent Frederick and Marcus ahead to infiltrate the temple. Ava and Bannon took to either side of Valdryn while a young knight by the name of Sir Brandon led the three other shield bearers in front of them. Each of the knights were broad-shouldered and at least six feet tall. Sir Brandon in particular was a mountain of a man.

"Are you confident in your decision, Jonas?" Valdryn quizzed.

"Yes. Master. They appeared to be the most level-headed of the teams and will follow your orders," said Jonas.

"Good. There's more at stake here than we previously thought." Valdryn did his best to hide his emotions when out in the field but this time wasn't as easy. "Verric is too hot-headed for the position he's been given. All we need tonight is a quick decisive strike but he seems to be preparing for a war."

"I had heard he was always quick to anger," Bannon said.

"He's trying to impress the General, no doubt," added Ava.

Valdryn stared at the temple and its decrepit state. Galadus restored what he could but some things are best left to their fate. The age of war scarred the temple to its core, destined to never return to its former glory.

"If we fail here, Verric will use the cannon and reduce the temple, and everyone inside, to ash." Valdryn gritted his teeth to push the anger down. Only a calm head would serve him tonight.

"He can't do that can he?" asked Jonas.

"As long as it serves the General, he can do whatever he pleases to bring the cult down." Valdryn let out a deep sigh, looking at the ruins before them. He remembered the paintings from when it was pristine. Such beauty between gods and mortals, and Verric is all too eager to see it erased.

"Then he's no different than Balvas," he blurted out. Jonas inherited much from his master during his training. He never could quite hold his temper though and it probably didn't help that Valdryn let his agreement show.

Valdryn's frustration subsided for the moment. He looked up at the night sky but the stars weren't as bright as they usually were. "I do believe your apprenticeship ends tonight, Jonas. Ava and Bannon, as the currently present battlemages, do you have any objections?"

"None from me, Blademaster. We could use more like you and Jonas in our ranks," said Ava.

"He'll make a fine battlemage," replied Bannon.

"Good. Keep your heads down and eyes open in there and we'll celebrate in the morning."

He saw his apprentice's eyes light up. Ever since Valdryn took him under his wing, all Jonas dreamt of was joining the ranks of his master. Ruvo was often intrigued by the dreams of mortals and did all he could to help them blossom. It'd be fitting to realize his dream in the home of such a god.

The group reached the temple entrance. They were greeted by a handful of guards but their armor wasn't quite like how Valdryn remembered. Darker tints, scarred armor, and torn tabards gave the sense of perpetual mourning. It was a stark contrast from Valdryn and his men. Shining steel armor with well-tailored blue tabards were awe inspiring to the downtrodden. Even young Jonas walked as a hero among the temple's denizens.

The temple had its own nightlife though it was far quieter than Ruvast's. The kitchens were still open for those who worked at night. Card and dice games ran throughout the night but more in good fun rather than gambling. Small teams of architects worked around the clock to find ways through the collapsed tunnels.

Valdryn looked around for his infiltrators. For better or for worse, he could not find any traces of them. There didn't appear to be many guards on the upper level. The balconies were restored and the scaffolding remained for further construction so it was possible they took the high ground.

"Follow me, Master Valdryn. Galadus has been expecting you," said their escort.

Valdryn and the others followed the guard though something was off in his voice. It was rough and distant. The posture of a young man with the voice of an old one and the stench of a barn mixed with the back alley of an inn.

They walked the long hallway a younger Valdryn once walked with Matthias. It was far more cluttered than Valdryn remembered. Chisels and hammers lay sprawled out along the floor. Chunks of stone were swept to the side in piles of rubble. The halls had drastically extended from the excavations, giving the appearance of a never-ending walkway into the pitch black.

Some of the posted guards smelled the same as their guide. The aroma swelled in the halls to the point where some of the others guards could hardly keep their composure. It would seem all of the once pristine aspects of the temple had fallen into disrepair.

"Do they not bathe?" Ava whispered to her brother.

"Apparently not," said Bannon, choking back a gag.

A robed man stepped out from Galadus's room holding an incense burner. The scent of lavender and blueberries filled the hall. It did not fully mask the foul stench but it did make it bearable.

"That's a relief," said Brandon. He sniffed at the air like hound on the hunt, trying to focus on the pleasant scent and block out the musk.

"You can say that again." Jonas breathed deeply though too eagerly. He got a strong waft of the foul stench and nearly gagged out loud. He shook his head and recomposed himself, not wishing to embarrass his master.

"Eyes open, everyone." Valdryn hadn't seen Galadus in over ten years. He was an old man last time they spoke and time slows for no one. When the prisoner mentioned Balvas, the first thing he thought of was that day with Matthias. Galadus is a strong and charismatic leader and Valdryn worried for his safety.

The room in which Galadus built his home seemed to have grown. Excavation cleared out the rubble behind the house and there were far more guards present than last time. The detail in the stonework of the pillars were restored and added a sense of extravagance to the room. It would appear that the temple guardian was making good on his promise, though at a slower pace than Valdryn expected.

"Here we are, Master Valdryn," said their escort. "You may choose two others to accompany you. The rest must stay here."

Valdryn nodded in agreement. "Jonas. You stay here with Sir Brandon and keep your eyes open."

"Yes, Master," Jonas replied, reluctantly. This was unfamiliar territory for him and being put in charge of the soldiers only added on to his stress. But he understood Valdryn was relying on him to keep a level head and secure the area.

"Ava and Bannon, you're with me." Valdryn and the siblings entered the home. The same scent of the incense overwhelmed them. Candles were lit all over while chests were bursting with flowers picked from just outside the temple walls. Herbalists and florists did what they could to mask the stench.

Galadus was sitting in a wheel chair, close to the fireplace. His shoulders were slouched and his eyes were mesmerized by the fire. Three other hooded men accompanied him. Valdryn tried to identify them but he could discern nothing from them. They looked more like statues than people.

"Greetings, Galadus," said Valdryn.

Galadus turned around from the fire. A long hood draped over, covering his face. Long white and wispy hair flowed out from under the hood, further hiding his face. "Ah, Valdryn. It has been quite some time since last we spoke." He motioned for the battlemages to take their seat.

As Valdryn took his seat, the hooded figures adjusted themselves. They did what they could to hide their faces. Valdryn still smiled, so as not to cause offense. "It has, Galadus."

"And how is our mutual friend Matthias these days?" Galadus asked.

"He now serves the Inquisitor's Guild as a combat instructor. He seems to enjoy it." Valdryn stared at Galadus. This was not the same righteous paladin he met years ago. The energy was gone and all strength seemed to have left him for some time. The Galadus he knew might as well be declared dead.

"That man never could appreciate the idea of retiring for good. I hope time has been far kinder to him than it has been to me." Galadus removed his hood. Deep dark circles formed under his eyes. His face had grown gaunt and his smile was missing teeth. "My apologies for the incense. I know the smell can be overwhelming but in our final days, all we can ask for is comfort."

"It's no bother. We do have official matters to discuss however." Valdryn pulled out a rolled-up note and handed it to one of the hooded men. In a brief glimpse, Valdryn saw his time-worn face similar to that of Galadus. This man differed in the fact that his lower lip looked blackened. *Are all of these men dying?* Valdryn wondered.

"Of that, I have no doubt my boy. Why else would knights in shining armor come to my door hmm?" Galadus took the note and read it aloud. "I, General Arven Barathel, hereby declare Balvas, associate of the Temple of Ruvast and advisor to Temple Guardian Galadus, to be a criminal. He is wanted for suspicions of treason, void practices, murder, and heretical activities. You are to surrender him until he's either found guilty or declared to be otherwise." Galadus lowered his head and rubbed his brow. "Oh dear."

"I know it can be a lot to take in at once but we need to see Balvas." Valdryn stared at the aged Temple Guardian, still trying to understand his sad state.

"I'm afraid that won't be possible." His tone had shifted and brow had lowered. A somber sigh overtook him.

"How do you mean?" Valdryn wondered.

"Balvas passed away a year ago." Galadus turned away from them to face the fire once more. "Unlike our gods, Master Valdryn, time is a sworn enemy of mortals. Age had gotten the best of him, taking him in his sleep. I never got to say goodbye to my friend."

The atmosphere of the room shifted. It was as though his funeral was still in process and everyone was too busy mourning to continue. It would explain the dreary garb of the guards and the less-than-ideal conditions of Galadus and his caretakers.

Ava and Bannon seemed disappointed. The plan was made around the prisoner's confession, now looking more like a lie. Valdryn studied the room. The overwhelming aroma made it difficult to collect his thoughts. The half-burned face of their prisoner came to his mind and her words rang in his ears.

"We have reason to suspect otherwise, Galadus." Valdryn had to see this mission through.

If he didn't bring out even a single suspect then Verric would level the temple and scorch the surrounding area.

"What reason might that be?" Galadus's head slightly perked up, like a hound out on the hunt.

"A prisoner. She confessed that Balvas was responsible for the cultist activity." Valdryn studied Galadus. Matthias always spoke highly of him and his fiery spirit. He had grown older but age affects all races differently. He knew Galadus to be one to take care of himself so even at his age, he shouldn't be reduced to this.

"Hmph. Didn't Matthias teach you that interrogation can have spotty results? And *she* confessed? What is her name?" There was disappointment, or perhaps anger, in his voice.

"She didn't say. It wasn't a priority," said Valdryn in a dismissive tone.

Galadus spun around to face them. "Now is that you or Barathel talking, hmm?" Galadus spat on the ground. "Let me guess. A young elf with dark hair and a burn scar on one side of her face?"

Valdryn froze, confused. "You know her?"

"Her name is Yvette. She and Balvas never got along. She was always an anarchist, deserving neither of pity nor mercy." Galadus stared Valdryn in the eye. There was something wrong about his stare, something hollow. "I had to watch the life leave his eyes. I will not let her tarnish his good name."

Valdryn was the first to break eye contact. He and the other battlemages stood up. Galadus's guards approached them to escort them out. The rotten stench began to overpower the incense. Valdryn's nostrils flared at the scent. "My apologies, Galadus. We will continue our investigations elsewhere."

"Yes. That would be wise." Galadus waved them out. Valdryn and the others made their way to the exit. "If you would like, Blademaster, my guards can escort you to the catacombs and you can see Balvas's coffin for yourself. We both know how Barathel would prefer a detailed report."

Galadus smiled a decrepit, toothy grin. He was a wrinkled shell of his former self, and Valdryn could sense it. This was not the paragon he knew. There was anger, not peace, in his voice. Valdryn turned around and merely offered a bow in agreement.

Upon leaving Galadus's home, a handful of guards rushed off into the lower depths of the Temple. Valdryn looked up at the scaffolding and balconies for signs of his spies but found nothing. He wondered about their haste but pushed it to the back of his mind to inform the others about the meeting.

"What did Galadus have to say?" asked Jonas. He was growing restless and uncomfortable with the all of the guards around. They were preparing for a fight they couldn't win but he didn't sense desperation. Instead, it was like a hivemind. They moved without fear or passion and simply set up defenses.

"Nothing good, unfortunately," said Valdryn. "Where are the guards running off too?"

"No idea. They're not exactly the most talkative people you'll ever meet," said Sir Brandon. "So, what now?"

"We're going to the catacombs." Valdryn motioned for the guards to escort them. He kept his distance from them so he could speak to the others without being overheard.

The room had grown eerily silent. Even the footsteps of the guards were muted, like shadows of death walking among the living. The sounds of the gathering by the entrance had faded and even the clangs of late-night mining had fallen silent.

"The catacombs?" Sir Brandon wondered. "What for?"

"To pay our respects." Valdryn followed the guards, resting one hand on the hilt of his sword. He saw the restored runes along the pillars outside the catacombs. Ruvo had taught the world various advance enchanting techniques. Most were for defenses or healing but few were ever for war.

He stared at the wall to his right for the moment. He could sense the cannon off in the distance with its aim fixated on him. It would take a weapon of magic and war to bring down the home of the god of magic and peace.

Chapter 10: The Storm

The catacombs seemed to go on forever. Long halls branched off of one another, creating a torchlit labyrinth of cold stone and hooded statues. Few guards were stationed here along each fork in the path. It was mostly caretakers, similar in appearance to the statues, that walked these halls. Their dark hooded cloaks helped them blend in with the shadows so as not to be too distracting.

Sir Brandon and his men stayed near the entrance. No one, not even the temple guards were to pass through. Valdryn could sense there was something wrong and he wasn't taking any chances. As far as he could tell, this was no longer friendly territory.

"So why are we really here?" Jonas whispered to his master. Only three guards made up their escort and they were far enough away to be out of ear shot but Jonas wasn't taking any chances.

"Something Galadus said." Valdryn kept his eyes on the guards ahead.

"What do you mean?" Ava followed to Valdryn's left. Her brother stayed close behind them.

"He said he never got to say goodbye to Balvas." Valdryn saw movement down the halls. They were being followed and were drastically outnumbered. "Then he said he watched him die."

Jonas tried to grasp the gravity of their situation. "Do you think that Galadus could—"

"I don't know, Jonas. It could've been a slip of the tongue but there is something wrong with Galadus and his guards. And there's no sign of Frederick or Marcus." Valdryn paused when he felt the temple shake. Dust and bits of stone fell from the ceiling. "Our plan derailed the moment we stepped foot in the temple."

"Don't mind the quakes," said a hooded caretaker in a shaky voice as he passed by. "The excavations have left parts of temple unstable."

"It'll take far more than a quake to bring the temple down," said another. It felt more like the dead were speaking to them. Only quick glimpses of the caretakers would show before their faces faded back into the darkness.

"A dwarven siege cannon with a fire core would do the trick," Bannon muttered under his breath. Jonas and Ava gave him a quick patronizing glance. "Did I say that out loud?" he wondered, genuinely.

Valdryn cleared his throat to silence the others. He pointed forward at the extravagant coffin. Most were sealed into the walls while Balvas's was left in the open, almost as a shrine to the late advisor. He bowed his head as he approached. Jonas followed by example while Ava and Bannon kept their distance.

The coffin was well cared for. Not a speck of dust laid on the surface and Phoenix Bell flowers pulsed with an illuminating orange glow. Small runes were etched all along the edges and a bust of Balvas sat on a ledge on the wall behind.

"I see Galadus spared no expense," Valdryn said aloud.

"Balvas was a great man and deserved far more for his services to the temple." The caretaker never looked back at them. She kept tending to the flowers and paid them little mind.

"I'm sure he was," said Valdryn. "How did he die if you don't mind me asking?"

The woman seemed confused, as if the wheels in her mind all paused at once. She stopped tending to the flowers and simply stared at them, searching for an answer in their glow. "I believe it was disease."

Valdryn stared at her. He could hear footsteps in the distance and the familiar stench from earlier was creeping in again. "Well, that's…strange."

"What is?" wondered the caretaker.

"Galadus said that he was poisoned," he replied, tightening his grip on his sword. "Presumably by a woman named Yvette."

Ava and Bannon didn't understand but Jonas knew all too well what he was doing. It reminded him of the day he met his master and began his apprenticeship. *Don't ever lie to Master Valdryn. He'll get you to reveal far more than you ever intended.*

"Ah yes, poison. My mind has withered with time unfortunately." The woman's arm began to shake as she looked away from the flowers and stared at Valdryn. Her tannish skin faded to a dark gray at the base of her neck. Her milky white eyes and toothless grin gave her the impression of a harmless old woman.

Valdryn unsheathed his sword. "Galadus actually said it was old age. On whose behalf do you lie?"

The guards brandished their weapons, forcing Jonas and the others to do so as well. The forced standoff in close quarters wasn't ideal but it was only a matter of time. The shadows among the wall were writhing, waiting for their chance. Valdryn was all too prepared.

"What are you doing, Valdryn?" Ava shouted.

"You wouldn't kill me over an honest mistake, would you?" The old woman fell backward, barely catching the edge of the coffin with her boney gray fingers.

Valdryn advanced towards her. "For an honest mistake? Never." The old woman sighed out of relief. "But this whole place is far from an 'honest mistake'. It is one big lie told by Balvas, no matter whose face he wears."

The old woman's brow turned from fear to anger. "That is unfortunate."

"Indeed, it is," replied Valdryn.

The woman pulled herself forward and leapt at Valdryn. One quick slash sent her head bouncing off the walls, black blood pooled around the body. Jonas and the others were stunned by the quick execution.

"What the hell is going on, Sir?" Bannon shouted.

"Undead. Burn them all," he commanded.

Streams of fire shot out by the twins kept the undead caretakers at bay. Valdryn and Jonas cut down any who made it past. The scent of charred flesh was a welcome replacement for the rotting stench from earlier.

A lanky caretaker leapt from the shadows and latched itself onto Valdryn's back. He saw a curved dagger come down from the corner of his eye. Valdryn quickly grabbed for the caretaker's wrist. He used his free hand to grab him by the hood and throw him into a nearby statue. It shattered and collapsed onto the caretakers in front of the group.

Valdryn tossed the tattered hood to the floor. The injured caretaker rose from the rubble, bones beginning to protrude through flesh and muscle. His skin was grey and cracked with various deep scars running down his body. His eyes turned black and hollow. His soul was gone. He let out a high-pitched howl before charging Valdryn again.

Valdryn slashed at his knees, forcing the undead to the ground. He grabbed him by the throat and held him suspended in the air. A blue aura formed around Valdryn's arm. A sudden pulse of energy sent the undead hurtling down the hall. The statue debris followed, like stone knives cutting through the air. The undead caretakers who weren't impaled by stone were thrown to the side.

"Keep pushing forward!" shouted Valdryn.

"I can see Sir Brandon," said Jonas. "They're surrounded too."

Sir Brandon and his knights were being overwhelmed by guards. Without magic, their only advantage was their shield wall. Valdryn focused his power on his fellow mages. An invigorating energy pulsed within them, heightening their own. Ava and Bannon felt the wave of power and unleashed a large pulse of frost magic. The side halls had iced over and the surrounding undead were frozen. Icy sculptures with arms extended lined their path.

The pair of battlemages took an axe in each hand charged through the frozen figures. With each chop, an undead would shatter and burst into icy shards of rotten meat. Their leaps and spins were mesmerizing to Jonas. Never before these two had he ever seen someone turn a battle into such a dance.

The group ran through the halls to regroup with Sir Brandon. The guards used spears to keep the knights at bay. Behind them were the caretakers with curved blades repeatedly swinging down on their shields. It was only a matter of time before they broke through their guard.

It was too risky for spells. Sir Brandon and his knights would be caught in the crossfire. Valdryn led the charge with quick arcing slashes, catching the caretakers unaware. The others kept their distance from the tight corridor and instead chose to guard the rear flank. There were still stragglers that survived the blast of frost and they were recovering rather quickly.

With each slash from Valdryn, the caretakers fell. Black blood stained the stone at his feet and covered the walls. He looked up to see Sir Brandon's shield covered in it. The halls were running slick, making it hard to gain footing.

"Good to see you're still with us, Blademaster," said Brandon.

"It'll take more than a handful of undead to stop us." Valdryn thrusted his blade down on one of the writhing bodies at the base of the stairs.

Brandon and his knights continued to push forward against the temple guards, slowly gaining more ground. Forming a shield wall, the knights could withstand the guard's spears. Every few moments, the knights would thrust their blades out above their shields at the closest guards.

"Ava! Bannon! Help clear the way up here." Valdryn shouted before joining his apprentice. "Jonas and I will keep you covered."

The siblings nodded and ran behind the knights. With their axes holstered, flames formed in their hands. Fireballs flew over Brandon's head, like miniature shooting stars lighting up the night sky. Some of the temple guards were set on fire, throwing their weapons down in a panic. They charged the knights but were immediately cut down.

From the catacomb halls, more caretakers staggered towards the group. Jonas felt the rush from combat. With ease, he sliced his way through them. His attacks were like scissors on paper. There clearly wasn't much holding these monsters together.

Valdryn traced his hand over his blade, engulfing it in a blue flame. As the undead fell one by one, their black blood caught fire. With the bodies piled up and the blood pooling, a barrier of blue flame began to repel the undead within the catacombs. Even the dead knew fear in the face of the raging inferno.

"Well, that should buy us some time, Master." Jonas stared at the bright blue flame.

A sudden roar let out from the darkness. Heavy footsteps echoed from the other side of the flames. Out of the dark and through the flames leapt a hulking undead with metal grafted to its skin. A spiked caged helm muffled its screams while it used its steel plated hands as weapons. The impact of the leap sent Valdryn and Jonas staggering backwards. Valdryn noticed Ava and Bannon turn around the face the screaming beast.

"No!" shouted the Blademaster. "Help Sir Brandon and make us an exit." He reignited the flame and faced down the giant undead. "We'll deal with this one."

Jonas nodded and entered a defensive stance. He stayed low and kept his distance. He called out to the beast, getting its attention. With a piercing roar, the creature charged quickly to Jonas. Its intense speed nearly caught him off guard. He quickly rolled out of the way. The creature's fist smashed into the wall, sending cracks in all directions and splintering stone through the air.

Valdryn slid forward and brought his blade down. The beast reacted faster than expected. In one fluid motion, it sidestepped the blade and kicked Valdryn back against the wall. It leapt at him with its fists raised. Valdryn quickly retaliated. He spun himself around and kicked off the wall, sliding just under the beast. A quick slash left a blue streak of flames flickering on its chest.

Valdryn looked to his apprentice. "Together, Jonas. We attack as one."

"Understood, Master," he shouted.

Together, master and apprentice charged the creature. Its agility allowed it to block both blades but their speed was also hard to match. It could block and dodge their attacks but it could not react quick enough to offer his own offense. Jonas found and opening and feigned an attack. When the creature went to block, Jonas sliced at its head. The cage helm protected it from a killing blow but the blade's tip slipped in and sliced open its cheek.

Blood poured out between the gaps in the helm. The pain fueled the creature's speed. It threw the pair against opposite walls. Before Jonas could recover, the creature kicked him back against the wall and kept him pinned with its foot. It was trying to crush Jonas beneath its weight. Jonas reached for his blade, barely touching the pommel with his fingertips.

Valdryn's impact on the wall formed a small crater. Blood dripped from his brow and he struggled to regain his breath. He looked up to Brandon and the others pushing through the guards. They had their exit. He looked over to see the beast leering over his apprentice. He reached for his blade, trying to summon the blue flames once more.

Jonas gave up on his sword and instead resorted to beating at the creature's leg to no avail. His armor was starting to give way. "Master! Help!"

The only thing Jonas could see in the moment was a blue flame protruding from the creature's gut. The blue light traced upward as the creature shrieked in pain. The fire engulfed the beast before Valdryn's blade split it up the middle and flipped it over his back. The creature collapsed into a bloody mess turned to ash. Valdryn picked his apprentice up.

"Master…" Jonas was struggling to catch his breath.

"It's okay, Jonas.," he said, struggling as well. "Let's get out of here."

They left the shadows of the catacombs behind them as they rejoined the others. Jonas winced and clutched his side every few steps but he was still able to wield his sword. There was still a handful guards to contend with. Together, master and apprentice would defeat them one by one. Valdryn would parry the oncoming attacks, knocking the guards off balance. Jonas would finish them off with a blade through the heart.

Sir Brandon and the others overwhelmed the others guards. Their armor and shield were caked in black blood. Ava and Bannon were in a frenzy, dismantling the undead, piece by piece. If a battlemage career fell through, they could easily find work as butchers.

A large group of guards blocked off the tunnel leading to the front of the temple. Valdryn and his companions were fatigued and surrounded. There was no escape through the front and they couldn't afford to retreat back to the catacombs.

"Shield formation. Now!" Sir Brandon and his knights fell in line in unison.

"We'll cover the flanks," said Ava, running to their left while Bannon ran to the right.

Valdryn and Jonas ran to support them when suddenly a swirling inferno crashed through the roof of the temple. It incinerated the guards and the makeshift house in the center of the room. Everything in its path was turned to ash.

"What was that?" shouted one of Brandon's men.

Valdryn looked up at the giant hole in the ceiling. Another one crashed behind him, collapsing the catacombs. *The cannon. All those people.* Valdryn shook his head. "It's the cannon. He fired the damn thing too soon."

"What do we do, Sir?" asked Brandon.

"Take your men and get as many of the civilians out as you can," replied Valdryn.

The temple was crumbling around them. Everything was catching fire and most of the guards had disappeared among the chaos. The crackling flames and crashing bangs from the rubble barely drowned out the screaming.

"What about you?" asked the knight.

"We still need to find Galadus. We can't afford to let him get away. Now go," ordered Valdryn.

Sir Brandon nodded and ran off with his knights. Valdryn ran with the others towards the newly excavated tunnels behind the ashes of Galadus's house. It was the only safe place out of reach of the flames.

"What do you think happened to Frederick and Marcus?" asked Bannon.

"If they're not already back at camp then their probably dead," said Valdryn. "We can't worry about them now."

The stairwell before them was dimly lit but unguarded. It was a moment of respite for them while the temple turned into chaos. They felt the walls shake as the cannon fired once again. The temple was coming down but the previous temple guardians would've surely created more than one exit.

The halls were littered with spiderwebs but otherwise remained seemingly bare. The stone rubble was pushed to the corners and small candles were laid out, following a wounding route towards the core.

"Where are all the guards?" wondered Ava.

"Galadus must have ordered them to attack Verric and the others," said Bannon.

Spiders the size of the average hand skittered along the floor. Tiny barbs covered their spindly legs. Jonas stomped on every one he could, leaving behind a crunch and thick green slime.

"Not a fan of spiders?" Ava chuckled.

"Not in the slightest." Jonas stomped on another. It made a nauseating squishing pop noise.

Ava laughed again to herself. A small flame sparked from her hands and scorched the surrounding webs. The flames crept up the wall, chasing the spiders into their nests. Another impact from the dwarven cannon sent quakes through the temple. The spiders and the ceiling began to crash down upon them.

"Not again," sighed Bannon.

The battlemages ran down the path closing before them, Ava's flames lighting the way. The temple hall was collapsing around them, trying to swallow the group into the darkness. Before they could be claimed, the group dove into the next chamber, narrowly escaping the collapse.

"By the gods, what has he done?" Valdryn wondered.

Everyone looked up to see what Valdryn was looking at. Thick streaks of blood covered the floor and led to a large wooden door. Scraps of savage butchery littered the corners and hung from the door.

"Ugh. Dammit," Bannon grabbed for the back of neck and pulled a spider away, it's leg wriggling, searching for an escape. He crushed it in his hands, the green ooze leaking through his fingers. "We're going to have a long talk with Verric."

"Agreed," muttered Jonas.

"Come here," said Valdryn. "Help me with the door."

With a few strong hefts, the group was able to open the door. A strong decayed breeze rushed path them. Jonas gagged at the foul stench. The buzzing noise of insects flooded the chamber. Among the piles of dead bodies stood a hooded figure, arms outstretched to the ceiling. Before him was a large hole in the ground. Swirls of purple light emanated from the hole, illuminating the chamber.

"Is this the best Barathel could do?" The figure pulled his hood down, revealing rotten flesh and bare bone. "Dwarven artillery is no match for dark magic."

"Is that Galadus?" Ava whispered.

"No," Valdryn replied. "Galadus has been dead for some time, hasn't he, Balvas?" Valdryn shouted across the room.

The figure smiled a decrepit grin. The flesh on his face had rotted and stretched with his smile, revealing a blackened tongue and cracked teeth. "Poor Galadus put too much faith in his light. He devoted his life to it, and yet it did not warn him of the poison awaiting him."

"You will pay for what you've done," said Valdryn.

"I will be rewarded for my service. My gods may have been defeated long ago but they are still very much alive, unlike yours. I will undo the Old Pantheon's actions and usher in the return of my Masters." Balvas extended his reach towards the pile of corpses. Black blood flowed along the ground in streams and pooled at his feet. Severed limbs and broken bones followed after.

Bannon started to scream uncontrollably. His veins turned black and blood leaked from his eyes. He writhed and shrieked in pain, as if his bones were being broken while he caught fire. He pounded on his own skull to relieve himself of whatever was taking over him.

Ava ran to her brother. "What's wrong, Bannon?" He shoved her away and pulled out his axe. He swung down at her but Jonas was able to block it just in time.

"It would seem one of my spiders got a hold of your poor dear Bannon. I'm afraid he'll never be quite the same again." Balvas laughed as the pool of blood grew larger. The bodies in the chamber were pulled to him. They were lifted in the air and revolved around him.

"What is he doing?" Jonas had never read of anything like this in his studies.

"I don't know, Jonas. But we have to stop him, no matter what," Valdryn responded with determination.

"You two go. I'll deal with my brother." Ava pulled out her axe and used magic in her off-hand to push her brother back. "I will save you, Bannon."

"You are all far too late. This world will be bathed in blood and shadow, born anew. Now, behold but a fraction of true power." Shadowy tendrils burst from Balvas and pierced the surrounding corpses, dragging them to him. Bones snapped and blood sprayed everywhere. A wave of shadows washed over the merged corpses.

From the large pool of blood, emerged an amalgamation of rotten flesh. Spikes of protruding bones covered the creature. Long jagged claws extended from its hands. Pieces of skulls held together by twisted muscles forged a larger skull, from which protruded a deep familiar voice. "This is no longer your world."

Valdryn and his apprentice stared in disgust. The towering creature before them was something out of the old legends. In the tales, it took multiple paladins just to subdue them. What could one Blademaster and his apprentice hope to achieve?

Valdryn shook his doubt away and summoned forth the blue flame on his sword once more. "Keep your distance, Jonas. Consider this the opportune time to test your fire magic."

"You don't have to tell me twice, Master."

Valdryn charged while Jonas hurled fireballs overhead. Balvas swatted them away, laughing. Valdryn slashed in a wild flurry but the creature was more agile then it appeared, dodging with ease. It flipped backwards, kicking Valdryn away. It let out a loud roar that shook the cavern. Parts of the ceiling began to crack and fall.

The roar sent Bannon into a frenzy. Slashing and spinning like a mad man, he pushed his sister closer to the hole in the center of the chamber. She tried to knock her brother off balance but his swings were too unpredictable. His speed and strength were somehow bolstered by the transformed Balvas. She could do nothing but dodge and block to keep her distance.

"Jonas. Use the new spell you've been working on." Valdryn slid under the creature's large claws. He extended his blade upward, carving into the large malformed arm above him. Jonas nodded and began to conjure a swirling flame around his arm.

"You try in vain, Battlemage. You will all fall—" A spear made of pure fire pierced his stomach. He stared down at the piercing flame, and laughed. "Pathetic." A large pulse of dark flames shot out from the creature.

Ava and Bannon were far from the blast, but were still toppled over. Ava took advantage and encased Bannon's arms in ice, pinning him to the ground. Jonas was sent backwards, rolling across the floor and towards the hole. Valdryn was the closest and received the brunt of the attack. His armor was slightly scorched as well as his tabard. He focused his magic to protect his body but the dark flames scarred his forehead and lower jaw.

"I told you all once already. You have no chance against the Abyss." Balvas summoned dark flames the engulfed his body. Flame covered tendrils protruded from his back and lashed out at Valdryn. The Blademaster cut them down but they kept growing back. One slipped past his guard and pierced his leg, forcing Valdryn to his knees. There was no visible wound but the pain was all too real.

Balvas stood over him, staring through him with hollowed eyes. He raised his claws, ready to strike, but reeled back in pain when Jonas shoved his sword into his shoulder. Blood splashed everywhere, temporarily blinding Jonas as it landed on his face.

"You little bastard!" shouted Balvas.

Bannon mirrored the creature's pain and broke free, knocking Ava to the ground. He pounced on her and wrapped his hands around her throat. She struggled to break free but to no avail.

"Bannon! Please!" She tried to reason with her brother, to reach whatever was left of him. She found nothing. With a single tear, she placed her hand on her brother's chest. Three bloodied icicles shot through his back. His grip on her throat loosened.

Valdryn summoned another barrier around himself, preparing for the final strike. Before he could make his move, the ceiling collapsed and the chamber was engulfed in flame. Another shot from the dwarven cannon brought the temple down around them. He looked around for an exit. He only found one.

"Ava! With me!" He pointed at the twisted creature Balvas had become. She wiped away her tears and nodded. Together they leapt at the creature. Ava drove her axe down into the creature's chest. Valdryn sunk his blade deep, piercing through the chest. Together, the battlemages and Balvas toppled over and fell into the hole at the center of the chamber. The darkness below swallowed them, leaving the storm above behind.

<u>Chapter 11: Dreams in the Dark</u>

Valdryn felt like he was falling endlessly, surrounded by the darkness. He remembered fire all around him as he drove the creature into the hole with Ava and Jonas but neither heard nor saw any sign of them. Isolated, he closed his eyes to center himself.

Where am I?

He tried to recall exactly what happened. He remembered the ceiling collapsing around them. The fire that engulfed the chambers and the wounds he sustained during the fight. He especially recalled the howling as Balvas was consumed by the darkness.

Where are the others? Where's Jonas?

He could see Ava leaping on top of the creature, driving her axe down deep. Jonas was clinging to the blade wedged into the creature's shoulder. They were swallowed by the darkness and lost somewhere in the nothingness.

Am I dead?

"Not yet."

Valdryn opened his eyes, startled by the voice. "Who's there?"

"My name…is lost to me. But I, too, find myself in a chamber of darkness yet I see it all."

"What should I do?" Valdryn asked.

"Remember where the light won't tread." The voice faded into the dark once more.

Valdryn slowly landed on his feet. It felt as though he was standing on water but there was still nothing in view. He swore he saw movement all around him but he was too focused on the voice. His memories drifted off to his childhood.

Kelvanon, the capitol of the Kalboria nation, was bustling with trade. Its location on the southern coast allowed for multiple harbors, promoting naval trade with the neighboring lands. The markets were packed with merchants peddling foreign merchandise. Silks and furs came from the far east while from the north came durable metals and exquisite gems.

"Exotic furs sure to set you above your peers!" shouted one merchant.

"Durable blades forged to bring down the greatest of giants!" shouted another.

Valdryn and his father always made their way to the market at the end of every month. His father brought him along for a chance to teach him about the different nations and cultures. A few lessons in history every once in a while, can go a long way. He studied events such as the rise and fall of ancient elven kingdoms as well as the growth of the southern empire and their line of warrior kings.

The pair passed through the crowds, nearing a small shop on the outskirts of the market area. A tattered banner hung from the door with a sigil of a diamond held by a dragon's claw stitched in the center, the sigil of the Delver's Guild. Some of the lesser valuables found in the guild's adventures were sitting in the window.

The inside of the shop had goods lining the shelves from one end to the other with pottery and strange figurines. Display cases held oddly crafted weapons by the counter while the tables in the center were covered in different cloths with foreign sigils. Young Valdryn once again found himself running over the armor stands.

"Good to see you again, Arcus." The grayed merchant leaned on the counter. A thick scar left him blind in his left eye. The hair on his head was receding but his beard grew thicker with each visit. "And you too, Little Valdryn."

"Hello, Uncle Harris." The young elf never looked away from the armor. He was too busy pretending he was a legendary knight slaying dragons and demons.

"Every month I see you, I could swear you've aged five years," said Valdryn's father.

"You've always been a cocky elf, Arcus," he waved his knife at him haphazardly.

The two stared at one another, leering. Both men tried to hold it back but couldn't help from bursting into laughter. Harris ducked under his counter and pulled up a small chest with the look of excitement overtaking his face. Though wrinkled, the wide-eyed giddy look he gave made him look young again.

"What's this?" asked Arcus.

"Open it," said the shopkeeper, in a half whisper.

He lifted the latches to reveal a blackened bracer with an empty gem socket in the middle. Runes covered the piece, seemingly etched erratically. Spots of what looked like polished bronze shone beneath the scorch marks.

"Is that what I think it is?" Arcus asked, awe-struck.

Harris's one good eye lit up. "These special weapons were wielded by the elite guards in the city of the gods."

"I thought everything was lost during the war?" Arcus mirrored Harris's excitement. Every guild member's dream was to uncover a relic of the gods. Many lost their lives in the Dragon's Crown mountains searching for this treasure but every once in a while, one lucky hunter would return, stoking the fires once more.

"As did everyone else. Then one day, a few rookie members stumbled into my shop, battered and bruised, and showed me this." Harris locked up the chest and stuffed it behind is counter. "You should come back to the guild. We'll get the old team together, maybe find another one of your swords. Remember that day?"

Arcus laughed. "How could I forget. Henley and Farris nearly fainted when they saw their first skeleton. But I have a family now, and they have to come first."

Harris nodded. "How is your lady, by the way? Haven't seen her in a while."

Arcus's smile faded. He looked at his son, forcing a smile. "Valdryn."

"Yes, father?" The little elf ran up to his father.

"Take this gold and find a good book from the markets." Arcus placed a pouch with the Delver's sigil in his son's hand. "Quickly now. We have to start heading back soon."

Valdryn ran to the door. Before leaving he looked back as his father said something to Harris. He couldn't hear what was said, but Valdryn noticed the merchant looked sunken with a faded smile.

The crowds were slowly beginning to disperse as the stalls often closed earlier than the shops. The merchants were shouting their final deals. Customers were arguing, trying to outbid their competition over fancy cloaks and shiny daggers. The book shop was a few doors down from Harris's. The faded image of a book was etched into the door with stacks of books blocking half the inside of the windows.

The shop was never all that busy. Not too many people cared for dusty tomes. Those seeking books of arcane interest would look to the university. Simple herbology books would find their way here but the shelves were often stocked with guides to the different nations and those detailing events of the past involving kings and their petty wars. While the books speaking of the gods would be found at their temples, other books of important mortals would be here for those interested in learning.

Arcus once brought home a book titled "The Sentinel Towers". It detailed the actions of each tower's knight-commander as the brave knights held their ground in the face of darkness, securing time for the nations to rally and overcome their greatest foe. Valdryn often dreamed of being a knight after reading that book.

The inside of the store was like a maze. Shelving running this way and that, statues and busts serving as markers for those who managed to get lost. Valdryn was looking for more stories on knights. He picked up a large book caked in dust with a faded title. After trying to make sense of the strange words, he put it back.

Another book that caught his eye was small and sported an orange cover, "Creatures of the Night, Vol. II". He flipped through the pages. Each chapter was dedicated to different creatures spawned by the darkness. The image of the chimera easily grabbed his attention. Never had he heard of such a beast.

"Strange and beautiful creatures," an elderly woman said. "But if you remain distracted for too long, it will eat you up child."

Valdryn looked up at the woman. She had strange jewels around her neck and faded marks ran down her arms. Upon closer inspection he noticed she was an orc. While her voice was more soothing than most, her green complexion and round ears with pointed lobes gave her away.

"Looking for books on creatures, child? Looking to be another knight famous for slaying monsters?" she asked.

Valdryn's eyes lit up at the notion, to become a hero. "Yes, ma'am."

The woman flashed a nearly toothless grin. "I can sense something in you, child, you are to become something great one day. Come, let me show you books worth your time."

The woman led him to the room with expensive books. A crystal ball rested on the table with a small pile of books. Each one looked unique and was in great condition. Some were covered in runes while others had small gems incrusted on the covers. The book keeper was running her fingers down the spines, looking for the perfect book.

Valdryn grabbed random books and read the title aloud. "Of Wings and Fire?"

"It's about dragons," said the orc woman. "But dragons are boring, child. They fly. They breathe fire, and they destroy things. A talented mage can do that with their little toe."

He put it back, disappointed. He grabbed another. This one was a blue book with gold trimming. A large amethyst rested in the center.

Something about the glow in the crystal was mesmerizing. "Beyond the Cosmos?"

"Theories on other worlds, where the gods came from, what else is watching us from beyond the skies. It's a bit out of your age group." She was too busy looking for a specific book to turn around.

A green book with pink leaves and vines down the spine rested on the table. "Nymphs of Nerros?" He went to open the book but the woman quickly snatched it away.

"That one is also out of your age group," she said, blushing. "Here, this one is more your speed."

She handed him a crimson book with a strange black symbol on the cover. An eye with an 'x' on top and a larger line running vertically down the middle. "Drovakai? What does that mean?"

"The symbol is that of an elite group within the Inquisitor's Guild, known for hunting down evil men and creatures alike," she said. "Not too long ago, one of their members, Isaac Kellen, hunted what he called a 'Drovakai', creatures of pure evil. This book details some of their hunts."

Valdryn picked it up in awe but was interrupted by the noise of the woman clearing her throat, holding her hand out.

"Right," Valdryn placed the gold in her hand but as her hand touched hers, something caused the woman to go wide eyed. She grabbed him by the wrist as she began to shake. Her jewels began to glow and her tattoos grew as vibrant as the first days she received them. Her grip tightened, bruising the boy's arm, then loosened once more as she fell back in her seat, breathless.

"Are you okay?" Valdryn ran up to the woman but she pushed him away.

"You are marked, Valdryn." The look on her face was exhaustion mingled with pain. It took what strength she had left in her frail body to regain some of her composure.

"How—"

"I see your fate, child," she interrupted. "A creature of darkness and destruction awaits you where the light won't tread. You will be broken and bloodied and shrouded in darkness before the end."

Valdryn backed away, stumbling towards the exit.

"The awakening of the soul within will mark the ending of this age. You will bear witness to it all, the beginning and the end.," she shouted.

Valdryn heard someone come through the front door. A familiar voice shouting, "Valdryn!"

"Valdryn!"

His hair was caked with blood and his armor was partly singed. Blood ran from his brow and down his cheek. His body felt stiff and bruised from the fall. He tried to stand but his head was pounding.

"Where am I?" He grabbed his head, trying to calm the ringing in his ears. "Under the temple?"

He looked at his surroundings. "Too dark." He calmed his breathing and raised his hand. "Need more light." He summoned a ball of starlight, illuminating the cavern. He jumped to his feet when he saw chunks of flesh and bone strewn about. He was alone in a pile of death. Ava and Jonas were missing as well as Balvas.

He reached for his sword but remembered he lodged it into the chest of that foul abomination. He heard the echoes of roars coming from deeper in the caverns. He pushed rubble and bone away, hoping his weapon had been removed in the fall. The roars grew louder but multiplied. There was more than just Balvas down here.

He heard shouting. "Come on you bastards. Is that all you got!"

Ava.

Then another voice. "Valdryn! Where are you?"

Jonas!

Valdryn abandoned his search for his sword. His people needed him. He picked up a large cracked bone. "I'm coming, Jonas! Ava!" He ran deeper into the darkness, with nothing but starlight to guide him.

Chapter 12: Where the Light Won't Tread

The cavern's paths were littered with bones from all manners of creatures. Streaks of blood and rotten flesh ran down the winding tunnels. Spiders made homes from the decrepit remains of the temple's ancient guardians. Bestial screams echoed all around Valdryn as he gathered his surroundings.

"Jonas!" Valdryn shouted repeatedly. He hadn't gotten a reply.

The noise of beasts grew louder and numerous, closer than ever. Even with mage light illuminating his path, Valdryn saw no signs of life. He chose to follow the freshest blood trails while keeping his weapon firmly at the ready. If he could find Balvas, surely, he'd find the others as well.

Valdryn came to a small open area with a large corpse in the center. All along the walls were remains of both man and beast. He noticed the hooves of the corpse, figuring it was a member of the local minotaur tribe from the southeastern part of the isle. Upon closer inspection, however, he noticed something was off. Unlike the standard minotaur biology, this one had razor sharp claws and teeth like a shark.

The Blademaster stepped closer to investigate when suddenly the body began to twitch. Valdryn backed up and raised the snapped bone he found like a club. He slowly approached the corpse, arms slightly extended. When he went to flip the corpse over, a large centipede-like creature burst through its back and wrapped itself around his arm. He felt it tightening, like a snake constricting its prey. The pain was overwhelming him when suddenly he heard his apprentice shouting.

"Master Valdryn! Where are you?"

He summoned forth the flame from his childhood once more, incinerating the strange creature. Nothing but ash remained, falling like snow. He charged forward towards the sound of Jonas's voice. He could hear the stampeding of hooves off in the distance. Much closer though, was the sound of skittering behind him. He had disturbed the nest of centipedes and they were now on the hunt for new food. One lurched at him from the wall with striking speed. Valdryn was able to roll out of the way, but just barely.

They ran along the walls and ceiling, hissing and chattering as they closed in on Valdryn. He summoned a wall of flame to block their path but they seemed unaffected. Nothing would come between them and their prey. These were much larger than the first one he encountered and pushed through the heat and the pain.

The ground beneath him began to shake. Sensing something large beneath his feet, Valdryn leapt to the side. The ground cracked up and the largest of the insects burst forward. It was of a dark crimson hue. Swirling vein-like purple lines ran along its head with thick spikes covering the length of its body. He could sense this was the queen.

The large creature lunged at Valdryn and crashed into the wall and disappeared. Valdryn sprinted down the tunnel, the walls rumbling all around him. The queen and her children broke through the walls in their attempts to catch their dinner. The bones of their victims scattered and ricocheted with each burst.

One of the insects lunged for Valdryn's legs, tripping him. It climbed on top and went for his throat but before the mandibles could reach their target, Valdryn stabbed a broken bone through its head. As he threw the creature to the side, the ground beneath him gave way.

He found himself in a pit with much smaller centipedes, hardly a threat. But as he looked up, he saw the queen burst through the ceiling. With their prey trapped, the hive slowed their pace and observed as their queen lowered herself, slowly approaching Valdryn.

"Come on then, beast. Come get your fill." Valdryn gritted his teeth and stared at the queen.

Her mandibles chattered as the body started to coil. Her children piled on top of one another to get a view in hopes of scraps.

"I'm ready to die," he whispered under his breath. He summoned his fire aura once more, his skin sporting a faintly orange glow. "But I'm not going to make it easy for you."

As the queen lowered herself around Valdryn, the fire aura singed her outer carapace. She was unaffected as she quickly healed. Valdryn had studied healing capabilities of diverse creatures before but this was unnatural. He sensed an energy pulse through its body. The purple veins had engorged and ran further down the length of the insect's body.

The queen squeezed around her prey, lifting him up. Valdryn freed his hands, trying to scorch the beast through its healing but to no avail. It was getting harder for him to breathe when the queen began to tilt her had back, preparing for a fatal strike. Valdryn closed his eyes, prepared to meet his end.

With a shaking boom, a loud roar echoed through the tunnels.

"Keep running, Jonas!" shouted Ava.

Valdryn opened his eyes with a sharp golden glow. The queen lunged at him but he caught one of her mandibles, holding her head at bay. With his other hand, he punched through her mouth and down her throat. A similar orange glow ran through her body and forcing her to shake violently. In an instant, her body exploded, spilling boiling blood everywhere. The remains of the hive fled at the sight of their fallen queen.

Some spikes from the queen remained intact. Valdryn grabbed two as a means to climb out. The spikes dug into the earth and stone with ease. He looked behind him but the tunnels seemed vacant now. The skittering stopped and a brief silence fell on the walls. Valdryn took a moment to breathe before breaking off into a sprint.

The next room he came to was a bloodbath. The remains of corrupted minotaurs and centipedes were strewn about. One minotaur was pierced from head to toe in bloodied icicles. Only one still lived but barely. It was sitting up, back against a pile of corpses. One of Ava's axes was buried in its stomach.

Valdryn approached it, ready to strike, but it made no motion to defend itself.

"What happened to you?" Valdryn asked.

It squinted up at him, confused. Minotaurs were often territorial but preferred peace over war. Through trade with nearby settlements, the majority of their tribes know the basics of common tongue, or so they should.

Valdryn crouched by the wounded creature. "Answer me."

Puzzled, it replied, "Ik'laeth numra."

"What?" Valdryn had never heard this language before. He never even saw it in his studies of ancient languages.

"Ik'laeth numra."

"I don't understand. Can you speak the common tongue?" he asked.

Its breathing was picking up as tears fell from its eyes. It reached for the axe in its gut. Valdryn jumped back. "Ik'laeth numra!" it shouted. "Ik'laeth numra, Molrog!" It wretched the axe free and shoved the blade into its throat, ending its own suffering.

"Molrog?" Valdryn stared in confusion. "What does he have to do with this?" Valdryn regathered his senses and pulled the axe free. He saw a fresh blood trail leading out through the back of the room.

"Where are you, Valdryn?" Ava's shouting was so close now. He didn't have time to worry about Molrog. He sprinted off though the tunnel, large claw marks raked along the walls. Bits of decayed flesh were scattered around along with tattered scraps of armor.

Something shined through the blood on the floor. He knelt down to find a broken sword. The top half of the blade had been snapped off and blood coated the base. Upon closer inspection, the hilt looked familiar. *Jonas*. A blood chilling scream came from up ahead. Valdryn clutched the blade and ran ahead.

Amongst piles of bones, stood Balvas. Valdryn's blade was still buried in his shoulder. There were fresh wounds still bleeding the black rot within. Ava and Jonas had managed to put up a fight but they were cornered. She stood between Balvas and a bloodied Jonas. She was wounded and her barrier was fading.

"I warned you what would happen." Balvas's new body was scarred and singed but still he lived. "Your end has come."

He raised his giant claw for a fatal swipe when suddenly he was caught off balance. Valdryn sunk the broken blade deep into his ribs and slammed the axe repeatedly into his shoulder, trying to hack off his arm.

"Get him out of here, Ava!" Valdryn shouted.

"But what about—"

"Now!"

Balvas let out a painful roar, blood spilling everywhere. "No one escapes here alive."

Valdryn hooked the axe into his shoulder, leveraging himself to pull the monstrosity back away from the others. He pulled the broken sword free and drove it deep into Balvas's eye. A shrill of a scream nearly deafened Valdryn.

"Enough of this!" Balvas reached up with a writhing claw. Clenching his fist, he slammed Valdryn down into the floor. Valdryn's axe was pinned against his body. He tried to free his arm but Balvas was crushing the breath from his body. "Why continue to struggle? Your gods gave their lives and even that couldn't stop the darkness."

"Correct me if I'm wrong," Valdryn coughed. "But I don't see your gods around either."

Balvas lowered to stare down at Valdryn, face to face. "That is because you are blind."

Valdryn smiled, eyeing the blade protruding from his eye. "Now isn't that the pot calling the kettle black."

Balvas tightened his grip, blood dripping down his skull. He flexed his open hand, the bone like claws caked in blood. "Is that truly what you want your last words to be?"

"Matthias always said it's not your words but your actions that matter." Balvas could feel something burning beneath his grip. "And you know how he loves to right all the time." Balvas loosened his grip, allowing Valdryn to grab the burning axe on his chest and slice through the claw digging into his shoulder. With both hands now free, Valdryn grabbed for the blade in Balvas's eye. Rather than pulling it free, he ignited it.

Screaming in agony, Balvas swatted Valdryn away with enough force to break through the cavern's wall. Balvas wretched the blade free, extinguishing the flames. He looked around but between the pain, smoke, and missing eye, he lost Valdryn. "If you won't die, then I'll settle for the ones you care about. Starting with your apprentice." He ran off, tracking Jonas's blood trail.

Valdryn looked around the chamber he had been thrown in. It was far different than the rest of the caverns. There were skeletal remains in here but they were evenly lined up, their weapons placed on their chests. Most of the blades were caked in rust or broken, most likely from a battle long ago.

He reached for one of the swords. It seemed sturdy enough but upon tapping it on the ground, it shattered. In the center of the chamber was a pile of armor and other relics. Through the dust and rust, Valdryn could make out the emblem of the Burning Sun. The other garb closely resembled that of the temple guards. "All of this is from the last war," he muttered to himself.

Among the relics he found a blade not nearly as rusted as the others. There seemed to be nicks in the blade but was otherwise in good condition, all things considered. As he grabbed the hilt, he felt a sharp pain in his shoulder. His wound needed to be tended to before he could effectively fight again. An image of Balvas flooded his mind. *He needs to die. No matter the cost.* "But first, I need to save Jonas."

Valdryn climbed out of the chamber. The familiar scent of burnt flesh filled the air. Rather than shaking in disgust however, Valdryn smiled. "I hope it hurt." He stumbled through the chamber, one hand holding the sword with the other holding his shoulder.

Up ahead, Valdryn heard more shouting followed by a loud crashing sound of metal on stone. A sickening deep laughter echoed down the tunnels. "Come, Valdryn. Come watch him die."

Valdryn's eyes widened as his heart raced around his mind. "Jonas!" He kept shouting as he ran down the winding tunnel. "Jonas! Speak to me!" He never received a response. He came to another chamber with multiple paths. A woman was kneeling in the corner, crying. Valdryn recognized the armor. "Ava? What's wrong? Where is Jonas?"

Ava turned around. A large cut ran down her cheek. She tried to stand but she collapsed back to her knees. Her leg was broken. Beside her was Jonas. He was covered in blood and gasping for air.

Valdryn ran to his side. "Jonas."

"Master." Jonas coughed up blood. "I tried my best."

Valdryn could feel his stomach twisting and turning. "I know you did. Better than any other battlemage I know."

"Wait until we tell Tariv that." Jonas smiled; his teeth had turned crimson. "I'll have my own story to tell."

Valdryn saw the blood pooling beneath him. "It'll be pretty hard to top this one." He did everything he could to hold back his tears.

Jonas saw the pain in his master's face. "No magic can save me now, can it?"

Valdryn looked at Ava for an answer, anything at all. She merely shook her head. Valdryn shut his eyes, but a tear still broke through. He felt a hand on his, caked with blood. He turned to see his apprentice, tears washing away the blood.

"It hurts, Master." He coughed up more blood. Every breath, every motion brought him pain.

Valdryn barely heard him. In his apprentice's tears, he saw his own. He saw reflections of his home on fire. He saw his father bleeding out in his arms as the so called 'Heroes of the Plains' arrived late to save anyone. *What good is being a hero when you can't save anyone? You can still save him from the suffering. Bring him peace.* The words enveloped his mind. "I know, Jonas." He tightened his grip on the blade, waiting for an answer.

Jonas looked down at the blade, then back to his master and nodded. "It's okay."

Valdryn raised the blade, pointing it at Jonas's heart. "No. It's not. But it will be, and soon." He plunged the blade through his heart. The boy let out a few last breaths. Valdryn pulled him close and whispered in his ears, "I promise." His apprentice went motionless and silent when Valdryn pulled the blade free.

"I'm sorry—" Ava tried to speak through her own pain.

"Where is he?" Valdryn never looked at her. He simply wiped the tears from his face.

She pointed towards a dark corridor. "Please don't go. You're too injured."

"I have to do something, Ava," he stammered. "He needs to be stopped before anyone else gets hurt."

"And how will dying do that exactly?" A deep voice boomed from behind them.

Valdryn spun around, blade at the ready. "Show yourself."

A horned figure stepped forth from the shadows. A minotaur showing no signs of corruption with a warhammer capable of bringing down a giant in one swing. Clawed scars decorated his cheeks.

Valdryn lowered his blade, when he recognized the local chieftain. "Molrog? What are you doing down here?"

"Looking for you," he replied. "Sir Brandon asked for our aid when he saw the temple collapse."

"I am relieved to hear he made it out and I thank you for your concern but Balvas needs to die—"

"And he will, Valdryn." Molrog's voice shook the cavern like an earthquake. "But you won't be the one to do it if you chase after him now. Besides, there are more pressing matters to attend to."

"What do you mean?" Ava asked.

"Barathel and his lapdog, Verric, are planning a mass execution. He's going to kill innocent people and make a spectacle of it." Molrog spat at the notion.

Valdryn looked down the tunnel where Ava previously pointed. Every fiber of his being screamed at him. *Hunt him down! Kill him! For Jonas!* He looked down at his apprentice and the anger was replaced with remorse. The sorrow overwhelmed his anger. The flame in his heart died down, the embers patiently waited. "No more innocent die today."

Molrog nodded. "Allow me to help with your boy. You need to reserve your strength for what's to come."

"Thank you." Molrog picked up Jonas's body and Ava as well. Valdryn looked at the drying red handprint on his arm. Jonas's limp arm swayed with the minotaur's stride. Something changed in him the day he lost the man who raised him. He felt a similar shift now that he lost the boy he raised.

Chapter 13: Bloodied, Not Broken

Molrog's tribe occupied the coastal caverns on the southern half of the isle. Minotaurs were one of the few ancient races left after the war. Their homes were built into caverns, taking advantage of the natural protection from the elements. The guards of Molrog's tribe favored animal leathers and bones as armor to represent their successful hunts.

The tribe's healers were tending to Ava's injuries. They had given her medicine that quickly dulled the pain and sent her into a deep sleep. Her leg was wrapped in a brace and bandages covered her arms. Her injuries were bad but the healers were talented with an array of medicine. Given ample time and care, she would make a full recovery.

Jonas's body was in the bed on the opposite side of the hut. His bloodied broken armor still covered his wounds. His skin was as pale as snow and the blood on his face had dried and stained his cheeks. The pain on his face had faded, leaving behind only tear stained streaks in the blood.

Molrog was washing off the blood in a nearby pool of water. His mate, Galla, was helping with the clotted tufts of fur. They had matching golden rings adorning their horns and swirling paint on their shoulders. She had softer features than Molrog, but she was also accustomed to war.

"That poor boy," sighed Galla.

"Young Jonas is at peace. It's his master who concerns me," replied Molrog.

"Who is he?" she wondered.

"Matthias's successor," he replied. "He's seen death before and that's what worries me. Every death takes its toll. Every soul has its breaking point."

The pair looked over to the cliff. Valdryn was sitting, legs over the edge, looking out over the sea. A storm was forming in the distance and coming their way. The blood on his armor had dried, including Jonas's bloody handprint on his arm. *You had to do it.* His new sword rested in his lap. He shifted his gaze from the hand print to the blade.

Under the sunlight, it didn't appear to be as damaged as he first thought. The nicks in the blade were smaller than he thought and there wasn't nearly as much rust. *He was suffering.* He shook his head. "It was my fault."

"How so?" Molrog took a seat beside him, letting the air dry his upper body.

Valdryn looked over to Molrog, eyes bloodshot. "He shouldn't have been here. I should've known better."

Molrog exhaled though his nose, staring out at the waves. "Don't waste your heart on 'should haves' and 'could haves'. It will kill you faster than any battle."

"You get that from a fortune teller?" Valdryn huffed.

Molrog smiled. "Even if I did, it wouldn't make it any less true. And right now, there are people who need you to focus."

Valdryn stared at his new blade, looking for answers in the dark metal. "What am I supposed to do? Walk into the capital and execute Verric and Barathel?"

"If you have to." Molrog didn't look at Valdryn. He kept his gaze to the distance, perhaps even beyond the storm. "Ik'laeth Numra. I'm not sure of the direct translation, but 'Numra' references what we call the Abyss."

Valdryn caught his reflection in the blade. *The Abyss draws near*. The cracking of thunder grew closer as the water turned restless. Visions of Jonas and his father dying flooded his mind. He thought of temple residents being reduced to ash by the siege cannon. He remembered Gordok and that deadly machine of his. Surely Sandra enjoyed firing it more than she'd like to admit. "I'm going to need new armor if I'm to do anything."

"It's already been prepared for you. It's nothing an esteemed battlemage would wear but it will do." Molrog stood and motioned for Valdryn to follow him. Together they approached the hunter's hovel.

The hunters as well as their homes sported strange bones for armor and decoration. A skull with large fangs and four eye sockets rested above the entrance to the hut. Another skull, elongated with four mandibles rested on a shield with crossed curved swords behind it. These remains were not of this world, but perhaps from another among the stars.

Inspecting the various skulls, Valdryn was in awe. "What kind of creatures are these?"

"I wish I knew," replied Molrog. "These trophies are from a very long time ago and from tribes long forgotten."

Valdryn picked up a humanoid skull. It was thick like an orc's but the teeth were unusually sharp. There was a dried green residue staining the cracks along the skull. "Do you think we'll be forgotten?" *Surely.*

"Absolutely."

Valdryn looked back, expecting something more optimistic. He had many mentors who would say the same but perhaps he was still too focused on his apprentice. A wounded heart always seeks comfort.

"Everything is forgotten eventually. It's inevitable." Molrog opened up a trunk containing Valdryn's new armor. "But if you are quick enough, we just might get a few more centuries." Molrog smiled, but his eyes gave way to fear.

Valdryn took the armor from Molrog, investigating the new garb. It was flexible and mundane. It came with a single shoulder guard for his left arm and a series of leather bandoliers to keep daggers and potions fastened tight. Again, he paused when he glimpsed the bloody handprint on his plate armor.

Molrog saw this and went to take his leave. "Take the time you need, but don't take too long."

Valdryn had the hut to himself. Alone with his thoughts, he dropped to his knees. Tears ran down his cheeks, dripping down on his gauntlet. The dried blood started to flake and smear.

"...my fault..." Valdryn's stomach was twisted and hollow. He pounded his fists into the ground.

Not yours. Theirs.

"...he was there because of me..."

He was there because of Barathel. He died because of Verric.

Valdryn wiped away his tears, staring at the surrounding skulls. In death, he found nothing but chaos but now he found comfort among the ancient dead. The quiet calm was all he needed for reflection.

You prepared him for fighting. You couldn't have prepared him for them. For politics and paranoia.

Valdryn clenched his fists. He loosened his plate armor and replaced it with the thick leather. He grabbed his blade and tested the grip of his gloves. They were comfortable, durable, and flexible. His movement wasn't as restricted as before and the dark coloring would help him hide in obscurity.

A makeshift scabbard rested by the door. It was nothing extravagant. Standard wood wrapped in a similar dark leather had a crudely stitched tree at the top with growing roots. Valdryn ran his finger along the stitching before exiting the hut.

Ava was still in a deep sleep, recovering from her wounds. Her forehead was damp with sweat but the healers assured him that was to be expected. Valdryn grabbed her hand. "Hang in there, Ava. The fight isn't over yet."

He walked over to his apprentice. His possessions were kept in a trunk at the foot of his bed, the glint of the freshly cleaned armor shining through. The healers had replaced his torn armor with tattered clothing. His wounds were cleaned and sealed. Valdryn took his hand and knelt at his side. He placed an object wrapped in cloth on the floor.

"May the sight of Ruvo guide you through the dark. May the might of Kal'bore protect you on your path. May the grace of Allistara soothe your pain." Valdryn placed the wrapped item on Jonas's chest. He unraveled it, revealing the gauntlet with the bloody hand print.

"I never pictured you as a man of faith," groaned Ava.

"You should be resting." Valdryn turned to her.

"As should you." The two smiled at one another, clearly holding back tears. "I'm sorry."

Valdryn shook his head. "Don't be. We both lost someone in there. Verric, Barathel, Balvas…they'll all pay for it."

Ava grunted in pain and gritted her teeth. "You know there's no turning back from that, right? Our opinions of them mean nothing if they're still getting results."

Valdryn looked back at his apprentice. The stillness in the boy's face was all too familiar, beckoning the knots in his stomach to tighten. He remembered the day he buried his father along with half of his neighbors. "His 'results' often involve burying the innocent. Results don't mean a thing when everyone loses."

Ava smiled reluctantly and nodded. "Just be careful. One dead battlemage is too many, but three—"

Valdryn smiled. "I know, get some rest. I'll need all the help I can get when this is done."

"Yes, Sir." She laughed before closing her eyes and fading back to sleep.

Valdryn took the gauntlet from his apprentice's chest, whispering a final prayer. "Watch over me, Jonas. And forgive me for what I've done and what I must do."

Molrog was waiting outside with three of his hunters, studying the sky. The storm was growing closer and larger, the lightning crashing down upon the water. Most of the tribe was bringing their supplies into storage. An older minotaur had joined him as well. His fur was a mix of white and grey with black and blue tribal marking all over his body.

"It appears our savior is ready," the old minotaur said as Valdryn approached.

"I am no one's savior," Valdryn replied.

"That remains to be seen," huffed Molrog. "This is our shaman. We have been discussing the meaning behind the words of the Lost you encountered in the caverns."

"Anything useful?" he asked.

"Disturbing is more accurate," the shaman said. The staff he used for support was adorned with feathers and bones. One large fang at dagger length rested at the top. "Without proper context, the old tongue is hard to understand. But it's safe to say he was asking for forgiveness in the end."

"And should we succeed, he may have it," interjected Molrog.

"Indeed", the shaman continued. "Ik'laeth Numra roughly translates to 'Kingdom of the Dark Born'."

Valdryn felt sharp pain in the back of his skull. *The city of the gods.* "You mean Sotiras?"

"Perhaps. It has never been referred to as a city of the dark before," said the shaman.

Valdryn took a moment to understand this new information. "Why would a Lost be calling Sotiras, a city of light and life, a dark kingdom? Sotiras was built by the gods and was later sacrificed to keep the Abyss at bay."

"Either way, it does not matter," said Molrog. "You need to focus on the present problem, Valdryn. We'll continue deciphering the meaning behind these words."

"Agreed," said the shaman.

Valdryn nodded. The shaman took his leave while Molrog and the hunters led Valdryn to the border of their home. Their path took them down towards the coast and back up to an open field. From here, they could see the smoking rubble of the once beautiful temple. Barathel and Verric's war banners flown in the distance.

"Here is where we part ways, Valdryn," said Molrog. "My hunters will escort you to the camp. Be wary, ever since the temple fell, undead have been spotted along the Isle."

"I appreciate it, but a walk on my own will clear my mind." Valdryn traced the crude emblem on his scabbard once more. "Before you go—"

"You wish to know of sigil on your scabbard."

Valdryn nodded.

"It's a symbol of kinship. The tree represents the world and the roots symbolize the bonds we forge. Without the roots, the tree could not survive." Molrog closed his eyes, as though recalling a memory. "And so too would the world die, should all our bonds break."

Valdryn thought of his days as a soldier under Matthias. He remembered the days he spent as an apprentice, harnessing his inner arcane powers with Tariv. He thought of Sir Brandon, Ava and Bannon, and Jonas. He blocked out the image of Jonas's body and focused on the earlier years. It made him smile. "Thank you. I will remember your words."

The two nodded and parted ways. Molrog returned to his village. Valdryn made his way towards the camp for answers.

Chapter 14: Regret

Valdryn followed a path littered with corpses. Molrog's hunters had been busy, spearing the undead or pelting them with arrows. Some were pinned to trees while others were half buried in the mud. The once beautiful Isle was returning to a state of war, blood and death stretching for miles once again.

The wind had picked up, scattering the leaves and broken branches along his path. He looked around as he made his way towards the camp. The corpses belonged to both sides. Fallen soldiers from Ruvo, Balvas's corrupted guards, and risen dead from ages past were scattered about.

So many dead.

"We survived one war just to kill each other in another." Valdryn flexed his hand, feeling the scar brush up against the leather of his glove. The pain from the burns on his brow lingered, just enough to draw his focus elsewhere.

Such is the way of the world.

"It shouldn't be," he said to himself. "We should be better."

The words of every hero.

Valdryn shook his head as he neared the camp. "They're gonna think I'm crazy talking to myself."

Archers were stationed on the perimeter in case any undead approached the camp. Someone apparently thought impaling several of them around the camp would somehow deter the dead. Large piles of corpses were being burned down by the temple ruins. Far enough to not smell but the smoke could be seen for miles.

"Halt!" shouted one of the guards. "State your business."

Valdryn pulled down the hood of his cloak. He raised his hands so as not to startle the guards. One of them instantly recognized the bright green eyes though the new scars nearly caught him off guard. "Blademaster, apologies. We thought…we heard—"

"Not quite yet. Where's Verric?" Valdryn pulled his hood back over his head and approached the guards.

"The Captain returned to Ruvo with the traitors from the temple," the guard replied.

"What of Sandra? Sir Brandon?" quizzed Valdryn. He never broke his gaze on the guards, staring them down as if looking for more in their answers. It put them on edge but they were quick to regain their composure.

"Sandra is hunting down the undead in the forest with the other mages," answered another guard. "I believe Sir Brandon is with Ironveins in his tent."

Ironveins. It was his device that brought the temple to ruin.

Valdryn nodded and walked past the guards. Before he left, he turned to one of them. "Who reported my death?"

The guards looked at one another, muttering under their breath. "Well, Verric read the report aloud but Four-Fingered Fred and his criminal friend were the ones who gave him a list of names to review."

Valdryn turned from the guards and proceeded further into the camp. The smell of cooked meat and fresh pastries filled the air, a welcome change from the outer perimeter. Soldiers currently off duty celebrated by drinking kegs dry. Others were dancing and playing games. The older, more seasoned soldiers were off praying or dwelling on the memories of the dead.

They're so certain they've won, that they're safe.

Davon was sitting with a few of the older soldiers. There were trunks and piles of random memorabilia around them. They were making lists of each item and pairing them with names. A few of the younger fighters nearby had to take to drink, not in celebration but in sorrow.

"Darren Moser. Golden chain," muttered one of them.

"Louis Vaine. Spectacles," said another.

"Bannon Tollis. Family locket." Davon rubbed his brow.

Valdryn walked up to the gentlemen without their notice. He placed a torn tabard on the table. "Jonas Porter. Battlemage's tabard."

The soldiers looked up at him. Davon's eyes widened with a breath of relief. He stood up and embraced his friend. "I thought you were gone."

"So, I've been told." Valdryn grip wasn't as tight as the old man. He was here with a purpose and couldn't allow anything to slow him down.

"Jonas? He..." Davon waited for a response.

Valdryn motioned for Davon to follow him. He waited until they were out of earshot before saying anything. "Jonas died during our escape."

"What happened?" Davon wondered.

"There's a series of tunnels beneath the temple. We were hunting Balvas while trying to evade the fires," Valdryn replied, biting back the angry tone in his voice. "Balvas killed him before we could escape."

"I'm so sorry, Valdryn. I know you cared for the boy. He would've made a fine battlemage." Davon rested his hand on Valdryn's shoulder. He tried to flash a reassuring smile but the recent death toll

"He *did* make a fine battlemage." He looked to the dark clouds growing closer. None of the soldiers seemed to care, none of the younger ones anyway. It was their first victory, or so Verric and Barathel would have them believe. They just witnessed Ruvo's temple crumble on innocent people and the first they thing they do is drink and sing. "I need a favor, Davon," said Valdryn.

"Anything," replied the old fighter, eagerly.

"It's not going to make any sense right now, but I need you to get this camp back in order." Valdryn stared at his friend, a newfound fire in his eyes. "The war is not yet over. Gather those who can fight and prepare to march on Ruvo."

"On Ruvo? What's happening?" Davon was lost, ignorant to what truly happened, what will happen.

"Balvas survived and he's not human anymore. Furthermore, Verric is about to execute innocent people for the sake of his career. I won't allow that to happen." A group of guards were walking by. Valdryn eyed them down, wary of who might be under Verric's command. "Go. Get the fighters ready and get to the capital when you can."

Davon nodded and rushed off. Valdryn could hear him shouting at some of the more dysfunctional soldiers. He couldn't help but smile. Out of the corner of his eye, he spotted a man with a familiar brand on his arm.

Marcus.

Valdryn trailed him through the camp. Marcus barely acknowledged any of the nearby guards as he weaved through the celebrating crowds. Valdryn noticed a limp in his walk. His left leg was lagging with a freshly stained bandage below the knee.

Did you get that while running away?

Valdryn gripped the hilt of his sword, his knuckles growing tighter. From the corner of his eye, he glimpsed the smoldering ruins of the temple. The once proud and beautiful monument was now cast in the shadows of war banners. He loosened his blade, ever so slightly so as not to cause any alarm.

Marcus clutched his side as he passed the infirmary tents. Several soldiers were resting outside with bandages and burn scars. Some from within the tents were calling out, hoping somehow, somewhere, the gods would listen. Marcus took a vial from his pocket and handed it to a man nearly wrapped from head to toe in soiled bandages.

"Here you are my friend. This will help with the pain." The man thanked him and Marcus went on his way.

As if you really care.

They had come to a large tent on the edge of camp. The only nearby guards were those on patrol. Marcus disappeared into the tent, Valdryn staying close behind. The inside was dimly lit with a table in the center. The food on the table was barely picked at by the tent's occupants. Gordok sat at the head but was a stark contrast compared to the soldiers from earlier. His face was sunken. He was one of the few who saw this day as a loss, not a victory.

He was accompanied by a few others. Valdryn recognized Sir Brandon and his fellow knights. Their armor was replaced with simple clothes. They kept their swords with them but nothing else. There was another man, sitting opposite of Gordok. His arm was wrapped in bandages and he was missing a finger. Marcus sat down beside him.

Of course, both of them made it out.

"What are we to do?" Fred was swirling the cheap alcohol in his cup.

"What *can* we do? Let Verric have his parade and be done with it." Marcus clutched his leg, wincing in pain.

Sir Brandon slammed his fist down. "We can't just leave those people to die."

"You may be a knight and have a code to follow but in case you haven't noticed the brand on my arm, I'm under their thumb." Marcus spat.

The men began shouting at one another, like dogs circling a tree and barking at a squirrel. Forever loud, forever out of reach. Gordok massaged his temples, trying to block out the noise. "Enough," shouted the dwarf. His cup spilled over the table. "With Valdryn missing and the guards drunk and blind from 'victory', we are the only ones who can do anything."

Valdryn loosened his grip on his sword and took in his surroundings. These men aren't happy, they are broken. "I should have never brought that damn cannon here. This is all my fault, and now I have to make it right." Gordok was shaking from the fear and anger rising inside.

"How?" pondered Fred.

"I don't know." Gordok wasn't made for leadership. He could build and repair anything laid before him but he wasn't one to make the tough decisions.

Valdryn felt his own anger subside for a brief moment. Gordok was not responsible for any of this. Verric and Barathel used him for their own ambitions. He took a deep breath and stepped forth from the shadows. "You can start by pulling yourselves together," he said in a stern voice.

"Master Valdryn?" Fred had turned pale. "Is that really you?"

Gordok felt a weight lift from his shoulders. "It has to be. But Verric said—"

"Verric said a lot of things and very few of them were truths," Valdryn said. "I aim to cut that liar's tongue out once and for all."

Brandon looked at the other knights. They swore their oaths to principles and ideals, not the those in power. "We're with you, Valdryn."

Valdryn looked at Gordok though he knew what answer to expect. He replied with a simple nod and a fist on his heart.

"Good," he said, turning to the knights. "Find Davon and he'll tell you everything."

The knights departed in search of their instructor. Leaving Gordok, Fred, and Marcus behind. The two infiltrators looked on at the Blademaster nervously. Gordok refilled his cup and one for Valdryn. He thanked the dwarf but never took his eyes from Fred.

Marcus stuttered out a few words while trying to stand. "Perhaps we should—"

Valdryn unsheathed his sword and placed the point of the blade under Marcus's chin. "You will sit and tell me everything."

Gordok jumped back, confused. He knocked over his cup once again. "What are you doing?"

"These two left us behind. If they had stuck to the plan, Jonas and Bannon would still live and the temple wouldn't be a pile of rubble." Valdryn's temper was known to very few and it easily shifted the atmosphere in the tent.

Fred quickly downed his drink, gritting from the burn in his throat. "If we hadn't escaped, we would all be dead."

Fred and Marcus kept to the shadows, taking care to avoid the guards. The upper halls of the temple were fairly empty. Most of the crates had been moved into storage rooms as the rubble was cleared away. A few guards were on patrol but this was far from a challenge for the pair of infiltrators.

They weaved between the halls and upper ramparts. Below them they spotted Valdryn and the temple guards escorting him. Fred couldn't help but wonder about the lack of guards in the

upper reaches. Most of them were set along the
path to Galadus.

"This is all too easy," whispered Marcus.

"That's what worries me," replied Fred.

A heavy iron gate blocked their path with no
way of opening it from their side. They noticed
makeshift guard towers through cracks in the
upper wall. Scaffolding ran up towards a hole in
the top.

"Only one way to go." Fred pointed up,
sighing.

"You know I hate heights." Marcus felt the
hairs on his neck stand as his mouth went dry.

"I'll hold your hand, Princess." Fred
couldn't help but smile, holding out his hand.

Marcus swatted his hand out of the way and
clambered onto the scaffolding. Fred stayed close
behind, pausing every so often to see if any guards
had noticed. Beams of moonlight shone through
holes in the ceiling, dotting their path up the wall.
The scaffolding nearly took them to the top of the
wall. A hole, big enough for them to slip through
rested just out of reach.

"Give me a boost, Marcus."

Marcus knelt down with his hands together
to give his companion a foothold. As Fred reached
for a grip on the ledge, the wooden plank under
Marcus gave way. He was able to grab a hold of
the ledge but was too far for Fred to help.

"Dammit, Marcus," Fred half whispered half
yelled. "I told you to lay off the sweets."

"Really, Fred? You have to judge me at this very moment." Marcus pulled himself onto the nearby platform. "Just go open the gate. I'll meet you on the other side."

Fred nodded and slipped away. He kept pace with Marcus, glimpsing him through the cracks as he struggled to find his way back down to the gate. Most of the guards were on his side of the wall so he had to take care to not alert anyone.

"To be fair, Marcus, I'm always judging you," he smirked.

Marcus, startled, nearly fell again. "To be fair, Fred, I've always hated you."

Fred chuckled to himself, making sure he didn't make too loud of a noise. "And yet here we are. Together once again. Sneaking past enemy lines." The pair nearly reached the end of the scaffolding.

A guard was waiting by a rusted wheel near the door. He stood solid and focused. If Fred didn't know any better, he would assume the guard wasn't even breathing. Fred dropped from the ledge and rolled behind a nearby barrel. He spotted Marcus through the gate, holding his hand up.

Marcus pulled out his knife and ran it across the bars of the gate, getting the guard's attention. The guard, grunting oddly, turned to the gate with his weapon drawn. Fred caught a glimpse of the man's arm and its sickly pale tone. He pulled a chunk of rock from a nearby crate and chucked it down the nearby side passage. The guard quickly turned around and ran after the noise.

Fred ran to the wheel, lifting the gate just high enough to let Marcus slip under. "Not too shabby for someone missing a finger." Marcus grinned.

"Come on. Let's just make this quick." Fred never looked at Marcus. The two ran down the path leading towards an open area.

"What happened? What did you see?" Marcus looked confused.

Fred showed him his hand. The remaining nub from his severed finger was twitching. "The phantom itch," he whispered.

"Damn," he said with a deep sigh. "That's never a good sign."

Below them was a small cottage-like structure surrounded by guards. He noticed Valdryn and the others entering the room. Marcus pointed towards the back wall. Heavily armed guards were protecting what seemed like nothing more than a hole in a wall. A sudden faint snapping noise from their right got their attention.

"What the hell was that?" muttered Marcus.

"Only one way to find out." Fred pulled his knife out and approached the doorway at the end of the path.

In the middle of the hallway knelt a hooded figure. The two slowly approached the figure as the snapping grew louder. A few popping noises and wet drips nearly turned their stomachs. Fred took one step closer but stepped on something squished beneath his heel. The figure ahead stopped moving as Marcus looked down at his friend's boot. A half-smashed eyeball peaked out from under his foot, forcing Marcus to gag. The figure quickly ran off, leaving behind half of a bloody lizard corpse.

"After him!" Fred shouted.

The two bolted after the runaway, their boots splashing in the puddles of blood. The strange figure hissed at his pursuers, knocking over crates to impede their path. Fred was graceful, leaping over the crates and dodging thrown objects with ease.

They were gaining on their target when they wrapped around a corner and found more hooded figures. Behind them was door with a lit torch on either side. The figures all held crude tools as weapons from pick axes to sickles. They let out a loud screech before attacking. One pinned Fred to the wall but Marcus speared a shovel trough the figure's skull. Fred pulled one dagger free and launched into the eye of the next attacker. He pulled out his other dagger and plunged into another attacker's throat.

Marcus Kicked one in the knee, buckling his leg and slit his throat. Blood sprayed everywhere as the pair sliced through the mob. They both charged the last one, plunging their daggers through his chest and pinning him to the door. Through the window they saw dead bodies, strung up like livestock. Another figure was gnawing on a leg with the flesh on his face decayed.

"They're undead, Marcus!" said Frederick. "We have to warn Verric."

"But what of Valdryn?" Marcus asked.

They heard footsteps quickly traveling up the stair case to their right. The guards must have heard the screeching. The two ran off, retracing their steps. They made it out to the fresh breeze and left the temple behind them.

"Everyone who entered would be dead and Verric would still have burned it all down." Fred didn't show anger, only regret. "Yes, people died because of us. But you lived and that's what counts."

Valdryn knew he was right. One way or another, Verric would have had his way and destroyed everything regardless of circumstance. At least this way, there are survivors. A few broken survivors are better than none at all.

Fred placed his hand on Valdryn's shoulder, "I'm sorry for what happened."

You will be.

"It's not your fault." Valdryn turned away towards the map on the table. He saw the capital city and plunged a nearby knife into it. "But I still need your help with taking the city."

"What do you need me to do?" he asked, at the ready.

"Marcus will be useless with that limp so you'll have to go on ahead of everyone and try to evacuate the city." Valdryn studied the surrounding land on the map.

Fred looked confused. "How am I supposed to convince people to leave the execution of their enemy?"

"You won't be able to." Valdryn's expression was sullen. "You're going to have a very small window of opportunity to get whoever you can out of the city."

Gordok walked over to the map, eyeing up the knife. His gut was churning once again. "Are you planning on destroying the city?"

"No. Balvas is. He didn't die in those caves and he will easily overpower the guards." He moved a half-eaten apple by the knife and a handful of grapes just outside the city. "Our men will march on the city ready to aid the city's defenses so long as Verric surrenders the prisoners."

Everyone nodded in agreement except for Marcus. "Two problems with your plan. What are you going to about the soldiers here who support Verric? And what of Sandra?"

"I'll convince her to let us pass," he said sternly.

Marcus laughed. "Verric promised her a hefty position in his little entourage for her support."

Valdryn wasn't all that surprised but he was hoping to have all of the mages on his side for the coming battle. Tariv and others were deep in the city and cut off from communication. He was her best bet to save the prisoners without incident.

Just another traitor driven by selfish desires.

"I'm leaving you here to keep Verric's loyalists distracted." He flexed his sword hand around the hilt of his sword. "Leave Sandra to me."

Chapter 15: Immolation

The once beautiful forest was now tarnished from blood and fire. Sandra and her mages had scorched the earth in their efforts at stopping the undead horde. It was impossible to decipher from the burnt bodies who served the light and served the dark.

Sandra would always act as though she favored precision but Valdryn always knew the truth. She was often praised for natural talents and that would go to anyone's head. She came to favor power above all else and would never hesitate to show it off. Others would believe she was doing what was necessary but Valdryn understood he now found himself in her own personal paradise.

Valdryn was walking among the burnt bodies, struggling to find the words for what he saw. The once vibrant blue sap had turned to a brownish red wax that coated the bodies. He heard a sudden cracking noise as his boot sunk in the mud. He looked down to see a half-buried corpse, his foot stuck in the ribcage. The tabard was too scorched to find a sigil but the sword seemed fairly intact.

This man was on their side and still he burned.

Valdryn pulled his foot free as a charred living corpse dragged itself through the mud. When it saw Valdryn, it wrenched a knife from its shoulder and picked up its pace. Valdryn side stepped the corpse and crushed its skull beneath his boot.

More burnt warriors shambled into the clearing but collapsed into nothingness within the mud. Shadowy smoke escaped their bodies and disappeared in the direction of massive flames. Valdryn followed with his sword drawn and his anger returning. More walking corpses began to collapse and add to the shadow's trail.

"Is this all the Abyss has to offer?" shouted an unfamiliar voice.

A survivor?

An injured man was wielding a long wide blade, cleaving through the undead. The left half of his armor was torn off and exposed the burnt flesh. The adrenaline coursing through his body helped him fight off the pain of each swing. Gritting his teeth, he kept up the attack and slaughtered his foes.

"No wonder you hide in the shadows." He brought his blade down in a vertical swing, splitting an undead fighter down the middle. "You make piss poor fighters."

They began to surround the injured warrior when Valdryn joined in. Using his magic, he summoned an aura around the unknown man. He moved with a renewed vigor and cut through the horde with an incredible speed. Valdryn joined in and together they toppled the undead forces.

"I thought you were dead, Blademaster," said the man with a grin.

"Story of my life, soldier," Valdryn replied. "What's your name?"

The two mirrored each other as they carved a path through the dead. Kicked-up ash and shadows filled the air with each kill, a cloud of death with each swing. "Yurik, sir." A wide arcing slash cut through three undead at once.

"It's good to meet you, Yurik. How are those injuries?" Valdryn launched an ice spike, piercing another undead between the eyes.

"Nothing I can't handle. But that witch killed my men." Just the mention of the witch refueled Yurik's rage. With one wide arc he cleaved through a mob of the creatures like a knife through butter.

"Who?"

You know who.

"Sandra. She set the whole forest ablaze and watched as my friends were engulfed in flame." Yurik knocked his enemy's weapon to the ground before removing the upper half of its head.

Valdryn harnessed his energy and sent a shockwave crashing through the rest. "She normally wouldn't leave people to die." The forest grew silent again, aside from the crackling of the flames.

"She'll follow orders to the letter if it furthers her career," Yurik spat. "She doesn't deserve her powers."

We're in agreement there.

Valdryn looked around for signs of Sandra and her mages. The battle left everything spread apart and the flames destroyed any trail to follow. The smoke blurred his vision and he never knew Sandra to be a loud boaster despite her pompous attitude. "Where is she?"

"I lost sight of her by the edge of the forest." Yurik pointed to the north with his sword. "She had four mages with her and they're not looking to disobey her either."

The shadows also flowed to the north where spouts of flame can be seen rising above the trees. Valdryn pressed forward with Yurik following close behind. Black blood dripped from his giant blade but somehow still clung to Valdryn's. He didn't think much on it, focusing on the more important task at hand.

More undead appeared on their right, also heading towards the city. Creatures similar to Balvas's transformation also traveled north but their bodies seemed poorly held together. The seared flesh on their bones writhed in pain but the swirling shadow seemed to soothe their anguish. In an instant, they vanished. Consumed by a large wave of fire. Valdryn and Yurik dove to the ground, taking cover behind fallen charred trees. One of Sandra's mages walked among the ashes.

"The hounds would never stray too far from their master," said Yurik.

"Agreed. Let's make this quick." Valdryn stayed low on his approach.

Yurik flanked towards the right, using the trees to obscure his path. The mage made his way towards Valdryn when Yurik picked up a nearby skull and threw it at the mage. He quickly leapt backwards, scanning the area for the assailant.

"Show yourself and we can be done with this, cretin," shouted the mage.

Yurik stepped forward. "Remember me?"

"Should I?" the mage snorted.

"You and the one who holds your leash killed my men." He readied his sword, preparing to bring his full strength down upon the fledgling mage.

The mage spotted the burn injuries and laughed. "The knights who tried to play at hero and ran towards their end? You are no match for my power, let alone Master Sandra's." Flickers of flame flashed in and out around his hands.

Valdryn stepped forward and encased the mage's hands in ice. "So much for power."

"What? You're supposed to be de—"
Yurik's blade burst through the mage's chest.

"One down." Yurik used the mage's robes to clean his blade.

Valdryn wiped the blood splatter from his face. He stared at the body of the mage. He didn't know the man personally but he had seen him before. Sandra and her mages always put forth a visage of elitists but deep down they were just like everyone else.

Valdryn and Yurik followed the mage's path backwards. More burnt bodies were scattered around and despite the scorch marks, Valdryn could tell their armor was fairly new. The trees were blasted outwards like a crater. The stench of burnt flesh was strong here and the burnt faces of the victims were stuck in a painful expression.

Yurik stood among his dead friends. He removed their pendants and wore them around his neck. They were dull in luster and shaped like a shield. All distinguished members of Kalboria's military were awarded one for their deeds. The burden of these pendants around his neck faded as Yurik centered his focus.

"You will not be forgotten, brothers," Yurik muttered to himself.

Valdryn placed a hand on his shoulder. He noticed the collection of pendants had begun before their encounter. Beneath his armor were the pendants of other soldiers, perhaps some who fell during the siege. "They're close, Yurik. Let's end this now."

Yurik nodded and the two set off to hunt the other mages. Following the bodies towards the forest's edge, they found another mage. She was slumped down against a large tree stump clutching her leg. Layers of ash surrounded her on all sides.

Valdryn and Yurik flanked her on both sides, placing their blades on her shoulders to ensure her cooperation. On closer inspection, Valdryn saw the dagger in her leg. She was gripping it with a burnt hand. The flames had scarred her arm and traveled up to her face. She was struggling to breathe through the pain and blood loss.

"What happened here, little mage? Your spell fire back on you?" mocked Yurik.

She barely met his gaze. "Sandra...doesn't care..."

Valdryn felt the anger building up once again. He remembered how Jonas used to idolize her and her power. He was too young to know better but Valdryn always assured him power meant nothing without restraint. "Where is she?"

She turned to Valdryn and laughed. "She won't be happy...to see you..."

"The feeling will be mutual, I'm sure," Valdryn replied. He knelt down and infused her leg with healing magic. He pulled the dagger free and the wound began to seal.

This is pointless. Kill her and be done with it.

Valdryn shook his head, clearing his thoughts. "Now tell us where she is."

"You're too late..." she pointed off in the distance. "She found you..."

Valdryn and Yurik looked over to see Sandra and two apprentices approaching. Her robes remained remarkably white despite the field of ash she created. Her apprentices wore masks similar to the ones Ava and Bannon wore but they weren't nearly as clean. One of them had a particularly large red stain across their robes.

"Brought your little lap dogs, Sandra? Makes my job easier," shouted Yurik.

"More minions of the darkness I see." She didn't pay Yurik any mind. "I'm not surprised that you still live, Blademaster. Only a servant of the abyss would survive the temple."

Valdryn scoffed. "You know damn well I'm no servant. It was your magic that powered that cannon and killed everyone in there."

Her apprentices stepped forward, conjuring fire. "Watch your tone, traitor!" spat one of them. Sandra motioned for them to step back. Like trained dogs, they obeyed.

"When the master speaks, the hounds sit." Yurik smirked.

Sandra's stare was soulless and icy, a scowling statute amidst the dead. "Prove yourself then. Kill this man."

Valdryn looked at Yurik. "You want me to kill this man? An innocent man?"

"Far from innocent," she said. "He turned on my mages when the undead arrived."

"Nothing but lies from someone supposedly so powerful." Yurik dropped into a stance, ready to charge. Her mages matched his fury and were all too eager to deal a killing blow. Like most young mages, they fell for the lies of their master.

"I am your superior now, Valdryn," she proclaimed. "You will do as I say."

Valdryn paused, holding his blade at the ready. He looked at Yurik once more and laughed. "Superior? I am still Blademaster of this isle and no empty promise from Verric will change that. You're nothing more than an opportunist." Valdryn Stepped forward.

"Do not move," said one of the mages, sternly.

"We were sent here to help these people, not ourselves." Valdryn continued pushing forward. His steps kick up the still ash, polluting the air.

The pair of mages stepped back but Sandra stood her ground. "These people dug their own graves, Valdryn. They don't deserve our help." Sandra raised her hands, prepared to attack. A sharp glimmer shone in her pale blue eyes.

Valdryn studied Sandra down to the slightest detail. A small bead of sweat dripped from her brow. Her fingers let off a slight tremble while her escort started to do the same. He sensed a power growing from the opposite direction and sighed. "So much power and potential in you. Everyone at the academy saw what you could become. Is this truly how you want your *legend* to end?" he asked under his breath.

"I…I will not die here," she stuttered.
So be it.

Valdryn spun around, summoning a barrier around Yurik. "On your flank, soldier!" Flames washed over the barrier, obscuring Yurik's vision. The mages used elemental magic in an attempt to kill Valdryn. The Blademaster quickly slashed a large icicle out of the air. He summoned a quick blast of frost to consume the oncoming fireball. His blade absorbed the lightning and launched it back at his rival.

In place of Sandra, the contorted body of a mage laid smoking on the ground. Even Valdryn was surprised by the blade's durability and nearly forgot about the other mages. Yurik charged passed him, regaining his attention, and brought his blade down on another mage. A hastily summoned shield of ice blocked the blade but shattered nonetheless.

Valdryn dashed forward, dodging the oncoming spells. He went in for the kill but noticed something out of place and changed his target. He reversed his direction but a wall of flame blocked him off from the mages and Yurik. The flames formed a ring around him, with Sandra at the center.

"How did you know it was an illusion?" she asked.

"As icy as your stare is, I've never known your eyes to be blue," he replied.

"A simple error," she scoffed, preparing another spell. "I'll work on it once you're out of the way."

"I'm surprised you can admit you've made a mistake." Valdryn readied his sword, fully expecting her next move.

Fire swirled around one arm while ice encased the other. She was quick to master elemental magic while at the academy and she only get more powerful over the years. "It will be the last."

Valdryn focused his magic and bolstered his reflexes. Sliding and dodging, Sandra's attacks would barely miss as she picked up speed. The elements covered the field, forcing Valdryn to stay defensive. She knew close combat would seal her fate.

The Blademaster tried to advance but his opponent's spells were coming too fast for him. Spikes of ice protruded from the ground while spears of fire dashed towards him. He used the ice as a shield but they would splinter on impact, scratching and cutting at his face. As the shards fell, they swirled around his legs and held him in place.

Sandra knelt down, placing her hand on the scorched earth. Cracks of flame and magma scattered and reached out towards the ring of flame. "What use is a Blademaster who can't even reach his target?" she sneered.

"Come closer and find out," he spat back.

Sandra smirked. "Let's see just how skilled you really are." From the fire barrier, stepped forth beings of rock and flame. The elemental minions leapt towards an immobilized Valdryn. He parried each swing as they rushed past him. With a crouching slash, he severed the legs of a charging elemental. The creature wailed in pain but crawled back towards Valdryn.

How do I get out of this?

Another one charged. An upwards cut split the creature in half. A pulse of energy washed over him. At first, he thought the flames of the creature had enveloped him. The radiating heat was hard to bear but he regathered his senses and realized she had given him the advantage.

"They're made of an arcane flame, not nature," he muttered under his breath. He looked at Sandra on the other side of the ring, her hands still pulsing with frost and flames. Nothing about this ring is natural.

Her greatest strength is her greatest weakness.

He remembered absorbing the mage's spell earlier. He eyed the elemental crawling towards him. It reached out but Valdryn quickly grabbed his wrist and pulled him forward. Piercing what would be its heart, Valdryn saw his blade drink in the energy.

Need more.

One by one, Valdryn would thrust his blade into the oncoming elementals, absorbing their energy. He sensed the power building up in the blade. He used his own magic to raise the rocky debris left behind from the elementals. More were rising from the flames, double the previous wave. A smoldering hail of blue flame swirled through the air, puncturing any elemental that got too close.

Valdryn allowed the debris one more pass before launching it at Sandra. She summoned another barrier of ice to absorb the impact easily but she wasn't prepared for what followed. Valdryn unleashed the flames he absorbed with an arcing slash. Sandra tried to block but wasn't fast enough. It struck her arm covered in ice. While it wasn't with enough force to sever her arm, it did dispel her magic as well as send her reeling back in pain.

"You bastard, Valdryn!" she screamed, clutching her arm. "That blade of yours is unnatural."

"Because it can best your magic?" he mocked.

"Because no blade is that capable," she spat back. "You took it from the temple, didn't you?"

"I wasn't given much of a choice when you and Verric dropped the temple on top of us." He advanced towards her. He stared her down and watched her every move, prepared for anything she can throw at him now.

"For all you know that blade could be from the Abyss." She hurled another fireball, grunting from the pain.

Valdryn swatted the flame with his sword, feeling its power grow once more. "If that's what it takes to save the Isle." He hastened his approach, narrowing his vision on his adversary. The flame wall was closing in but began to fail as Sandra's power was waning.

"The selfless are always doomed to fall, Blademaster." She summoned her remaining strength and punched down into the earth. Large spikes shot up through the ground in a path towards Valdryn.

Her grand finale.

Rather than trying to dodge, he thrusted his blade into the ground and released the flames the blade absorbed earlier. A large pulse of fire blasted through the spikes and collided with Sandra and the flame wall faded away. Valdryn saw Yurik standing over the body of one bloodied mage while choking the other.

Sandra was laying on the ground, her robes scorched. Small earthen shards pierced various parts of her body. Her left leg was pinned with an array of spikes running up to the knee. Her already broken arm was bleeding profusely. She was clutching the large shard piercing her gut.

Valdryn approached her, observing her wounds. He almost felt sorry for her. "It didn't have to come to this. All you had to do was set aside your ambitions for just *one* day."

"A life without ambition is no life at all," she muttered. "May your Abyss take you, Blademaster."

Upon closer inspection, her wounds were fatal. She will bleed out before the storm hits the mainland. Her expression showed hatred and rage but her eyes revealed her sorrow and regret. He had never known Sandra to express anything beyond overwhelming arrogance. The once proud sorceress, bested by her own power.

"It surely will before the end." He placed the tip of his blade above her heart. "But not before I help those people."

"This will be the end of you, Blademaster." Her weary eyes met his.

A dying animal, grasping at her final moments.

He gripped his hilt with both hands, meeting her eyes with his own look of regret. He remembered his younger days at the academy. He remembered the first day he met her and Tariv. She wasn't always so cold and ambitious, merely a child with something to prove. Memories are all he had left now.

"Farewell, old friend." He thrusted his blade down and pierced her heart. Her body went still and her pain released. Valdryn let out a deep breath before yelling at the top of his lungs. His eyes began to water but he blinked away the tears. He collected himself and went to pull his blade free, but it would not budge. He tried using both hands but to no avail. A voice echoed from the back of his mind.

Mourn not the loss of the wicked and ambitious. The world will live on from their loss.

"Who are you?" replied Valdryn, startled.

I...don't recall my name, or much of anything for that matter. The last thing I remember is Burning Sun and their siege of the temple but even that memory is hazy at best.

"The Burning Sun?" Valdryn was confused. "That was centuries ago."

Centuries? It's really been that long.

"Who are you talking to, Blademaster?" Yurik startled Valdryn.

"You don't hear the voice?"

Yurik shook his head.

Valdryn stood there, pondering the voice's origin. It could be a dying illusion of Sandra's, a final mockery. In the back of his mind though, he knew such a trick would be beneath her.

I assure you I am no illusion.

"Then what are you?" demanded Valdryn.

An ally. A tool. An equalizer.

Valdryn stood there, contemplating the nature of the sword. It was clearly designed to combat magic, something paladins would value when hunting rogue mages. *Could Sandra be right?* It's not unheard of for the soul of a warrior to be trapped in their weapon. Perhaps some things are better left undisturbed.

The more time you waste here, the more heads that will roll from the executioner's block.

Valdryn knew the words to be true and time was not on their side. Valdryn went to free the blade once more but the voice flooded his mind.

No. Not yet. This one is gone and she won't be needing her power anymore. We can use it.

Valdryn looked at Sandra's lifeless corpse. The blood had pooled and stained the earth. Despite the resentment that formed between them, he could not deny how powerful she was. She was certainly a boastful mage, but she earned it. He knelt down by her body to mourn her loss one last time.

"Do it," he muttered.

Place your hands on the blade then.

As soon he grabbed the blade, he felt pain wrack his chest. It was as if the blade was piercing his body instead. Sandra's body twitched and pulsed as the blade drank in her power and bestowed a portion of it into Valdryn. Her body had grown pale with discolored veins. Valdryn pulled the blade free though it looked different than before. The nicks in the blade had been repaired and the rust had been replaced with a reflective darkened steel.

"That's one hell of a weapon you have, Valdryn," said Yurik.

"That's one way to put it," replied the Blademaster. Its unique enchantment was hard to dismiss but he couldn't shake the fear it instilled in Sandra. However, he was sworn to defend this Isle and he would do what he must to see it through.

"What do we do now?" asked Yurik, awaiting orders.

Valdryn looked back at the storm. The lightning was raging and wind had begun to cast aside the ashes. He turned to face the capital, the arcane tower off in the distance. "Return to camp and find Gordok. Tell him to meet me in the fields just before the gates. Bring everyone."

Yurik nodded and ran off, leaving the Blademaster to his thoughts. Valdryn approached the open fields. He noticed the increase in archers on the ramparts and the various barricades outside the gates.

There are a lot of soldiers between you and your goal. A lot of people will die.

"Only Verric *has* to die. Barathel will see reason, he has to. I'll make him if I have to." Valdryn thought of the innocent people inside the city walls, cheering for the executions. He wondered if they'd still cheer if they knew the truth.

Spoken like every hero…before every tragedy.

Chapter 16: The Price of Ambition

"Liars! Traitors! Scum!" shouted the voices from the growing mob in the city streets. Verric led his prisoners from horseback through the city, putting them on display for all to see. Some had already been severely beaten. Bruises and cuts covered their limping bodies. Children threw stones from the alley ways while the sick and elderly tossed rotten scraps of food from their bedroom windows.

"Please! We are innocent!" shouted an older man with a young child close behind.

"No mercy for traitors!" squeaked a child as he threw a sharp stone. It missed the old man but left a gash above his son's eye.

Seeing his son's pain broke the man. He shouted and cursed at the mob. "You're nothing but cowards! You would never venture past the city walls but attack a child the first chance you get!" Another stone flew through the air but this time the man was ready. He caught it and threw it back, striking the young man who cast it.

A guard struck the man in the back of the head, driving him to his knees. His rage numbed the pain. "I hope even just one true traitor still lives to see this city burn." The old man spat at the guard.

The guard unsheathed his sword and went in for the kill. He raised his blade high but a voice intervened. "Enough!" shouted Verric, his voice booming over the crowd. "They will be dealt with according to our laws, not mob rules."

The guard sheathed his sword and pulled the man to his feet. The injured boy clung to his father as they were marched to the recently erected executioner's block. The city was drowning in fear and hatred and Barathel did nothing more but oversee the preparation for a mass execution.

A long line of over one-hundred prisoners was marched into the construction district. Verric would personally start the proceedings by escorting a rather muscular pale figure in chains to the stage.

"Our ancestors fought alongside the gods to vanquish the darkness." The shouting from the mob began to fall silent. "When the dark proved too strong to be beaten on the field of battle, they made the ultimate sacrifice to ensure our world would remain protected long after they're gone." Verric kicked his prisoner's leg, forcing him down. From beneath the black hood, a muffled growl could be heard.

"These traitors would undermine the sacrifices of those brave men and women. They would see to the fall of our world and usher in tyranny of the Abyss once more!" The shouting from the mob picked up again. Verric smiled at the cheers and shouts raining down around him, knowing it would soon fall silent once more.

He removed the prisoner's hood, revealing a captured temple guard. His eyes were pale and skin an ashy gray. Black blood stained his lips and rotten teeth. As he strained for his release, the chains tightened and scraped against his skin. Droplet of black blood dotted the stage. "And yet for all their powers," continued Verric. "They are easily bound in chains." With one quick motion, Verric unsheathed his sword and sent the prisoner's head rolling.

"And easily put down like rabid digs," interjected Barathel.

The crowd cheered as the headless body twitched before them. A handful of prisoners made a break for it but Verric's archers proved quicker. Arrows quickly pierced their legs as they fell on top of one another. Verric smiled as he found his first volunteers.

The injured boy and his father were towards the center of the line. Despite the growing crowds, they could see perfectly what awaits them as their friends were lined up on the stage. "What are we going to do, papa?" The young boy clung to his father's tattered robes.

The old man looked around, hoping for a sign of escape. He found nothing. The world darkened and his heart sank. From the corner of his eye, he saw a scout talking to one of the captains. While he couldn't hear them, they seemed on edge. The captain summoned a few nearby guards and sent them off towards the main gate.

"We just need to wait," he said, comforting his son. "We'll get our chance."

A small caravan approached the main gates, barely ahead of the storm. Injured soldiers were in the front wagon while the rear one appeared to hold dead bodies. Soldiers still capable of fighting despite possible injuries guarded the caravan on both sides. At the head was a brawny soldier with severely damaged armor. Bandages wrapped the left side of his face and he walked with a limp.

A guard with a winged helmet approached the caravan with six more guards following close behind. "State your name, soldier. And your business here," shouted the captain.

The bandaged solider approached the city guards. "Murray," grunted the soldier. "Ironveins is trying to clear the field of the dead and injured. He's tasked me and a few others to see it done."

"Grim task there," replied the captain.

"Someone's gotta do it," said Murray.

The captain nodded and turned to his men. Two of them approached the caravan to inspect its contents. The captain approached Murray to get a better look at him. "How is Ironveins doing out there anyway?"

Murray handed the captain a rolled-up parchment. "He's doing well enough."

The captain unrolled the parchment. Ironvein's anvil signet lay at the bottom. When he rerolled the parchment, a pouch full of coins surprised him as it dropped into his hand. "What's this?"

"To cover inn fees. It would be unwise for us to try beat the storm back to camp," said Murray. "Ironveins said it should be enough and a guard could point us in the right direction."

The captain seemingly ignored Murray and looked to his guards inspecting the caravans. He could hear the grunts and moans from the injured in the first caravan. The guards approached the second caravan but upon opening the canvas, the stench of death overwhelmed them. There were scorched bodies from the burnt forest and fallen soldiers from the temple fields. One of the guards reeled back and removed his helmet before vomiting on the road.

The captain felt his own gut churn when the wind carried the foul stench towards him. "Follow me. Leave the dead inside the main gate. I'll have some guards take the injured while the rest of you can take care of your affairs at the inn."

Murray nodded then whistled for his men to follow. The wagon full of corpses was left by the main gate, blocking off an alleyway. The guards escorted the wagon of injured soldiers towards the infirmary.

"Thank you, captain. We can find our own way to the inn," said Murray.

The captain nodded. "If you're feeling up for it, we're carrying out the executions before the storm hits. I figured you would enjoy watching those bastards get what they deserve."

"I'll certainly be there." Murray shook the captain's hand.

With most of the guards gone, Murray walked over to the other wagon. He knelt down, resting his forehead on the side. The nearby gate guards paid him no mind, giving him time to mourn his fallen friends. He made two soft taps by a small hole in the wagon's side. He received two quick taps in reply.

"The guards are gone, but they've already started the executions. We might be too late," whispered Murray.

"Too late to turn back," replied a voice from within the cart.

Murray nodded. "Aye. Follow the alleyway to the north. The rest of us will catch up when we can."

Murray left the cart and joined with the rest of the injured soldiers. The guards appeared none the wiser to Murray's conversation with the dead. The howling winds and their growing nausea kept them distracted.

A knife cut the canvas of the wagon on the side facing the alley. Two hooded figures climbed out with drying red stains spotting their cloaks. Frederick removed the hood and tossed it back in the wagon. "That stench alone almost killed me."

Valdryn did the same. "And that was the easy part." He stretched his arms and legs, limbering up for their next task. He wiped the dried blood that crusted on brow and inhaled the fresh air deeply.

The pair walked down the alley, pulling up cloth masks to help conceal their identities. The cracking of thunder grew closer as the wind began to rush over the city. The alley and streets were empty because of the executions. Only a handful of guards were out on patrol but there wasn't much going on with everyone focused on the executions.

"I'm still not so sure about this plan," said Fred. "Murray is capable enough but Marcus's injury will slow him down."

"We don't need Marcus to fight, just to take the gate guards by surprise," replied Valdryn. "As long the men he chose are capable, we'll be fine."

"I suppose, but it'll be difficult for him to escape the infirmary. Not to mention Gordok and Yurik were still trying to find enough capable fighters before we left." Frederick sighed, eyeing the windows to ensure no one was spying on them.

"They'll get it done. They have to." Valdryn focused his hearing. Under the howling wind, he could hear the scurrying of the rats in the sewer system. The sniffling and coughing of the sick let him know that some people could not be bothered to see the executions. The sudden cheering of a mob broke his focus. "We're running out of time."

"Knees to chest then, Blademaster," said Frederick before picking up speed.

The pair rushed through the alley, racing against the cheers. Each roar from the crowd marked another life they failed to save. Valdryn was focusing his power to heighten his senses while following close behind. He could pinpoint most nearby guards and quickly redirect his course to avoid them. There were far too many people huddled together to determine the amount of guards, but it was safe to assume that direct conflict would not be the best of ideas.

Frederick tapped Valdryn's shoulder and pointed up to the guard tower. "There's a good vantage point up there," he whispered. "I'm not the best archer but I'm good enough to get you close."

Valdryn clasped Fred's shoulder and nodded. The pair split up, with Valdryn staying low and Fred taking the high ground. Valdryn crept around various storage crates, slowly making his way towards the crowds. Three guards stood between him in and his chance to slip in unnoticed. He looked up towards the tower, waiting for a signal.

Frederick positioned himself just before the top of the stairs leading up to the top of the wall. He was listening for the pacing of the guards as their steel boots stomped along stone. He was more than capable of dispatching one or two guards at a time but if he wasn't careful, he'd be overwhelmed in mere moments.

As two guards passed one another, he crept between them. As soon as they were at a safe distance, he ran for the one nearing the tower. He kicked the back of his leg and forced the guard to his knee. Before he could retaliate, a dagger slipped under his helmet and slit his throat. Fred quickly disposed of the body by tossing him over the wall.

The loud thud the body made as it impacted the ground caught the tower sentry's attention. He went to the rear window to investigate but couldn't see anything, even with his helmet removed. Suddenly, he felt an arm wrap around his throat and squeeze the air from his lungs.

"Sorry 'bout this," said Frederick. "But you bet on the wrong horse." With a quick twist and snapping noise, the guard's body went limp.

Fred gathered up every arrow he could find and stacked them on the nearby table. He grabbed the bow and tested its flexibility. Satisfied, he looked down and saw Valdryn staring up at him making gestures towards the three guards in his path.

"Alright, Blademaster. I'd say I've bought us a little more than two minutes. Let's make this count." He let loose the first arrow.

Using his heightened senses to follow the arrow, he saw it land in the darkened alley, clanging off of something metal. Two of the guards took notice and went off to investigate. The last stayed behind to hold his position. Seeing an opening, Valdryn ambushed the lone guard and snapped his neck instantly.

One of the guards turned to see Valdryn standing over the body. He unsheathed his sword but a swift arrow silenced his shout. He fell to the ground, clutching his throat and struggling in vain to alert his fellow guards. The third guard turned to face Valdryn but the Blademaster threw one of his knives and pierced his shoulder. The force of the impact made the guard spin just enough to expose his face to Frederick. A swift arrow pierced deep through his eye, killing him instantly.

"If he considers his skills 'good enough', I'd hate to see what he considers a master," Valdryn muttered under his breath. He quickly hid the bodies in the shadows but there was nothing that could be done about the blood. He had his opening now and he wasted no time taking advantage. He disappeared into the crowd of onlookers, leaving Frederick to cover his escape.

Valdryn squeezed through the initial crowd just to be cramped shoulder-to-shoulder with the bulk of the mob. Another head rolled from the executioner's block, frenzying the mob once more. One man was holding up a severed head, mocking the prisoner with cheers from the bloodied pale lips.

Animals. Makes you wonder if they were ever worth protecting.

"It's not them. It's the ones in charge fueling their passion," Valdryn whispered.

"Kill them all!" shouted an older woman.

"Kill them! Kill them!" chirped the children. Specks of blood stained their clothes and dotted their faces.

Keep telling yourself that.

The executioner's posture was slouched, exhausted from the near endless slaughter. His tabard was stained crimson beyond recognition. Those looking to make a few extra coins had rags and mops to clean the stage of all the blood. Half-dried streaks ran down the front boards and the bodies were dragged behind the stage to add to the burning piles.

Valdryn pushed his way through the crowd, slowly reaching the stage. The commotion from the crowd helped him blend in. Guards flanked both sides of the stage, blocking off access and leaving only the front exposed. Barathel's personal guards were wearing a heavy set of plate armor with gold and blue filigree, combining fashion with practicality.

The general was leering down on everyone from his perch. He looked right at Valdryn but the grime on his face and thick leathers made him look like just another mercenary. Despite the oncoming storm, the people remained determined to see this through and cheered at every fall of the axe.

"Bring out the next one," commanded Verric.

The guards ushered out another prisoner. This man was older with a fresh wound on his forehead. His face was bruised but he stood defiant and fearless. The small child next in line was crying and screaming but the cloth gag muffled his pleas.

It's now or never.

Valdryn forced his way to the front of the crowd. Clutching a knife in his belt, he kept his focus on the executioner. He was simply a man doing as he was told but such is the way of war. The crowd of civilians were the ones calling for death. He just happened to be the one swinging the axe.

"You are all monsters," shouted the older man. "We have done nothing."

"You're traitors!" shouted members of the mob.

"According to Verric and his cowardice followers. Individuals acted against this world but you all act in unison against the innocent." He spat at the mob and stared them down with an intense fire in his eyes.

Verric himself pushed the man to his knees, clearly angry at being called a coward. He was always quick to anger as though he had something to prove. Even if no one else would admit, Valdryn always believed his ambition was akin to unbridled chaos.

"It is you who are the traitors." The man closed his eyes, waiting for the drop.

The executioner brought the axe above his head, waiting for his command. Verric nodded and the axe began to drop. Valdryn focused energy into the knife and launched it with enough force to break the blade off the shaft.

"Enough of this!" shouted Valdryn. "These people are innocent."

"And who are you to say so?" demanded Verric with his blade unsheathed.

He removed his cloth mask and hood. He had more scars since they last spoke but he knew instantly who he was faced with. "Someone you left to die, coward," he said, pointing at Verric and Barathel.

The crowd grew silent. The old man stood to meet Valdryn's gaze with hope. Verric gripped the hilt of his sword tight and used the blade to the keep the old man in place. "You were in the temple when it collapsed. How is that everyone is dead but you still live?"

Valdryn didn't bother answering him, barley acknowledging his presence. "Balvas led the cultists from the shadows. There were only a few who lived among the Temple's population. The bulk of his forces were made up of from the tombs within."

"Answer me!" shouted Verric.

Valdryn continued, ignoring Verric's order. "It was Verric who betrayed us when he gave the order to destroy the temple, with all of us still in it.

He killed innocent men, women, and children. He is the traitor and you've all blindly followed him."

"Guards! Arrest him. He's either deranged or he works for the enemy." Verric and his men pulled their swords.

Barathel looked down at his Blademaster. "In these trying times, we must act without hesitation. Kill him, mercifully."

Valdryn unsheathed his sword. "If we continue down this path, it will destroy us all."

"Not if we destroy you first," Verric shouted. He ordered his men to charge but Valdryn did not fight alone.

A swift arrow pierced the first guard's throat. Two more quickly pinned themselves into another's shield and knocked him over. The guards formed around Verric and Barathel, trying to find the archer.

Frederick was a smart choice after all.

More guards surrounded Valdryn. The mob of angry civilians blocked off the exit to the main street while the guards blocked off the alley way. Barathel and Verric had their personal guards forming a shield wall on the platform.

Another arrow came in low and pierced a guard's leg. Valdryn quickly slashed at the man's throat as he dropped to his knees. He shot flames at the guards closing in, impeding their progress. Another arrow flew but missed its mark. The Blademaster ducked an oncoming swing and spun his blade, slashing the guard's back.

"Find that damn archer already!" shouted Verric from his well-fortified position.

"The general and his favorite lap dog hide while you risk your lives," shouted a familiar voice. Marcus and a handful of archers appeared on the nearby rooftops, pelting the shield wall with arrows.

Valdryn slammed his fist in the ground. A wave of energy knocked over the nearby guards and Frederick took advantage. One by one an arrow would pierce the open slits in their helmets. Frederick used the last of his arrows in a barrage and leapt from the shadows, swinging his bow into the back of a guard's head. Disoriented, the guard was easy to put in a choke hold using the bow for leverage.

"Out of the way ye' cowards." Gordok and his men pushed a burning cart from the main street towards the stage. The mob immediately dissipated and screamed as the rolling inferno rushed past them. Valdryn rolled to the side and Fred abandoned his hostage to be run over by the cart. The loud crash muffled the thunder from the sky above as a massive inferno engulfed the guards.

Barathel and Verric managed to escape the fire but some of their personal guards weren't so lucky. With most of the guards now either wounded, dead, or fully distracted, the prisoners made their escape. Gordok and his men fortified Valdryn's position, readying for battle.

The old man and his son approached Valdryn. "Thank you, Blademaster. You were truly meant to defend this land."

Valdryn smiled. "I do only what I must. Go with Marcus, he will lead you to safety."

The man left with his son as Valdryn approached the General. Barathel was coughing from the smoke and Verric was clutching his shoulder with blood trickling down his cheek. The guards that survived the explosion reformed their wall.

"Traitors. The lot of you," muttered the General.

"I didn't want this, Barathel. I only wanted to stop this façade, the slaughtering of innocents." Valdryn readied his blade.

"No one is innocent," spat Verric.

Valdryn narrowed his focus on Verric. "Least of all you."

Verric was the first to initiate combat. Letting out a rallying cry and charging Valdryn. The clang of metal on metal echoed out from the area with the crackling of embers in the background.

Verric used all his rage to strike out at Valdryn but the Blademaster kept his calm, focusing his rage rather than unleashing it. He kept his guard up, blocking each strike even though they seemed endless.

"You will die, forgotten!" shouted Verric. "You will be nothing more than yet another stain on the Isle's history."

Valdryn paid his words no mind. He simply retaliated with a quick strike to Verric's cheek wound with his pommel. Valdryn always preferred action over words and he wouldn't let Verric's insolence change that now. He was taught to remain professional but he always longed for putting Verric in his place.

This Verric relies too much on his opponent's pride. Perhaps a reflection of his own soul.

Barthel showed no signs of hesitation in cutting down his enemy, but no joy either. He knew what he had to do but he took no pleasure in it, unlike Verric. He was all too eager for his chance to kill.

Gordok proved to be a skilled fighter as well. The burly dwarf was more agile than most would assume, sliding past his opponents with ease. He sliced one guard's leg and drove his dagger up under his chin. He carried small explosives that forced more guards to the ground, ringing their ears and potentially breaking the bones of those who strayed too close.

Yurik and Frederick kept the left flank busy. Yurik's broad swipes kept the guards on the move and off balance. Frederick moved quick, slashing away at each opponent just as they jumped out of Yurik's reach.

Smoke and embers filled the area hindering everyone's sight. Valdryn stayed on Verric, not allowing him to relent. He didn't have to best Verric, just out last him. To his surprise however, Verric showed no signs of tiring. If anything, it was as though he was gaining more stamina as his attacks picked up speed.

Something is wrong. We cannot rely solely on defense.

Valdryn bolstered his own energy and retaliated with his own slashes. This new sword differed in weight and shaped from his father's. He had grown accustomed to it, adapting his own style with it. This foreign sword's weight didn't allow for it to be swung relentlessly, so Valdryn had to shift his stance to take advantage.

He's wearing something enchanted. A ring? An amulet perhaps? Find it.

"Wearing some enchanted gear, Verric?" he wondered. "I thought you hated such things."

"I did. That is until I watched one of your precious 'innocents' cut down ten of my men with ease." Verric locked his blade with Valdryn. "After I carved out his heart, I took his armlet for myself."

Valdryn looked down at the rusted silver piece around Verric's wrist. Though it was old and worn, he could see luminescent specks of the residual magic. Had this been in pristine condition, this might've ended much sooner.

"Not just a coward but a graverobber as well," mocked Valdryn.

Verric picked up his pace, his swings becoming more erratic. Even Valdryn began to struggle against the speed. Verric was driving him back, away from the others. More guards appeared in the streets but Gordok planned for this, having the bulk of his forces keep them busy. A few of the prisoners also joined in, supporting their saviors.

I have a plan. Keep him busy a little longer and do exactly as I say when I say.

"Easy," Valdryn blurted out.

"Easy?! I'll show you easy." Verric unleashed a flurry of slashes and strikes. Even as his anger grew, he managed to maintain accuracy. Valdryn could do nothing but stay on the defensive, waiting for the blade to carry out its plan.

Get ready. As soon as he reels back, finish it.

While guarding against the onslaught, Valdryn noticed a small ember swirling around the blade, like a butterfly looking for a flower to rest upon. Verric didn't notice till it was too late. As his blade struck one last time, it ignited the ember. An outward explosion burned half of his face, forcing him back. He continued to flail his sword around, slowing Valdryn's advance. He overextended his reach and Valdryn took full advantage.

"You son of a bitch!" shouted Verric as his forearm fell to the ground, blood spilling from the severed limb. He lost his balance and landed on his back, holding the crimson stump and squinting with his half-charred face.

"You deserve worse." Valdryn stepped forward, boot on his defeated opponent's chest. He placed the tip of his blade above Verric's heart. "Any last words?"

"The Isle will fall because of you." Verric spat on Valdryn's boot.

Without hesitation, the Blademaster plunged his blade through the heart and silenced Verric forever. But the world kept spinning and the battle raged on as no one even noticed his death.

Valdryn moved to support Gordok when suddenly the ground began to shift and crack. Before he could react, the street opened up and he fell in. A hulking beast crawled out from the hole, laughing. Balvas had grown in size exponentially and repaired himself from the previous altercation. Tied around him were giant boulders with tunnel running through them like the centipede hives.

"You all sought to end me and my mission but you merely brought my army within your walls." The bodies of the fallen begun to twitch. Guttural banshee wails filled the streets as the fallen warriors began to rise and lash out at their old comrades.

Chapter 17: The Stench of Death

Thunder boomed around the city above. Screams of slaughter were carried on the whistling wind as the heavy rain pelted the cobbled roads. Valdryn's vision was hazy and shouting from the soldiers above were muffled. A necrotic husk crawled towards him but a chunk of stone fell from the ceiling and crushed its skull.

Valdryn was laying on a pile of shattered stone, his boots in the water. He looked around for his sword among the rubble and bodies. The longer he took, the more bodies started to rise. He pulled a knife from his belt and thrusted it through the base of their skulls. As he searched the water, he felt hands on his boots. From beyond the stone debris came a cluster of undead. They charged into Valdryn and pushed him under the water.

The Blademaster struggled under the weight of the horde. One kept trying to tear at his throat but Valdryn kept his head at bay. His sword had fallen from his hand when the ground caved in and he made frantic attempts to find it. His chest began to ache as all the breath was expelled from his lungs.

From the murky water he heard muffled whispers to his right. He reached out and felt the edge of a blade. He found the hilt and raised the weapon above the surface of the water. Repeated quick thrusts found their targets with ease. He could sense the magic channeling through his body and let out a strong pulse.

The undead were scattered along the tunnel from the blast. The Blademaster rose from the water, sword in one hand and a flame in the other. "If you want a meal, you'll have to work for it," he spat at the creatures.

In an instant, the creatures were on him again but even quicker were they cut down. One by one they were dismembered and left to rot in peace. The flames he summoned scorched the bloodied corpses, ensuring they would never rise again.

There. On your right. Verric's armlet.

Valdryn found the enchanted metal in the muddy waters. He placed it on stone and knelt over it, feeling the impulse in his mind to take Verric's strength. He thrusted his blade into the armlet, crumbling it into pieces. The blade drank in the arcane energy and gleamed in the dark. A spirit appeared before Valdryn, his attire was a mix of robes and armor with a mask bearing two horizontal eye slits.

"I'm free?" asked the spirit.

"It would appear so," said Valdryn, confused. "Do you remember who you are?"

The spirit pondered the question for a moment. "No, but I do remember the day I died. Outnumbered and surrounded by creatures of shadow. We followed him, full of pride and hungry for glory, to our demise."

"It wouldn't be the first time," Valdryn said, his mind lingering on Verric.

The spirit laughed. "There's still work to be done. No one else needs to share our fate today."

The spirit faded back into the blade once more as Valdryn pushed on through the tunnels. The awakened blade's spirit rejuvenated Valdryn. He could feel his connection to the sword growing stronger and in return, his own power. An unfamiliar power coursed through his body as he cut his way through the infesting horde.

It's like I can breathe once more. I can sense the world around us.

"What are you sensing now?" Valdryn cut one undead in half, from shoulder to hip. The blade's edge had been refined and had no trouble cutting through the rot.

Everything. But the pain above is overwhelming. That monstrosity has brought too much ruin as is.

Valdryn summoned a flame upon the blade and unleashed it in wide arc. The next wave of undead were incinerated almost instantly. A handful reeled back from the heat of the flames, feeling the intensity consuming the very air.

As the flames died down, the darkness grew again. Valdryn focused on the sound of their footsteps and swung through the dark. He could feel the blood striking his armor while the sound of their bodies crashing into the water echoed through the tunnel.

Fighting in these conditions is ill advised.
Allow me to lend some assistance.

The blade emitted a bright orange glow.
Small wisps of flame weaved through the air and
pierced through the closest undead. Their bodies
petrified into contorted statues of ash. From the
crumbling husks sprouted butterflies made of pure
fire. Most landed on the walls, illuminating a path,
but some landed on more undead and lit them
ablaze.

Beautiful and terrifying, isn't it? A mere
parlor trick to amuse children can be used to
decimate your foes with the right knowledge.

"I think I feel safer knowing you're dead,"
Valdryn replied, awestruck by the beauty in
destruction.

Given the current situation, I share that
sentiment.

Valdryn laughed and walked through the
cloud of ash, like a thin veil of blackened mist.
Though they were probably the corpses of warriors
long dead, he still felt a sense of remorse over lives
lost. A restless afterlife at the mercy of the power-
hungry is a fate no one deserves, least of all those
who swore to stand against the dark. Despite their
contorted faces, he clung to the imagery and
imagined what they looked like in life.

What remained of their souls still clung to
their past identities. The yearning for life brings
with it the fear of death, even if it's not the first
time. There were still undead that lashed out at

Valdryn, but they were cut down with ease. The others did not wish to die again after witnessing the fire spell that consumed the masses. Some crept backwards, waiting to see what Valdryn would do next while others simply fled.

Black sludge began flowing underneath the city, overtaking the already muddied waters. The undead coated in sludge stood their ground, staring blankly like statues. From the center of the mass stepped forth a familiar figure. The severed stump where his forearm would be was caked in coagulated black blood. The drips were quickly solidifying, replacing the limb.

"Verric," Valdryn muttered under his breath.

Most of his soul is still intact and yet, he seems stronger. There's something about that sludge...

Verric tried to speak but only black goo came out. It trickled down his chin and dripped back into the source. The mess that trickled from the stump formed into a distorted obsidian limb. In place of fingers grew jagged knifelike claws.

"I killed you once already," Valdryn readied his blade. "I'll gladly do it again."

Make quick work of him. There's something about that sludge that I need to inspect.

The spirit appeared again and knelt down by the black pool. The creatures didn't notice but Verric looked in his direction, sensing a shift in the air. Verric attempted to speak but only more sludge came out.

"I see not much has changed," mocked Valdryn.

The sludge-coated creatures moved surprisingly faster than their counterparts. Before he knew it, Valdryn was surrounded, though they didn't go in for the kill. Instead, they were more focused on dragging him in the darkened water. He nearly sliced one of their arms off. Dangling from strings of flesh, it was almost instantly repaired by the sludge.

"What is this stuff?" Alarmed, Valdryn leapt to the opposite side, building what little distance he could.

Another one leapt with him but a quick slash sent its head rolling into the water. The creature kept fighting on though, swinging with precision. Valdryn thrusted his blade through its heart but his blade was stuck and the creature showed no signs of slowing down. It gripped Valdryn's shoulder tight and tried to drag him down into the sludge.

"Any help would be appreciated," he shouted.

Ice.

"What?" Valdryn was nearing the edge of the sludge and the others were closing in.

Ice can kill them.

Valdryn channeled his magic through the blade, freezing the creature from the core. The creature was frozen nearly instantly and with one quick twist of the blade, it shattered. He combined his pulse aura with ice magic. It wasn't as powerful as he hoped but it was enough to regain the upper hand.

The frozen corpses cracked and shattered with each strike. But as one fell, another would rise from the sludge. Verric slid between the rising masses, closing his distance to strike out at Valdryn. To his surprise, Verric was holding his own against the magic. While the pulse would set him off balance, the ice magic left only a thin layer of frost on his skin.

"It's not working, Spirit!" Valdryn shouted.

We must stem the flow. The river of sludge gives them their power so we must take it away.

"How do we do that?" Valdryn backstepped just out of Verric's reach. His sludge claw shattered two of the frozen corpses.

Use the sword. Thrust it down into where they rose and channel all your energy to freeze it.

Staring at the growing mass of sludge corpses between him and his target, Valdryn knew there was no easy way through. He wasn't getting through them without receiving a few new scars. He took a deep breath and readied his charge.

"I hope you're right about this," he said.

You don't get to die here. Not until you finish what you started.

He launched himself into the mass, knocking over a few on impact. One latched himself onto his back and held his free hand in place. Another tried to grab his sword but had its head split in half with a counter slash.

Valdryn cut wildly, slinging sludge though the air with each attack. It was all he could do to make his way through. To get the creature off his back, he slammed backwards into the wall. It was a risk but it paid off. The creature loosened its grip and was tossed into the other ahead. The gap in the mass gave the Blademaster all he needed to reach his target.

When he was just out of reach of the mass, Verric closed the distance. His hardened claw tore through the leather armor and raked up his back. Valdryn fell to his knees and yelled out in pain. Before he could turn and react, he felt the claws dig deep into his shoulder as he was lifted up in the air.

"I'm getting tired of this dance, Verric." Valdryn lifted his blade and laid the flat side on his shoulder to aim his strike. With all his strength, he thrusted his blade back into Verric's mouth. He twisted the blade and wrenched it forward, tearing off Verric's lower jaw and slicing the claw in half.

Freed from Verric's grip, he crawled forward to a bubbling pool in the river. He slammed his blade downward and felt it pierce something, perhaps another corpse. Ignoring it, he focused his power into the blade and with the spirit's help sent out a large pulse of ice.

With a bright flash, the sludge river was frozen solid along with the mass of corpses. Valdryn breathed a sigh of relief when he saw

Verric's frozen statue but his respite was cut short when the immense pain overtook him again.

"What…is this…?" Valdryn writhed on the ground, tearing at the leather pieces on his shoulder. Where Verric's claw made contact with the skin, what looked like black veins spread. An overwhelming burning sensation emanated from his shoulder and his back, completely preventing any magic focus.

The spirit knelt beside him, frantically trying to identify the cause. "Stop moving, Valdryn. I need to see the wound."

"It's like there's fire running through my veins, spirit." Valdryn gritted his teeth, his jaw tightening.

The spirit could see the black veins, writhing like tentacles. They began to grow, covering his arms and nearing his neck. "There's only one thing I can do and you're not going to like it."

"Just do it. We need to get up there and stop Balvas," he shouted.

The spirit placed both his hands on Valdryn's shoulder. The spirit's form grew translucent and dissipated before Valdryn's eyes. The pain grew into an inferno and then everything suddenly turned to black.

"What the hell is going on out there?" shouted Tariv.

"There's some sort of creature, Sir," replied an injured guard. "I've never seen anything like it."

"There are undead everywhere. Barathel and his guards were lost in the confusion," replied another. "We need to get back out there."

"No," said Tariv, to the soldier's surprise. "The keep will be our last bastion. We cannot risk losing our position."

In the distance, Balvas's guttural and maniacal laughter could be heard. A strange looking boulder soared through the air and crashed through the upper levels of the keep. Rubble from the impact scattered over the courtyard like hail. A smaller boulder speared into the ground outside the main gate.

"Get into the keep and check on the upper floors," Tariv ordered a handful of soldiers eager to get inside away from whatever evil was taking over the city. "The injured need to get inside immediately and the rest should take to the ramparts."

Tariv approached the boulder, hammer at the ready. It was riddled with large holes like a hive. A chattering noise could be heard from within the core. Tariv raised his hammer, ready to strike, but the noise grew louder. A giant centipede sprouted from the core and coiled around the hive. Black venom dripped from its mandibles but otherwise this beast was pristine.

Its loud hissing summoned forth the hive's inhabitants. Agile undead with smaller centipedes coiled around their bodies burst forth. These undead wielded weapons unlike their lesser counterparts and appeared capable of basic communication. Their insectoid protection hissed among each other while the walking corpse clicked their jaws and made gestures.

"Drop the portcullis!" Tariv shouted. His hammer struck one of the undead. It was sent flying backwards but it rose back to its feet just as quickly. The centipedes absorbed most of the impact and barely budged. Tariv pressed any advantage to buy the guards some time.

Using the length of his warhammer and his own magic, he kept the undead at a distance. Each impact was strong enough to shatter a man's ribcage but this enemy felt no pain, no fear. His next strike decimated a creature's head and it collapsed. Though moments later, the centipede's own head burst forth and took control of the corpse.

"Sir, what the hell is going on?" panicked a young guard.

"Merged creatures, soldier. Necromancy isn't the only distasteful form of magic." Tariv summoned his magic into his weapon. The strength of his impacts was increased tenfold. He sent another undead flying into the hive, leaving a larger hole at its base. Despite his capabilities, each swing of his hammer took a toll on his body and drained his stamina.

The large centipede lunged forward and snatched one of the archers, biting him in half immediately. One by one, the guards above were picked off with each lunge form the creature. Tariv retreated beyond the gate but found himself to be the hive master's next target. It coiled itself around his legs and dragged him back.

With his hammer out of reach and the enemy closing in, he resorted to his amplification magic. His reinforced punches began to crack the chitinous plates on the centipede's head. The undead could sense its pain and ran to its aid. Surrounded and pinned, Tariv was no match for the overwhelming force.

"Fire!" shouted a familiar voice. A hail of arrows rained down on the creatures and slowed their advance. A lithe hooded figure ran past and up to the gate. The damage from the centipede left the chains exposed. With two crescent daggers, the figure sliced the chain. The gate crashed down on the larger centipede and pinned it in place.

The lesser ones felt its pain and were losing control of the corpses. With Tariv free, he harnessed his strength and tore a centipede from its host corpse. The separation of the two creatures resulted in their instant deaths.

The hooded figure climbed onto the back of the giant centipede, using the daggers to claw at its chitin. When they reached the head, they hooked the blades into its mouth. With a struggled pull, the head of the creature was split in half, stilling the writhing body. The lesser ones died along with it, shriveling and drying upon death.

"Now we know how to kill them," Tariv spat. He breathed deep to calm his mind but the chaos around him made that more difficult than usual. He looked at his savior with a hint of distrust. "And who let you out, Yvette?"

"Technically speaking," she said as she removed her hood. She bore her scar proudly but there was a shift in her eyes, something about her had changed. "The bigger horde in the heart of your keep let me out."

"I was worried you'd say that. You have my thanks but what are your motives?" he wondered, not too eager to be near death once more and so soon.

"I'll explain everything on the way." She stepped past him and towards the keep, moving with an unnatural speed.

"On the way to what?" he yelled. He tried to keep pace but his armor and weapon slowed him down.

"Our only chance at survival," she replied.

Valdryn woke up in the darkness. The flame butterflies had begun to fade away, allowing the frozen corpses to be swallowed by the dark. He peered at Verric's frozen, jawless face as it faded into the nothingness. He remembered the pain he felt and checked his shoulder. The wound had healed and scarred over. The black veins had shrunk in size, now looking more like body markings.

"Spirit?" he whispered. "Where are you?"

He did not get a reply. As the darkness grew, so too did the silence. An eerie isolation underneath the city would've worried most but he enjoyed the brief silence before he marched on toward the battle ahead.

Valdryn reached for his blade cased in the ice. He caught a glimpse of his reflection in the blade. Similar veins rested around his left eye which had now faded from his famous green to purple. Upon grasping the hilt, the spirit appeared to him once more.

"I'm glad you survived," said the spirit.

"What happened?" Valdryn asked.

"A unique poison consisting of demon's blood had infected your system," replied the spirit. "You are fortunate I was here."

"Demon? I thought they were long gone." Valdryn looked down. Beneath the ice he could see the head of the creature where his blade had struck. "Another centipede?"

"Someone has managed to infuse these creatures with the poison," said the spirit. Valdryn could sense his concern. "It's not unheard of but this level of infusion takes skill."

Valdryn pulled his blade free. Any sensation of pain from before had faded completely. A cracking noise could be heard from the darkness. Verric leapt from the shadows but was suspended in air. Out of pure reflex, Valdryn held his hand out. An unfamiliar power coursed through him

"What is this?" He stared in disbelief at what he was doing.

"My power," answered the spirit. "It took a lot out of me to save you, but what's mine is now yours."

Focusing on Verric's twisted form, he tested his new magic. A faint orange glow emanated from within his throat. Even in his decrepit state he could still feel pain. A great fire grew from inside him. With one quick flash, the flesh had been incinerated. Only a smoking charred skeleton remained.

"This power…what exactly did you do?" Valdryn asked.

"Demon's blood doesn't just poison the body," the spirit said. "It attacks the very soul. Your spirit is strong but still struggled. So, I took some of the pain onto myself."

"A soul meld," Valdryn sighed.

"Yes. It will keep the poison at bay but it will linger until we find a definitive cure." The spirit's voice was exhausted. "I'll focus on regaining my memories so you can gain more of my power. For better or worse, we're stuck with one another now."

Valdryn made his way to the exit, leaving behind the darkness and the stench of death that grew within. The idea of being bonded in such a manner weighed heavy on him. The spirit has helped him thus far however, and if it meant saving the city then he would take that extra step to see it done.

Chapter 18: Brotherhood

The sounds of battle rang out from beyond the top of the stairs. The clanging of metal and the shouting voices were a welcome return to Valdryn's ears. With his sword drawn, he charged up the steps. The cellar room was brightly lit with torches on the various pillars. Barrels and crates were stacked to form barricades but to little effect.

The guards were dealing with more undead, outnumbered three to one. The captain, marked by his crimson half-cape, was leading the defense valiantly. Their defense training was being put to good use as they held their ground. They were holding their own until the centipedes attacked.

"These damned things again?" shouted one of the guards.

"Master Tariv said separating them from the body kills them both," said the captain.

One of the larger guards gripped the head of the creature. With it held in place, the others were quick to cut it from the walking corpse. A locked heavy door stood between Valdryn and the guards. He tried to force it open but brute strength wasn't for him. He centered his focus as an overwhelming surge of power rushed through his body.

"What do we do, sir?" panicked one of the guards.

"We bring these bastards down with us, solider," the captain rallied.

They prepared themselves for the end, ready to do their duty. A hurling mass of fire suddenly barreled through the masses and scorched all in its path. Even some of the centipedes could not withstand the power. Ash and embers filled the chambers but the guards were luckily unharmed.

"Death is not an option for us," Valdryn shouted. "Today, we live and our enemies will die."

"Blademaster?" The captain was wide eyed and hopeful. They had a chance to survive this after all. "Come on, men. If Valdryn says we don't die today then who are we to defy him."

The soldiers rallied around Valdryn and dispatched the invaders. Valdryn's mighty renewed blade sheered through the centipedes, even their carapace was cut clean. Though he clearly didn't need the assistance, the soldiers were glad to join in.

"Show them no mercy!" shouted the captain.

The insects were torn from their hosts, one by one, with ease. Valdryn's speed and power was unlike anything they've seen. The men have seen Valdryn in training but this was like an entirely new being to them. One centipede coiled itself around the blade to disarm him but Valdryn leveraged his blade tore creature from its host. These mindless creatures had walked into a slaughter.

Forced on the defensive, the beasts pulled back from the guards and forced them into the center of the room. They formed a wall to hold the guards but never closed the distance. The ceiling above began to crack and rumble. Falling trails of dust grew closer to the center as the cracks grew larger.

"A hive master is here," said the captain.

"A what?" asked Valdryn.

"Larger creatures that control these ones. Kill it and they'll all fall." The guards formed their own wall around the captain and Valdryn who were standing back-to-back. They were waiting for the moment to strike, knowing they would not get another.

The hive master burst through the ceiling above them but before Valdryn could react, the lesser creatures leapt at them. They threw themselves onto the guards' swords. With their weapons pinned, they could not fight back.

Valdryn struggled to keep the large monster's head at bay. The chattering mandibles repeatedly reached for his throat. He could feel the anger swelling and the magic on the verge of exploding but it put the guards at risk. All seemed lost when two figures rushed into the cellar with their weapons drawn.

The one with a large hammer barreled through the creatures, freeing the guards. The other hooked her glowing crescent daggers into the hive master, holding its head in place. Valdryn didn't hesitate to drive his blade through the creature's mouth and into its brain. The creatures screamed and lashed out in a painful panic as its blood poured from its mouth.

"Why are they not dead?" said the captain.

"There are multiple hive masters. We've killed two already," Tariv replied, nearly out of breath.

"They're vulnerable for the moment," said Yvette as she wiped the blood from her face. "Kill them now."

Everyone cut their way through the remaining creatures, carving a path to the exit. The group had made their way up to the first floor. The interior had been broken and bloodied, contrast to its once stunning beauty. Tapestries depicting Ruvo and his history were torn to unrecognizable shreds. Corpses littered the floor and blood painted the walls.

"Captain. Take your men to the second floor and hold your position until Yvette joins you," Tariv ordered.

"Yes, sir." He turned to Valdryn, wiping the blood from his blade. "It was a pleasure to fight with you, Blademaster. We're forever in your debt."

"Likewise," said Valdryn.

The guards left for their new position, unaware of the tension growing. Valdryn did not take his eyes off of Yvette and she understood why. They waited for others to fall out of earshot before breaking the silence.

"What the hell is she doing here?" spat Valdryn.

"Saving your life evidently," mocked Yvette.

The two were prepared for a rematch before Tariv stepped between them. "Enough. Valdryn, she's on our side."

"How can you say that? She started all of this." Valdryn felt his anger growing once more. He bared his teeth and clenched his fists around the hilt of his blade. Any more pressure and one would feel sorry for the weapon.

"I regret what I've done but this was never my intent." She lowered her weapons. "I only ever wanted Barathel dead."

Valdryn paused, intrigued by the common interest. "Why?"

The sounds of battle grew louder, matched only by the thunder and wind around them. A storm within a storm consuming everything. Even nature itself seemed to want the city reduced to rubble.

"We don't have time for the full story," she said. "All you need to know for now is I lost *everything* because of him."

Valdryn remembered the men he led into the temple. He remembered the look on Jonas's face when he was told of his advancement. His mind focused on the proud warriors who walked with him into the darkness. He remembered how all of that was swept away with one hasty decision.

"She can sense arcane power, brother," Tariv said. "You're the only one who can match that creature." He nodded to Yvette, motioning for her to take her leave.

"For what it's worth, I'm glad I failed my mission," she said. "Were I successful, we'd all be as good as dead."

"Perhaps a change in occupation is required then," he said, his anger subsiding.

"Perhaps," she smiled.

She left for the captain while more guards filled the main chambers. They took up positions overlooking the main entrance. No matter what happened, this room was to be defended to the last man.

"I sent scouts into the city," Tariv led Valdryn to their own destination. "I don't know how you rallied them but Ironveins and Yurik have been leading the defense well. Even the bulk of civilians are standing their ground."

Valdryn laughed with a sense of pride. Gordok wasn't much of a fighter despite some experience. He would rather be tinkering away with siege machinery. To see him on the battlefield letting his instincts take over was a sight to behold.

Yurik, seemed to only care for the lust of battle and avenging his fallen brothers. Valdryn pondered the notion that perhaps there was something after vengeance. If Yurik could become something more after avenging his men then maybe so could Valdryn.

"Yvette was able to locate the remaining two hive masters. She's dealing with one while we handle the other." Tariv pointed at another handful of guards, motioning for them to join. "It will buy us the time we need to deal with Balvas."

"I'm not even sure how to kill him, Tariv," worried Valdryn.

"We'll find a way," Tariv smiled, placing his hand on Valdryn's shoulder.

Valdryn and Tariv led twenty guards towards the prisoner wing. Corpses were piled high and rot filled the air. Valdryn hardly recognized the path he walked when he went to interrogate Yvette just a few days ago. Never had he seen so much blood. Even the raids weren't this horrendous.

"I'm sorry about Jonas," said Tariv in an effort to break the silence.

"How did you find out?" Valdryn could feel the emptiness in his gut.

"That boy was your shadow. Just the fact that he's not here and that look of anger hasn't left your face yet tells me everything." Tariv kept his eyes to the walls and ceiling. He was waiting to take on the next ambush, ready for a fight.

Valdryn looked at his sword. It was the source of his new power but it was the same one used to usher Jonas out of this world. "It was—"

"I don't need the details, brother," Tariv interrupted. "Just make sure the ones responsible pay."

Valdryn nodded, reassured that his friend still lived. He had grown far too accustomed to losing people. Tariv was the last one on the Isle who knew him before his promotion to Blademaster. He was the last representation of his past. The brotherhood forged through trials and training was a bond meant to last.

The guards with them walked with confidence. They were, by all means, experienced fighters but they understood the added benefit of having the Blademaster and the Hammer standing with them. These were men who earned their place and whose reputation spread, and rightly so.

A mangled corpse was thrown into the wall before them. The sickening crack and splatter of blood caught them off guard but they regained their composure instantly. Valdryn and Tariv took lead while the guards fit into a tight defensive formation behind them. With their flanks covered, Valdryn and Tariv could make their advance to the hive.

Peering around the corner, they saw the dead guards being consumed by the centipedes. Their host bodies would hold the fallen in place while the insects tore the flesh and muscle from the bones. A river of blood flowed through the halls and to the hive structure that now rested at the center of the cells.

"What do you see, sirs?" asked the captain of this unit.

"Harden your hearts and sharpen your minds," said Valdryn. "This isn't for the faint of heart."

Tariv concluded, "Nothing you have witnessed has prepared you for this. But you are Ruvo's finest for a reason."

They turned the corner as quietly as they could so as not to alert the hive too soon. Though the gorging was sickening, it was the perfect distraction. These creatures would be sluggish on a full stomach as well so Valdryn was prepared to wait as long as he could before going in for the kill.

Tariv and Valdryn turned to one another. Without a word they understood what the other was thinking and motioned for the guards to hold their position. Staying light on their feet, they approached the creatures. Tariv's boots were heavy still, so he avoided what puddles of blood he could. The leather supplied by the minotaurs allowed Valdryn to approach more quickly and quietly.

The Blademaster was in position to strike while Tariv was on the opposite side of the hall waiting for their moment. Attacking in unison, Valdryn severed the head of the insect while Tariv infused his hammer and flattened his target. The two waved the guards forward and they followed this strategy down the hall. Their speed was efficient enough until they came across a mound of bodies. The abundant food supply enticed the majority of the creatures.

"What do we do now," whispered Tariv.

"It looks like the perfect opportunity to test out some fire magic," said Valdryn.

Tariv smiled and fell back to the guards to prepare them. Valdryn got as close as he could, immersing himself in the foul stench and stomach-turning noises. He placed the tip of his blade in the center of the large pool of blood. Even though not everyone could wield magic, most still had a modicum of arcane energy in their blood.

Valdryn used his blade to summon every ounce of this energy from the fallen and began to amass it into a single ball of energy. An intense heat radiated from his body and blade, boiling the blood around him at his feet.

The creatures could sense the power generating behind them. The hosts turned with spears and shields ready. The insects coiled around the bodies, keeping their heads low. One stepped forward to study Valdryn. They were unsure on whether he was predator or prey, friend or foe.

An inferno swirled around his sword. With a horizontal slash, he bathed the chamber in flame. The front line of creatures was incinerated and the hive was engulfed in flames. Valdryn charged first and cut down one of the frantic creatures.

Tariv led the charge with the guards and made quick work of the injured. He grabbed one of the creatures by the throat and hurled it through the charred outer husk of the hive. "Don't give them a chance to recover!" he ordered.

The guards split and took to each side, forming small shield walls. A few took positions behind them and slowly pushed forward. Tariv guided the right and the captain took the left. Each creature they came across was far too injured to put up a fight. Valdryn held his position and stared at the charred cracking husk before him.

Well, that was certainly something.

"I thought you were resting, spirit," he said quietly so as not to alarm the others.

I was until a felt a massive surge of energy. I see your making use of our combined strength.

"Does it drain you still?" Valdryn wondered.

Not as much. Our spirits are growing accustomed to one another. Rather than consuming the energy, we are able to recycle it.

The guards were slaughtering the hive protectors. Yelling and cheering at their victory while Tariv focused on cracking open the hive. The hive master could be heard hissing inside but hesitated at the immense heat surrounding it.

"How are your memories?" continued Valdryn.

They're coming along. I remember riding out with my companions. The sensation of an impending battle is strong.

"There was a great siege of the temple a long time ago. Considering where I found your sword…" he trailed off.

Perhaps. But I can't recall any temple. There's this gaping black hole in my thoughts I can't see beyond.

Rain poured in from the hole in the wall the hive boulder created on impact. The howling wind turned this side of the keep into a wind tunnel and began to blow out the flames. The walls began to shake as something else made impact.

Valdryn was following the movement as it got closer the giant hole in the upper wall. A giant hulking creature stared down upon the guards. A mocking laughter was carried on the wind as he jumped and landed on two of the guards, killing them immediately. A giant crimson centipede unraveled from the creature's arm and swiped its way through the captain and the remains of his shield wall.

"I'm glad you live, Blademaster," said Balvas. "I wish to see the look on your face when this land is brought to ruin."

"Let's end this here and now, Balvas!" A thin veil of blue fire wrapped around his blade.

"Tempting, but I have more pressing matters to attend to." A black beam shot out from the crimson centipede's mouth, boring a hole through the hive. "As do you," laughed Balvas.

An immense ear-shattering roar emanated from the hive, cracking it on all sides. An enlarged minotaur, twice the size of his kin, burst forth. The hive master had embedded itself within the creature's mass. Its body had protruded in various spots to offer armor while its head had acted like a scorpion's tail from the minotaur's back.

Before anyone could react, the beast charged Valdryn. The remarkable speed nearly overtook him but the spirit helped him dodge out of its path. Pure anger and bloodlust fueled this monster on its path of destruction. The creature dropped to all fours like a feral beast and pursued Valdryn as he fell back to the others.

"Good luck, Blademaster," said Balvas. He made his way down the blood-streaked hall as the centipede around his arm picked at the corpses.

The guards quickly moved to cover the beast on all sides. Their blood drenched spears ready to take another evil creature from this world. The centipede lunged at them, keeping the distance it needed. Its speed was unmatched no matter how coordinated the men were.

Tariv and Valdryn stood before it within the circle. The beast did not care for its opposition. A giant bladed axe was buried into its ribcage, a sign of the battle it faced before turning into a slave of Balvas's magic. It pulled the weapon free with ease, the coagulated black blood still sticking to the blade.

"An undead minotaur with a sentient tail and a giant axe," sighed Tariv as he gathered his energy.

"And just when you think you've seen it all," said Valdryn. He stepped to the beast's left, dividing its attention. "It won't be enough to just kill the insect, I fear."

"A hunt then?" asked Tariv as he readied his hammer.

"A hunt," Valdryn smiled in agreement.

Valdryn attacked without warning. Two clean slashes left its mark on the beast's neck before it retaliated with its own slashes. With Valdryn on the defensive, Tariv closed in. His strikes were quick and decisive. One blow to the shoulder and one to the head which cracked the left horn in half.

Repeated alternated strikes kept the beast in place. Valdryn's quick slashes would draw its attention while Tariv's hammer would break the beast, piece by piece. The centipede was occupied with the soldiers. The melding of the two minds hindered the creatures' coordination which only fueled its rage in frustration.

Tired of this game, the beast spun wildly. Its tail whipped through the air, its clenched fist pounded the floor, and the axe scraped and slashed the ground. The tail was able to catch a guard and pulled him close. It constricted his body and bit down on his head. Another guard threw his spear and pierced the beast's gut. It retaliated by launching his axe, leaving behind a bloody mess of the guard.

"This thing can't be killed!" screamed a guard as he turned to run.

"Hold your ground!" ordered Valdryn. But that order fell on deaf ears as the beast tore through the remaining guards.

It ran for its weapon but Valdryn was faster. He charged into the beast and knocked it off balance. He drove his blade deep into an exposed part of the centipede's underbelly. The insect reared its head to strike but Tariv brought his hammer's full might. The chitin cracked on the head and the minotaur felt the pain as it let out a wail. Valdryn tried to bring his sword down on its head for a killing blow but was thrown against the crumbling wall.

"Valdryn!" shouted Tariv, his heart racing.

The beast reared its head and charged at full speed, ready to gore him with his remaining horn. Valdryn was dazed but rolled away just in time. The wall behind him crumbled and fell to the base of the keep. The beast picked Valdryn up by his neck and held him in place for the centipede. It lunged for the kill but tasted steel instead. Valdryn shoved his blade into its mouth and it pierced up and out of the centipede's head.

The minotaur roared, spewing blood and spit everywhere. Its legs grew weak but its grip remained. It clenched its other fist around the spear in its belly and pulled it free. It raised the spear high above Valdryn's head.

Death comes for us all I suppose.

"Not today!" bellowed Tariv. He charged headfirst into the beast. The spear missed its target and snapped on impact as it hit the wall. Tariv held his hammer reversed and stabbed repeatedly with the sharp pommel, forcing the beast to the edge.

Valdryn's vision was hazy but returning to him quickly, just in time to see his friend fall with the beast. As the minotaur lost its footing, it reached for Tariv. It pulled him in close and dragged him down into the darkened depths of the city below.

"No!" howled Valdryn, frantically searching for his friend, his brother.

The storm had blocked out the sun and shrouded the city in darkness. From this height, he couldn't see the bottom of the keep. It was as though the city floated within the abyss and anyone caught outside was lost forever.

"Tariv!" he screamed at the darkness, but the wind carried his words away. Slumped to his knees, Valdryn's heart grew heavy and the world around him grew bleak. His mind wondered down the memories of his fallen friends and family. Among the chaos, he was alone.

You are not alone, Blademaster.

The spirit appeared before him, nearly complete. The design of his armor was complete with robes and plate. The filigree on his mask and the sigil of a tree above his heart marked him as a high-ranking battlemage from a bygone age.

"Another memory has come to me, my friend." The spirit knelt down by Valdryn, placing a hand on his shoulder. "They are but fragments but I remember the faces of my comrades, my brothers and sisters. There were nine of us and we rode out against armies."

"What's your point, spirit?" Valdryn's eyes met the hollow gaze of the spirit's mask.

"We all met each other when we lost everything. Before we fell in battle, we ensured the ones responsible fell first." The spirit stood up and peered into the darkness through the broken wall. "The ones responsible for your friends' deaths are still standing and put everyone at risk."

Valdryn felt the power pulsing from the blade. The same energy radiated from the spirit and only grew stronger. The warmth washed over him and transformed his armor, mirroring the spirit's, with the exception of the mask.

"You have my sword. Now you have my armor." The spirit faded back and his voice echoed in Valdryn's mind. "Now stand up and finish this."

<u>Chapter 19: Follow the Blood</u>

Valdryn stretched his arms and legs, getting used to his new armor. Much like his sword, it had become unblemished as though it was just forged. He was a gleaming blend of silver light and obsidian metal among the crimson floor and walls. Most of the corpses that were being fed on were gone. Only scraps of flesh remained to litter his path back to the main hall.

"Everyone who dies just adds to his army," stuttered a voice from the shadows.

"Show yourself," Valdryn demanded.

An unarmed guard stepped forth, the same one who abandoned him and the others earlier. Valdryn did not hesitate in his movement towards the man. He slammed him against the wall with enough force to knock the breath out of him. He held his blade pressed to the guard's throat, his bright green eyes piercing through the man's soul.

"Of course, you still live. You ran and left us to die," spat Valdryn.

"We were going to die either way," cried the guard.

"We are all going to die someday. You knew the risks when signing up for the guard so why does your cowardice give you the right to live while others die?" Valdryn never blinked. He wasn't sure what answer he was really looking for, only a reason to take the man's life.

"It doesn't!" the man shouted. "Just kill me already and be done with it."

Valdryn gripped his blade tightly, his arms shaking. Every part of him wanted to take his life. He raised his blade high, screaming at the top of lungs, before plunging it down. It landed a mere inch away from the cowering guard.

"Killing you is a mercy you don't deserve." He took the knife from the guard's belt and carved a 'C' into the man's forehead. The man's screams were muffled by his own sobs and tears. "You will be known as a coward until the day you die. Accept that fate or redeem yourself through action. It does not matter to me."

He threw the whimpering guard to the side, tossing the knife back into the chamber Tariv fell from. Something in him was broken and his heart was set ablaze. He couldn't put it to rest but he knew he could put it to better use than punishing others. Balvas was still on his rampage and Valdryn needed to save every ounce of hatred for him.

Stepping into the main chamber, he found nothing but chaos. The guards were overrun with undead. They held their own but it would not last. Valdryn wrapped himself in arcane energy and leapt into the fray. The flames he commanded were precise and completely under his control. Each undead he struck down turned to ash and dust.

"It's the Blademaster!" cheered some of the guards.

"This battle is ours!" he rallied back. "Form a line and hold them back."

The guards fell back and reinforced the rear position, forming a phalanx between the undead and the stairs leading to the upper levels. Valdryn looked for a captain but found none. Instead, he looked for the bloodiest guard and pulled him aside.

"Did you see Balvas come this way?" asked Valdryn.

"If you mean that giant creature then yes, sir. He said something about Barathel before he…"

"Before he what, solider?" demanded Valdryn.

The guard swallowed the lump in his throat. "Before killing our captain, sir." He pointed at a fresh blood trail leading up the stairs.

Valdryn shook his head. The Isle was meant to be a new beginning for so many. Now it only represented the end. "You're in charge now. Hold the line and don't let anything pass. Once Balvas falls, his army will too."

"As you command, sir." The guard joined the line and rallied the others as the undead threw themselves on their wall.

Do you think they'll survive?

"In truth, no." Valdryn followed the blood to the upper levels. "But their deaths could buy us enough time to stop Balvas and the sooner he's dealt with, the more lives we'll save."

Its oddly comforting to be running towards the battle once more. Let us hope it ends better this time.

Yvette clawed her way through the masses. She destroyed the hive master but its spawn only grew frenzied. Most of her guard was still alive but scattered. The library had many rooms for study but were repurposed for holding corpses when the hive masters spread. The fight was in their favor until the mass of corpses ambushed them.

The undead moved sluggish due to their time buried in the grave or the wounds they suffered when they were alive. The insects had torn out chunks of flesh and the muscles in their legs had deteriorated, forcing some to crawl. Most of the librarians and historians were older too so their bodies were weakened from time.

Yvette climbed to the top of a shelf to build space and catch her breath. She could hear the guards in the other rooms holding their own but she was alone here. The hive master's body was slumped in the corner with its dark blood staining the floor. One of the corpses climbed up after her but her attacks were too quick. She hooked one blade into the temple and used the other to sever the head.

"I have to get out of here," she said, wiping the blood off on her pants.

The horde began to rock the shelf back and forth. Yvette hooked her blades into the shelf to hold her balance and search for a way out. She looked down and saw a barred door where the corpses used to lie. She recalled studying the layout of the keep a few weeks prior.

"That door could mean only one thing," she sighed.

As the shelf tipped over, she leapt through the window behind her. Shards of stained glass soared through the air and crashed down with her onto the balcony overlooking the city. The wind was strong this high up but the rain was refreshing. Parts of the city were on fire and towers of smoke joined with the dark clouds above.

"Is this all my fault?" she wondered. "I never wanted this. I just wanted Barathel to suffer for what he did."

She had no time to grab armor when the hive first crashed through the keep. She had leather padded boots and gloves. Loose padding covered her shoulders and chest but a simple shirt was underneath. Her legs were only protected by a thin layer of cloth pants.

She could hear the horde breaking through the door behind her. Even with the howling wind she could still make out the unmistakable sound of gnashing teeth. The frenzied hosts were coming for her. She readied herself into a low position, like a panther waiting to strike.

Time seemed to slow as the door began to give way. She spied the cracked telescopes the librarians would use to pass the time during their late-night studies. Leftover scraps from their last meal were scattered from the wind. She tuned the wind out and heard the screams from the city below. Beyond the holes in the door, she saw the faces of the corpses of simple folk frozen in anguish.

"I deserve this," she whispered, closing her eyes and readying herself for the end.

She flinched at each break of the wood until it finally fell. She was too deep in her thoughts to notice a shift in the sound. Where she was expecting an enraged charge, she heard a voice. "Glad to see you still live."

She opened her eyes to see the guards standing before her, covered in blood. It reminded her of a time when she was a child and she ran away from home. Upon returning, her mother said those same words with a smile and an open door. She caught the tears before they could fall. No need to show weakness now.

"Thanks for the help," she said. "Figured I'd keep them distracted for the rest of you."

The guard laughed. "I expected nothing less." Their laughter was cut short when the library floor burst into a storm of splinters.

###

Valdryn followed the blood trail to an open chamber with a spiral staircase leading up. The lower half of a body rested in the center, blood pooling and staining the floor. Decapitated bodies were piled along the wall. Yvette and the others made quick work of the undead along their way.

Where's the upper half of this body?

"Nearby," said Valdryn.

Valdryn felt a shift in the air and ducked. Elongated claws barely missed his head as the upper half of a captain lunged past. It leapt in for another strike but Valdryn caught him by the throat and incinerated him instantly.

"We don't have time to waste," Valdryn said, sternly. "Balvas is close."

I sense him as well. He's weakened however.

"How can you tell?" wondered Valdryn. He sprinted up the stairs hoping to close the distance soon.

That creature around his arm. It's both empowering him and draining him. It'll only be for a moment, but killing that thing will leave him exposed.

Valdryn thought about the creature. It wasn't as agile as its smaller counterparts but its strength made up for it. And if it was draining Balvas's magic to make itself stronger than a battle with it could result in the destruction of the keep.

Valdryn would have to be quick and efficient. Catching Balvas off guard would be best.

A few rooms ahead came a loud shattering sound. It felt like a barrage of canon fire crashed through the library and brought the walls down. Perhaps it was too late to save the keep from destruction.

Yvette held her side as she tried to drag herself to safety. When Balvas burst through the library floor, the damage shattered the wall and collapsed the ceiling above. Barathel's chambers were just out of reach but the falling rubble struck and weakened him.

"I've got you, Captain," whispered a guard. He pulled Yvette behind a chunk of the wall to keep her out of sight.

"I'm not your captain," she coughed.

"Yeah, well you're close enough." He covered her with his tower shield to keep her hidden. She tried to push back but he wouldn't let her. "Regain your strength, Captain. We'll deal with the big one."

He charged the chamber, sword drawn, and joined his comrades. Yvette wasn't as well versed in healing magic as she would have liked but it was enough to seal her wounds. She knew that guard had no intent of surviving. He believed in her enough to sacrifice himself to buy her time.

She couldn't see it, perhaps that was blessing, but she could her them being slaughtered.

One by one, Balvas tore through the guards. The giant insect coiled around his arms would swallow soldiers whole and spit out partially digested walking corpses. The guards had seen what the darkness had to offer and now, they had nothing left to fear. They cut down their risen brothers and continued their fight.

Silence suddenly fell on the room. Balvas wasn't tearing apart the guards. The men weren't shouting or clashing with the fallen. It was pure silence, broken only by the thunder and wind. Her heart was pounding as she tried to listen for anything. The mangled corpse of the guard who helped her landed by the ledge. His distorted lifeless face stared at her.

"You cannot hide from me, little one," said Balvas.

Valdryn was nearly crushed when the upper half of the tower collapsed. Balvas was tearing through the keep and its defenders. His undead army would be far more numerous had he not completely decimated the guards.

With the standard path now left in ruin, Valdryn was forced into the servant's quarters. He didn't expect to find any survivors but nothing remained in the rooms aside from ash and embers.

There were very little signs of conflict and Balvas would want to maximize on his army's potential. Only one other thing could have happened.

"He did this," coughed a voice in the far end. An older man was slumped in the far corner. His brown robes turned red on his side.

"Barathel," said Valdryn. He knew from the moment he stepped into the room.

The old man nodded. "Some of us were infected by the black blood. He didn't want to risk further infection." The old man coughed up blood, catching it with his sleeves. "He corralled us. Told us it was for our protection. Some knew better and fought back. Everyone else was burned in their rooms."

"Let me see your wound," said Valdryn.

The older servant moved his hands, exposing the wound to his side. A short thrust from a spear left a large enough wound. Had the man been a few years younger, perhaps it wouldn't be so severe.

"The cowards left me to die," he spat. "I gathered what water was left from the washing basins and put out the flames before they grew too great."

Valdryn knelt down and placed his hand over the wound. "I'm not an expert with healing magic but I'll do what I can." He summoned his energy and gifted a small portion to the man, sealing the wound.

"I don't know how to thank you, Blademaster," cried the old man. He looked away from Valdryn and to the rooms where his friends now lie. Everybody lost something from the actions of a few selfish men.

"Survive," Valdryn said before hearing a familiar voice bellow nearby. He could tell it was Balvas though he couldn't make out the words. All he could gather was that he found more guards to kill.

The old man nodded in agreement and hid among the burnt corpses of his friends. If the undead made their way up here they wouldn't bother with the charred remains. Better to hide among the dead than to join them.

Valdryn left the servants' quarters and found the main corridor to be completely devoid of any guards. No walking corpses, no blood, no death haunted this hall. Barathel was making a vain attempt at starving Balvas and his army. The bulk of the guard was either down in the entrance hall or spread throughout the city.

"Rather than joining us, he hides in his room with his personal guard." Valdryn said aloud, regardless of who may be in earshot. He no longer felt fear and the anger in his heart was emboldened by his sense of duty.

He and my lord certainly have that in common.

"What happened to your lord?" he asked.

I believe I killed him.

Valdryn paused, unsure if he was surprised or not, but did not wish to press the subject. He could hear the wind from beyond the doors ahead. He could smell Balvas's necrotic golem flesh. And he could hear Yvette's voice, defiant as ever, and couldn't help but laugh.

What's so funny?

"Just the other night I nearly killed Yvette in the forest," Valdryn said. He realized it was the last time he and Sandra cooperated, perhaps even the only time. Tariv and Jonas were gone now and he started a war in the city he swore to protect. "Now she's the only one left who help me finish this."

Chapter 20: Wrath of the Fallen

Valdryn stepped into the devastated section of the keep. The heavy rain soaked the floor boards and puddles had begun to from. The strong wind was a welcome change from the heat of the floors below. He half expected the keep to fall by now when he came to a large hole in the wall. He readied himself when he saw Balvas was holding Yvette over the ledge, dangling her above the burning city.

The Blademaster was sticking to the shadows to close the distance. Parts of the floor were still sturdy enough to walk on, forming a splintered walkway overlooking the room. He saw most of the guards who went with Yvette dead in the center. He looked up at the damage in the ceiling and spotted something familiar.

"Barathel's new war room," Valdryn said under his breath.

How can you tell?

"That giant slab peeking over the edge was something he had specially commissioned for his new position here," replied Valdryn. "An enchanted war table to impress all of the other generals."

A bit of a boastful bastard, isn't he?

"He's got twice the skill of most fighters, I know, but not even half the heart to be a leader." Valdryn remembered his first year under Belmont.

He showed him what it meant to lead. He put his men before his own life. He mourned for them before he even sent them on a mission and mourned them again if they never came back. But he assured Valdryn that Barathel wasn't liked by most and yet he earned everything he had.

Valdryn was close enough now and ready a strike but the crimson centipede was moving too much. It was inspecting Yvette, studying the small elf at Balvas's mercy. The serpentine motion made it too risky for him to attack.

"Betraying me was foolish, girl," boomed Balvas. Bones now protruded from his flesh, covering his body like armor. Interconnected bones shielded the entire front of his body, a lesson learned from his encounter with Valdryn in the tunnels.

"Betraying you implies I was on your side," Yvette choked. "You and your little cult were nothing more than a temporary asset."

Valdryn stepped in closer to ready a fatal attack but a misstep snapped a floor board. Balvas was too busy to notice but the centipede reacted immediately and reared its head to investigate.

Yvette noticed a silhouette above and hoped for the best. "You're nothing, Balvas. And you're going to die here." She reached out towards her sickles. A vibrant green energy washed over them and sent them spinning through the air. On their path back to their owner, the crescent blades carved through Balvas. His grip loosened as they sliced through his arm. Yvette caught her weapons and hooked them deep into his hand so she wouldn't fall.

The centipede reacted to Balvas's pain and coiled back towards Yvette, giving Valdryn the opportunity he was waiting for. He leapt high and brought the blade down into the creature. It thrashed through the air to throw him off but Valdryn only tightened his grip.

"You don't know when to quit, Blademaster. It will be the death of you!" Balvas declared.

Yvette saw her own opportunity and started ripping apart Balvas's bone armor. Chunks of bone and flesh fell to the floor before Balvas kicked her away. She didn't stay down for long however. The rush of the battle overtook her and she started carving away at his defenses once more. Her bladed frenzy grew in ferocity as she looked at the fallen guards who followed her.

Valdryn missed his mark and his blade pierced just behind the creature's head. He twisted his blade, causing as much damage as he could before its body began to glow a bright crimson. He tried to leverage his blade to split its head but a strong pulse of energy was released. It threw Valdryn off and pushed Yvette back once more. The debris in the room scattered and ceiling above cracked and splintered even more.

A long scythe-like blade of energy protruded from the centipede's mouth. Balvas whipped the creature through the air like a wild glaive. Endless swipes and slashes kept the pair on the move. Yvette had her natural reflexes to rely on while Valdryn had a helpful voice in his head to watch his back.

Yvette moved with such grace as each swing in her direction missed by a mile. This was her element, Balvas was her prey. Valdryn understood her strategy from the moment they fought and was able to counter with his years of experience. Balvas was full of primal rage and too blind to realize she was letting him waste his energy.

Valdryn wasn't as quick but far more powerful. He could read the creature's movements and predicted his path, always three steps ahead. He tried throwing fire and lightning at Balvas but he shrugged them off. If magic won't hurt him than brute force will have to tear him apart.

Balvas emitted a loud, ear-piercing howl. Spears of bones peeked out from his body, tipped with a dark orange flame. "You will all die."

"Get behind me!" Valdryn shouted to Yvette, surrounding himself with a strong aura of magic.

Yvette bolted behind Valdryn as the spears exploded outward. His barrier was strong enough to repel the spears but he soon understood that wasn't Balvas's intent. The spears that embedded themselves into the wall shifted from an orange flame to black. Obsidian needles burst from the spears, putting the pair on the move once more.

Balvas himself had grown weary and the parasite around his arm looked sluggish. Valdryn was almost crushed when a chunk of ceiling fell but Yvette's reflexes kept them out of harm's way. The room was collapsing with every movement. Looking up, he saw the war table teetering after Balvas's last attack.

"How's your accuracy?" He asked Yvette.

"You should already know the answer," she replied, spinning away from the black needles.

"Fair enough," he laughed. He created another barrier for a quick reprieve. "Can you bring that table down?"

She looked up and quickly noted it's positioning. "Shouldn't be too difficult if you watch my back."

The pair broke off, dividing the needles. Valdryn ran to his embedded blade and used it to get a hold of the centipede's head. As he dragged the head forward, he could feel his strength rising from the blade leeching the energy. His barrier grew with each passing second.

"Now, Yvette!" he shouted.

Her sickles absorbed the wind and glowed with bright green energy once more. She spun both blades towards the war table and brought it down with the first attempt. Barathel's extravagant prize will finally serve a purpose. Its crushing weight crashed into the centipede and wrenched it free from Balvas's arm.

The sudden burst of pain enraged the creature but it was too late. Valdryn pulled his blade free, leaving a giant gash in its head. He followed it up with a wide vertical swath of arcane energy, easily splitting the creature down the middle. The blade had consumed enough energy to awaken its full power. The energy blast burned the insect as it split and erased it from the room.

Now is the time to strike.

"Agreed," Valdryn said aloud.

Yvette followed his approach on Balvas but noticed the bone spears changing. They faded to black pulsating spikes. "Valdryn," she said, trying to get his attention.

"What now?" His advance did not slow. Yvette had to grasp his arm to get his attention.

Balvas's all too familiar mocking laughter echoed all around them. A giant obsidian axe of pure energy appeared in his hands. Flickers of black flame appeared and faded around him. "I really should thank you."

His power is growing. Something's wrong.

Valdryn grabbed Yvette and leapt backwards, narrowly dodging a row of black spikes. The spikes that pierced the floor and walls combined into five large crystal and floated around Balvas.

Conduits. The source of his new power.

"We need to destroy those crystals, Yvette." He summoned personal auras around Yvette and himself to ward off the energies. His breaths where now shallow and hastened, beads of sweat dotting his forehead.

"I'll take care of them," she said before charging. "You deal with the abomination."

They charged Balvas but he quickly reacted with a downward swing of his axe between them. The force sent them flying to either side of the room. "That creature was getting greedy and gluttonous, taking more of my energy than it gave back. But now that you've severed the connection…" He summoned pillars of dark light. The pure dark energy was a stark contrast to the black flame. Immense cold filled the area while an intense heat pulsated from Balvas's aura.

Valdryn tried to close the distance but the crystals pulsed with the same heat. Balvas had rendered an up-close fight impossible against his adversaries with limited range. This spell was meant for Valdryn. The necromancer knew what he was doing and they walked right into his trap.

Valdryn tried his energy arcs from his sword but the energy washed over the crystals. They only seemed to empower them, increasing the range of the pulses. Balvas's aura reacted in a similar way but he unleashed his own energy arcs. The concussive force was too much for Valdryn to absorb and they pushed him back.

"What the hell are we supposed to do now?" shouted Yvette, watching the crystal and waiting for another new trick.

"I don't know," he replied, regrettably.

I do. But it's what you've been fighting against.

"Will it stop him?" Valdryn asked, nearly muted. He stared the beast down hoping for a different option but to no avail.

It will distract him long enough for you to stop him.

Valdryn's mind was filled with glimpses of undead hordes made up of fresh corpses, walking bones, and restless spirits. Towering armored giants fell to these unnatural swarms. Orc clans attempting to claim territory were decimated. Conquering human armies were brought to their knees. At the helm of these hordes were warriors wearing similar armor to the Spirit's.

My ancestors. They mastered a spell which should only be used sparingly.

When the opposing armies fell, the undead were granted their rest. The corpses turned to ash and the spirits dissipated into a blinding light. But there was always a war. There was always someone trying to lay claim to something that did not belong to them. With war, came ruin and death. With victory came new life and the continued cycle of grudges. The ancient warriors would harness such death to hasten the end of the war. With their blades raised and directed towards the enemy, they would shout their incantations to wake the dead.

The images ended and cleared his mind. The barrier he crafted was beginning to shatter. He nearly didn't notice his blade raised and glowing. He paid it all no thought and simply acted. The energy swelled within him and he could sense all eyes were on him. "The wrath of the fallen will not be ignored! Bare witness to the fury of the dead and the sting of vengeance!" he shouted, though paired with another's voice.

Pulses of light radiated from his sword and washed over the entirety of the keep. Sprits in all forms of armor found on the isle appeared. Most of them had gaunt hollow faces but Valdryn was able to recognize some of the guards. Even the captain that joined him earlier was here.

"Why do only a few of them have faces?" he wondered.

"They say you can only recognize the spirits of the people you once knew," replied Yvette. "Where did you learn that spell?"

Valdryn was too busy looking for another familiar face in the ever-growing crowd of spirits. He saw the guards who joined him at the warehouse raids. He saw the men and women who worked in the keep that he would interact with from time to time. He saw everyone but the ones he wanted, the ones he missed the most.

The fallen are awaiting your command.

"I don't know, Yvette," he replied. "And it doesn't matter."

"I knew there was something different about you, Valdryn," shouted Balvas. "But your new found power won't be enough."

"We shall see," said Valdryn. Sprites of flame surrounded him like little guardians. "Fallen! Take your vengeance and destroy Balvas!"

The spirits charged Balvas like a swarm of insects looking for their next meal. Their spirit blades glided through his flesh with ease. They left no wounds but his pain was impossible to ignore. He dropped to his knees and screamed in agony. He lashed out but he couldn't focus his magic through the pain. His axe was able to cast away each spirit it hit but it was beginning to fade and flicker.

"Now, Yvette.," shouted Valdryn. "We go for the crystals."

Together they charged the crystal conduits. One by one they shattered, sending out waves of dark energy. Balvas was helpless as he watched his plan fall to pieces right before his eyes. As the last crystal exploded, his axe hardened and shattered with it. Splinters of crystalized dead energy littered the floor. His aura had faded and the mass of angry souls descended upon him.

"He's finished," Yvette smiled.

Not yet. What you see is just the shell of the man inside.

"Be at peace," said Valdryn as he waved his blade. The souls departed for the realm of the dead, leaving behind a slumped maimed Balvas.

"You...can't...stop this..."

Two of the flame sprites disappeared into the ground by Balvas. Before anyone could react, two flame spears shot up from the ground and pierced his hands. His only means to defend himself was diminished with his arms overextended above his head.

"This...world...will..."

Balvas attempted to stand up but two more of the sprites intervened. They turned into spinning blades and severed the legs above the knees. His energy was too far gone and his regeneration along with it. The black blood pooled beneath him and ignited. His body was beginning to cook but he would not rest.

"Darkness...comes...for—"

The last sprite shot into his mouth and expanded into shrapnel of pure flame. His lower jaw unhinged while his left eye socket was blown out. He tried to speak but only gargles came out.

"You talk far too much," said Valdryn. With one arcing slash, he carved down the middle. Like a breaking damn, the blood poured from within. Valdryn waved the flame away and reached into the broken corpse. Deep to the core, through muscles and organs, he found what he was looking for. With all his strength, he pulled a body through the wound.

"What in all the hells?" Yvette had never expected this.

The upper half of a young man dangled from the large corpse. His skin was somewhat translucent and fresh veins branched throughout his body. His eyes were a never-ending pair of voids. He gasped for air, ignoring his surroundings.

Valdryn grabbed him by the throat, stemming the flow of air but allowing him to live for the moment.

"Is that—"

"Balvas," said Valdryn. "This creature served as a cocoon for his rebirth."

"Just a mere display of true power," Balvas said, haggardly.

"Power," Valdryn said with a fire in his eyes. He pierced his blade into his shoulder and twisted. The arm fell limp but Balvas didn't show an ounce of pain. "With all this 'power', you still failed."

"Failed? Hmm perhaps in my original design." He took a deep breath, welcoming the fresh air. "But as I look into your eyes, I see now that I was never the true herald of the dark age. I was merely the messenger…the catalyst."

"What are you talking about?" asked Valdryn.

Balvas laughed, not mockingly, but perhaps relieved at the nearing end. "In the coming years, you will know. You will hear. You will see. And it will stem from your failure, not mine."

Valdryn clenched his fists around the hilt of his sword. He drove his blade through Balvas's wicked smile, down to the guard. His body went limp and the hulking mass he controlled quickly began to decay. The flame spears holding it up softened and washed over what remained.

"For Jonas," Valdryn muttered to himself.

"I can't believe it's finished," said Yvette.

"Not yet, Barthel still remains," he said. He turned to see her slouched over and clutching her side. "Are you hurt?"

She fell to her knees. "You've done worse" she smiled.

Valdryn held her up and helped her over to a pile of rubble she could rest on. He checked for her wounds. A small amount of blood stained her side from a reopened cut. He sealed it but couldn't remove the pain.

"See, it's not that serious," she winced.

"No, but it is enough to slow you down," he said, trying to hide his concern.

"I can still fi—" she tried to stand up but Valdryn quickly set her back down. Tears began to run down her cheeks but not from the pain. "I have to kill him. I made a promise. He has to die by my hands."

"What did he do to earn your hatred?" Valdryn asked.

"That's a long story and this isn't the time or place," she said through the tears. "Short answer, he's the reason my family is dead."

Valdryn knew that feeling. Even if Barathel didn't wield the blade, his actions were equally responsible. Barathel hardly had a hand in

Valdryn's final moments with his father but he was responsible for what happened to Jonas and Bannon. His mind wondered to how Ava was holding up. She was bed ridden and incapable of avenging her brother so he had to be her vengeance.

"Please, let me fight," Yvette pleaded. "Everything I've done, to the Isle, the people, to you. It can't be for nothing."

"If you go, you will die. You will be another casualty in his story," he said. "You set me on this path that night. So, I will keep your promise for you." He stared at her, seeing her now in a new light. Before him wasn't the assassin he dueled in the forest under the moonlight. She was now just another wounded soul among the many.

She looked deep into his eyes. She expected the same fire and fury she experienced in her cell. Instead, she saw emptiness. Where once there was a vibrant green there was now a dullness mixed with a darker sheen. She simply nodded in defeat.

"He will be brought to justice for all that he's done." Valdryn climbed up the rubble and left Yvette to recover. What remained of the floor above, was sturdy enough to support him as he made way out of the destroyed library.

"If I set you on this path…" Yvette wondered "What have I done?"

Chapter 21: A Promise Fulfilled

The highest level of the keep remained untouched from the battle that raged through the city. The interior was decorated with tapestries and carpets made of fabrics from the mainland. Statues and paintings had fallen from the rampage but there were no bodies, no blood, no decay in the air up here. The war room was gone and the guards were nowhere to be found.

Valdryn kept his sword unsheathed, ready for an ambush. Balvas's death meant the end of the undead siege but Barathel knew his Blademaster had come for him. He was well aware of the unfavorable opinions people had of him. Valdryn saw firsthand what Barathel was willing to do, or to be more precise, what he would have others do.

The valorous general hides like a coward.

"You sound different, spirit," said Valdryn.

The spirit appeared beside him, walking along and performing his own investigation. "Barathel and that creature of his provided more than enough sustenance to regain my strength. My name still eludes me but it will come to me, once I delve through the memories."

"That's good to hear." Valdryn peered down the long hall, looking for any movement, any sign of life.

"I have you to thank for it," said the spirit. "I would be withering away in that tomb if it weren't for you. I will find a way to repay you."

Valdryn groaned, unconcerned with a reward. "Just help me see this through and we'll call it even."

"Acceptable terms," replied the spirit before fading once more.

The lack of barriers and other defensive positions made Valdryn uneasy. Barathel was a confident man but he wouldn't be so careless as to leave his halls undefended. He was an experienced fighter and had picked up more than his fair share of tactics on the battlefield. Surely, he was planning something.

"Do you insist on hiding forever, Barathel!" Valdryn shouted. "The people no longer support you. The city guard no longer support you. The mages no longer support you." His words echoed through the vacant halls.

Valdryn approached an archway which lead to Barathel's office, the last place they ever spoke. It was cleared out but he could sense a power lingering nearby. Down the long hall, a pair of doors opened and two guards stepped out. Barathel stood between them.

"You have no idea what is happening, do you?" Barathel asked. "You are too consumed by your anger and vengeance to see."

"And have you ever asked yourself why so many around you hate you?" retorted Valdryn. "I seek justice, not vengeance, and I am not the only one."

"People will always hate those in charge." More guards stepped forth from his office to form a shield wall. "I do what I do for *them*, in spite of their disdain. If their hatred makes them sleep better at night, then so be it."

Valdryn stepped forth but stopped inside the entrance. He closed his eyes and sensed his surroundings. He knew what waited for him. "You could have been something great, Barathel. I am not too proud to admit it. But your decisions have brought nothing but ruin to everyone around you."

Barathel pointed his spear at Valdryn. A silver gryphon cradled the base of the long blade with runes swirling down the haft. "Just as you did with your mission into the temple? Just as you did with Jonas?"

"If those are to be your last words," Valdryn felt the fire inside grow, his teeth now bare in a slight snarl. "Then so be it."

He charged forward, throwing a blade of pure blue fame to his left and impaling the guard waiting to get the jump on him. Another stepped forth from the right but Valdryn cut him clean in half. The guard was crawling on the ground before he even knew what happened. Another charged him with his shield raised but Valdryn quickly enveloped the man in flames.

Two guards with halberds stepped forward but the Blademaster did not hesitate. With a burst of speed, he closed the distance quickly. A hard boot to the chest knocked one down. As he fell, Valdryn grabbed his weapon and used it to block an incoming swing from the other. He disarmed his opponent with the halberd and sank his blade into his chest.

"Are you so eager to die for another's cowardice?" he asked the guards. Another charged and blocked Valdryn's attacks but was ill prepared for his magic. Multiple blades made of fire pierced his chest and through his back. "Are you so willing to serve someone who would execute unarmed civilians?" Two more charged but were quickly cut down.

The others who formed the shield wall saw their fellow guards cut down with such ease. Barathel could sense their doubt creeping in though he wasn't surprised. Valdryn was clever enough to wage a war on multiple fronts. His words were a weapon in their own right, making quick work of the psychological battle.

"They are here because they understand loyalty, Valdryn. They can put their duty above their emotions," he said with hint of rage. "They know there is more to this world than just *their* view."

"My oath, my loyalty, was never declared for you. I serve the people. My loyalty is to them and this city." Another guard attacked but instead of killing him, Valdryn threw him aside. He could sense that it was fear that guided him, not any loyalty to Barathel. "You have shown countless times that you are loyal to no one but yourself, Barathel. If their deaths served you in any capacity, you would not hesitate to have their throats slit."

Barathel noticed the posture in his guards shifting, growing weaker. They did not want to die today and especially not for him. But he will make them. "Attack him now! All of you! Bring me his head!"

They did not move right away. The tension in the room was weighing everyone down as their two superiors argued. They took a moment to understand their situation. Instead of charging though, they moved to either side of the room. Not all of the guards were eager to follow him blindly to their deaths.

"What are you doing?" asked Barathel.

"They have chosen observance. They do not know the right course of action," said Valdryn. "They know their oaths but your actions conflict with their morals."

"Morals? This is treason!" Barathel shouted.

"No one, not even you, are above consequences." Valdryn readied his sword. "One of us will answer for our actions today and they will follow the victor."

"So be it," Barathel said.

The two charged one another, clashing in the center of the guards. For all of Barathel's faults, he earned every victory of his career. Rumors claim that when he was young, he trained with various elven communities. The forest elves taught him how to move swiftly and quietly. From the eastern mountains, he learned to harness brute strength. He even learned to master what magic he could from the elite members of the Kalborian royal court.

His speed wasn't overwhelming like Verric's but Valdryn was still caught off guard. Expecting Barathel to keep the distance, he was surprised when he wielded his weapon so efficiently at close quarters.

Valdryn was still countering with ease. The amplified magical energy in his system had him performing at top speed and strength. The pair seemed equally matched which worried Valdryn and his spirit companion. Barathel should be no match for either of them. He's either far stronger than he lets off or he's using enchantments like Verric.

I'll investigate this further. He must be wearing something.

"You're faring better than I expected," said Valdryn.

"I've been preparing for a fight such as this for longer than you know. I cannot fail here, not when there's still so much to do." Barathel picked up speed but Valdryn was able to match it.

The General slammed the pommel of his spear into the ground. The small pulse was enough to create distance between the two. Suddenly his spear split in two, as though it was never one whole weapon. A spear tip of arcane energy formed on the second half.

His weapon. It's like a conduit but different. It doesn't absorb surrounding energy. It amplifies his own.

"What does that mean for us?" Valdryn asked in a hushed whisper.

It means we underestimated him. Our only choice is to stay on the offensive and finish him without hesitation. Without remorse.

Valdryn charged Barathel with nothing else in his thoughts but the intent to kill. The force behind his swings drove Barathel back but his dual weapons gave him the speed to recover quickly.

It became a battle of attrition. With each attack, the opposition would defend and retaliate immediately. Blurring strikes and amplifying magic wasn't enough to solidify a victory. The spirit gave what aid he could, pushing Valdryn's body beyond its limits. The Blademaster grew unrelenting in his attacks. One swing broke through and caught Barathel's cheek.

"Well, it's about time, Blademaster," he mocked.

Valdryn followed up with a quick pommel strike and kick to his gut while he was caught off balance. He pressed his advantage and smashed into him with his shoulder. He continued with a horizontal slash. Barathel blocked with both weapons but wasn't prepared for a left hook. Valdryn grabbed the middle of his blade and used

Barathel's weapons as a leverage point. Forcing it downward, Valdryn left another cut down Barathel's cheek.

Kill him, Valdryn! Finish this.

Valdryn followed his adrenaline. He thrusted for a killing blow but Barathel narrowly avoided the attack. Valdryn quickly followed up with an upward arc. The General spun with the attack and tried his own slash. It missed but Valdryn's dodge left him exposed.

As he tried to move backwards, Barathel stabbed forward with his other weapon. The blade sunk deep into his gut. Barathel went in for his throat with his other weapon but Valdryn caught it and threw him back before collapsing on the ground.

Valdryn was wide-eyed as the sinking feeling of failure took hold. Even the guards didn't expect this outcome. The spirit stood above him though no one else could see him. A deafening ring blocked everything out but the spirit's voice.

You have not failed. Not yet.

"I told you I could not fail!" shouted Barathel. His tone was of a declaration instead of a boast.

We can still end this but you'll have to do one last thing you won't like.

"Now do your duty, guards. Kill the traitor and I will overlook your ineptitude," the general commanded.

The guards surrounded the injured Blademaster. They moved without hesitation but when they prepared to strike, their weapon grew heavy. Nothing about this day felt right and killing the one who saved the city only diminished their spirits.

Let me take control.

Their weapons were raised and ready to fall. Valdryn looked past them and met the spirit's gaze. He nodded in agreement. The last thing he saw before blacking out were the weapons of the fallen guards rattling on the ground.

With a blinding flash, Valdryn was back at his childhood home. He stood on the hill overlooking his house. Everything was frozen in time, just before the moment the bandit stabbed his father. He saw his younger self reaching out in vain as though somehow, he could stop the killing. To his left were the other bandits stuck in their guttural mocking laughter.

"What is happening?" his voice echoed.

He turned and saw the raging fire that consumed most of the farmland. Belmont and his men were charging through the bandit hordes while the mages tried to diminish the flames. Something about them seemed off though. Like a muddled painting, their faces were blurred and smeared.

"They look like that because you didn't actually see it." A hooded figure appeared beside him.

Valdryn jumped back and reached for his hilt but found it empty. "What? Who are you?"

"You never saw what happened over the hill. Your mind filled in the blanks from the stories of the soldiers and survivors," the hooded man said. "And as for your second question, well you will learn soon enough."

"What do you mean?" Valdryn asked.

"Awaken, dear Valdryn. See your mission to its inevitable end." Everything grew dark once more. His home faded into nothingness. "We will speak again."

Valdryn awoke on his knees, covered in blood. Barathel's guards were cutdown by their own weapons. His wound had healed but his armor had changed. The armor had blackened and purple runes seared into the plating.

"What is this? Dark magic?" he wondered.

"Ah so you're awake. I wasn't expecting that." The spirit's voice seemed different. What was more unsettling, was how the voice came from his own mouth. "Yes. It is dark magic."

Valdryn stood up and walked towards the broken doors of the office but it was not his own movement. Each step felt heavy and forced, as though he was made of stone. He could feel his breathing but he still wanted to gasp for air.

"Something's wrong," Valdryn said.

"Everything is going according to plan," said the spirit. "Together, we shall see this through."

A corpse with three swords through his back laid by the office door. His arm was outstretched, in a final call for help. Valdryn looked around at all the blood. An unease churned his stomach when he tried to reach out for them but couldn't move a single muscle.

"Do not mourn for them. They did not hesitate to come for you when you were wounded." The spirit offered no remorse in his words.

"I don't mourn them," Valdryn said. "It's the nature of their deaths that bothers me. The brutality."

The office was dark beyond the doorway. The golem heart from Barathel's desk glowed like a firefly in the darkest night. A shifting of metal could be heard in the back of the room. The heavy steps of metal boots were unmistakable.

"I can't see a thing," said Valdryn. The world looked different now, darker and still. He could feel an unfamiliar chill in the air but to his surprise it didn't bother him at all.

"We should change that." The spirit charged the blade

"Another light spell?" he wondered.

"Not quite." Valdryn could feel his own mouth involuntarily curling into a wicked smile.

The blade unleashed a wide swath of power. The back wall crumbled and shot out along with various pieces of Barathel's collection. The blast from the magic and the wind of the storm scattered the lighter pieces and collected novels. Barathel was the only thing in that room unaffected.

His spear was reformed and siphoning the magic in the area. An arcane blade three times the size of the spear tip enveloped the edge. Even his armor appeared to have arcane pieces attached to it. He emitted a bright light that dissolved the darkness in the room.

"That is ancient magic," said the spirit. "Where did you learn of it?"

Barathel looked on, confused. He met Valdryn's eyes and studied his gaze. His posture had changed and glimpses of pain washed over his face. "You're not him."

"I'm not who?" asked Valdryn.

"I don't know who you are but I will destroy every last spec of ash that remains when you're gone." Barathel dashed across the room, bringing the full weight of his spear towards Valdryn's heart.

The Blademaster swatted him away without even realizing. A similar spell enveloped his blade and increased both its length and width. The simple longsword had become something even a minotaur would struggle to wield. Valdryn used it with such grace and speed, it had worried him what he was becoming.

"You will tell me your secret before the end and I will grace you with a name as you choke on your blood!" shouted the spirit.

Valdryn's body ached as the duel continued. Where once he felt like a warrior with true power, he now felt like a puppet thrown about on a stage. He was now nothing more than a piece of someone else's game.

Even Barathel moved differently. His dedication and resolve had been mixed with regret and remorse. He struck with the intent to kill but he could not hide the apologetic look in his eyes. A reverse spin of his spear slashed across Valdryn's face but he didn't feel the pain, only the quick healing that wrapped his body.

"You can't win this, General," said the spirit. "You will die before ever seeing the final war."

"You know nothing of this new world, Spirit," said Barathel. "This world will survive you and your masters."

The pair each put their weight into their swings. They locked their blades in an effort to overpower the other. Small arcane flares shot out of their weapon extensions like sparks on a grindstone. Both weapons enhancements began to break and fade but the two warriors were too focused on one another to notice.

"What masters?" Valdryn asked, his voice breaking free.

The General was caught off guard but quickly regained his composure "Your companion serves the darkness," said Barathel. He was losing this fight and he knew it. "You have to put aside your anger towards me and cast him out."

"Don't forget all the deaths he's responsible for," said the spirit. "Your father would still be alive had he fully committed to saving lives instead of taking them."

"Don't listen to him, Valdryn," shouted Barathel as his spear began to break. "Everything I've ever done was with purpose."

"He's a murderer," the spirit yelled.

"He's a deceiver," replied Barathel.

"Enough," Valdryn shouted. Time slowed to a near halt. The Spirit and the General were silent. The only noise came from the cracking of both weapons as their enhancements began to fail. A sudden shattering turned everything to black.

Chapter 22: The Scars That Make Us

Valdryn stood at the center of an abyss. He shouted but no words, not even a noise came out. Darkness, silence, and an overwhelming chill expanded infinitely into nothingness. It was a humbling state of nonexistence.

Is this death?

He could hear his voice in his head, though that brought little comfort. He shouted again but the abyss would not allow it. He spotted a flicker in the distance like a dimming flame of a candle. It appeared to grow larger when the silence was suddenly broken by muffled voices. He couldn't make out the words but he could sense the violence and rage.

In an instant he was consumed by the flame but he didn't feel any pain. Instead, the flame brought life to the darkness. The abyss spread across the sky but he found himself in the fields outside his home. On the hill rested an army of decayed corpses with their weapons at their side. Before them stood their leader with a hole in his chest and half of the flesh on his face rotted away.

"Death would be a mercy," a voice echoed over the plains.

"Who are you?" demanded Valdryn.

"I am what haunts your dreams," shouted the bandit leader. "I am the one that set you on this path and turned your world upside down." The rotted bandit lifted up the corpse of an older elf.

Valdryn froze when he recognized the face. It was one thing to see him die as a child but to see his body, desecrated and taunting. His father's eyes flitted open and stared through him. Valdryn reached for his sword out of impulse but found nothing.

"What have you done, Valdryn?" His father asked with a single tear of blood trickling down his cheek. "What have you done?"

"What have you done? What have you done? What have you done?" The bandit army repeated these words, over and over. The words rung out around him like crows on the wind, circling their next meal.

Valdryn's heart sank and his legs grew weak. The hooded figure from before appeared but didn't say a word. He simply pointed towards the horde, singling out the leader. Valdryn stared but didn't understand. Not until he noticed a familiar glint beside him. Impaled in the corpse was his father's blade. The jewel in the pommel was unmistakable.

He reclaimed his resolve and readied himself got battle. The bandits made their way towards Valdryn but he only met their pace. "I kept my promise," he said before launching himself into the nearby bandit. He wrestled the axe free and used it to split the rotted flesh and skull in two.

He reached out to summon a fireball but nothing happened. He parried an oncoming swing and disarmed the broken sword. He grabbed the bandit's head but he couldn't summon his magic to burn him. The bandit smiled a decrepit toothy grin. "So be it," said Valdryn, before ripping its head off. With an axe in one hand and broken sword in the other, he charged the horde.

He carved his way to the leader, ignoring the deafening words roaring over the plains. It had been a while since Valdryn fought without any magic. To most, it would be debilitating, but it was a welcome reprieve. Here he was, in his element and fulfilling his purpose as Blademaster. He tore through the enemy in a whirlwind of steel.

He dreamt of this moment every night during his time in the military. He dreamt he was older and stronger. He would cut through the laughing bandits with ease, silencing them until the next night brought them back to life. He had trained for this moment for so long it had become a simple routine for him.

He slaughtered the army of bandits, leaving nothing behind but shattered bones. He swung the axe around and struck the leader in the shoulder. It lodged itself in his armor but Valdryn didn't slow down. He abandoned the axe and used the broken sword. He stabbed it into the leader's neck, waiting for the screams of pain he grew accustomed to.

"What have you done?" was all he said. He raised his weapon but was kicked away.

Valdryn used the momentum from the kick to dodge back towards his sword. He grabbed for the hilt but the decayed arms gripped the blade. With all his strength he tore the blade from the body, slicing the hands in half. He charged the leader the same as he did so many years ago.

Valdryn put his full weight in as the blade pierced through the heart of the bandit leader. He collapsed to his knees in defeat. "You can still win," the leader and his father said in unison before turning to dust. The army followed and the land around Valdryn turned to a sea of ash. He choked on the remains as he felt an intense heat all around him. His vision cleared only to find a field of burnt corpses.

"Run!" screamed a voice in the distance.

"She's gonna kill us all!" screamed another.

Valdryn recognized the forest from the Isle. Even with scorched warped wood, the trees were unmistakable. Burnt corpses were frozen in time. Some were running away while others seemed to be begging for mercy. Yurik's sword was plunged into a pile of corpses in the center of the nearby clearing. The man himself was holding mage by the throat, crushing the life out of him.

"Yurik? Are you really here?" Valdryn wondered.

He slowly turned to face Valdryn. "This is your fault, Blademaster." His eyes glowed a bright orange before combusting into a cloud of flame.

"Yurik!"

"All your fault," echoed the corpses. "All your—"

Valdryn sliced one in half and decapitated another. "I'm not going through that again." He cut down the mocking corpses. He took note of their blackened attire. Some were guards of the temple or the city. Others were mages or civilians trying to escape the battle.

The hooded figure appeared once more. He kept his silence but pointed to the burning pile of bodies where Yurik stood. A charred corpse pulled itself up through the large blade. The sword's guard tore at the flesh as it stood up. The body was mangled and the robes were in tatters but the icy stare was all too familiar.

"You always did enjoy getting the last word, Sandra," said Valdryn, a hollow feeling in his gut.

"You've had your fun, Valdryn. You've finally gotten the chance to make dear old daddy proud and play hero." She picked up Yurik's blade though she lacked the strength to wield it properly. "And all at the cost of the people you swore to protect."

She charged him with remarkable speed but her attacks were far from impressive. Valdryn didn't even bother to parry. Merely sidestepping was enough to maintain distance. She went for an overhead swing but couldn't find the strength to raise it. She laughed and dropped her weapon.

"You were always the top student in martial combat," she said in a mocking voice. "The poor sad Valdryn who lost everything as a young boy and had to fight tooth and nail for his life."

"And you were the best of all of us at the academy," he said. "But nothing was ever enough. Ever driven by ambition, the end you met was inevitable."

"We all get what we deserve," she said, lowering her gaze.

"In that, we agree," concluded Valdryn.

Sandra attacked first with a stream of fire. Valdryn projected a ward to retaliate but it wasn't absorbing the energy. Valdryn could feel his own energy fleeting while hers grew. Beyond the flames he could see her wicked charred grin.

"The ruin you brought to the Isle will consume you too," she screamed.

Valdryn could sense the power rising and quickly rolled out of the fiery beam. It decimated everything in its path, removing the trees and stone from existence. Everything around him began to crumble and fade, the debris clouding the area. He became stranded in a grey wasteland of nothingness rendering his senses useless.

Valdryn couldn't see more than a few feet in front of him but neither could Sandra. Her attacks were random and striking near him but never made contact. Perhaps she was toying with him, enjoying the moment before going in for the kill.

"For all your talk, you never did find yourself in a position of power," Valdryn shouted.

Sandra summoned flames from the earth near where she heard his voice. The light from the flame was swallowed in the ash storm. It was enough for him to catch a glimpse of her before the vision cluttered once more.

"So much ambition and yet you always found yourself following another," he continued to mock.

Sandra snarled and fired off two beams of flame. She crossed them in a slashing motion to maximize on her damage. It cut through the wall of ash but only for a moment as the impact kicked up more.

"I've had enough of this!" she screamed. She summoned beams from the sky. Each strike radiated heat and blew away a portion of the ash. The battlefield was a burning wasteland bathed in the fire and light of her magic. The remaining land began to break away, leaving little space for Valdryn to hide. "Where are you—"

Valdryn burst forth from the ash and sunk his blade through her chest, though he didn't feel the same way as the first time he killed her. He held her and gently laid her down upon the fading earth. "I'm here," he said with sadness in his eyes.

She reached up and caressed his cheek. "You can still beat the darkness."

The ground beneath him dispersed and the darkness consumed him once more. Valdryn found himself falling with stone debris. In the distance he saw a blackened sun hurtling towards him. As it grew closer, he realized it was no sun, but the blast from a dwarven siege cannon.

He reached out to stop his fall and found a nearby ledge to grip. A faint light emanated from the blast frozen in time, like the fading glow of dusk. He looked down as he failed to find his footing. The dark abyss where he once fell awaited him. He heard the darkness calling but a familiar grip kept him clinging to the ledge.

"You have to be more careful, Blade Master," Ava said. Her smile was a welcome sight.

"Ava?" he said, worried. "I'm glad you're here."

She smiled back. "You won't be for long."

Valdryn looked at her, confused. Her deep eyes and sincere smile left no trace of violence or distrust. But it was not her he had to fear. In a flash, she was incased in ice. Her expression of joy was replaced with one of pain. The hooded figure was frozen as well with his arms stretched over Valdryn, shielding him from the blast.

Ice coated every inch of the room. All of the warmth from the cannon blast was replaced with a bone-chilling bite in the air. Breathing became painful and movement was staggered but the masked figure before him was unmoved. The mask was frosted over but familiar. The frozen wound in his chest only confirmed Valdryn's suspicion.

"We all believed in you, Blade Master," said Bannon. "We followed you and you failed everyone."

Valdryn clutched his chest as he shivered uncontrollably. He kept his distance from Bannon, trying to summon a flame for warmth but his power was still drained. He looked around to get a better sense of surroundings but there was nothing beyond the ice. Rushing in head-first would've been a mistake he was trying so hard to learn from.

"You think you saved my sister but you left her, bedridden and stranded with the minotaurs," Bannon said. "Stuck behind enemy lines, perhaps they all died too. Maybe they, like us, trusted the wrong person and it got them killed."

"I did everything I could!" Valdryn shouted.

"It wasn't enough!" Bannon summoned a howling wind that blew Valdryn across the room. He disappeared into the frost-stained air, becoming one with the elements. Each gust of wind cut at Valdryn's flesh. "How are you any different from Barathel?"

Valdryn felt the impact of a frozen fist on his cheek. It knocked him off balance and sent him sliding across the floor. He tried to stand up but felt a kick to his ribs. Coughing up blood, he tried to crawl away but felt the weight of Bannon's boot on his back.

"Everyone around you dies while you pursue your own goal," Bannon spat. "You are just as destructive as the General but at least he can admit it."

Valdryn gritted his teeth and spun his blade into a reverse grip. He stabbed backwards and pierced Bannon's leg. Feeling the weight on his back lessen, Valdryn pushed up with all his strength. He spun as he stood up and knocked Bannon's mask off. The skin beneath was blue and coated in frost. Two frozen streams slowing from the eyes.

Bannon's wounds quickly froze over, only adding to his armor. He teleported across the ice and kicked Valdryn in the chest. With his opponent off balance once more, he pressed his advantage. Bannon's speed and strength were far beyond his own and he quickly understood might would not win this fight.

Valdryn was barely able to keep his defense up. His strength was leaving him and breathing only grew more painful. When he blocked the axe, a frozen fist would impact his ribs. Valdryn pushed away to create distance but Bannon would simply reappear before him and continue his assault.

"You had everything." Bannon took him by surprise with a left hook to the jaw. "You had a life, a career, people who looked up to you and you threw it all away. And for what?"

"Balvas and Barathel had to be stopped!" Valdryn shouted in reply.

"Wrong!" Bannon grabbed him by the throat and threw him against the wall. "Killing Balvas was your duty. Bringing Barathel to justice is your duty." Bannon threw his axe, barely missing Valdryn's shoulder. He teleported to him and knelt down to look him in the eyes. "But you did all of this because of a promise you made as a child. No matter how righteous the cause, it is all lost with the wrong reason."

Valdryn tried to punch him but Bannon caught his fist instantly. Ice enveloped Valdryn's hand and slowly crept up his arm. He used his free hand to reach up and place it on Bannon's shoulder. "I'm sorry for what happened to you. But the only thing Bannon would regret is failing his sister. You are not him." He gripped the back of Bannon's neck and applied pressure.

Bannon let go of Valdryn's fist to grab his other arm but recoiled in pain as Valdryn tightened his grip. The ice around them began to crack as Valdryn ripped off a chunk of frozen flesh. Buried within the rotted chunk was a frozen spider.

"You will suffer before the end," Bannon screamed.

Valdryn stood up, free from the ice. With Bannon's axe in one hand and his sword in the other, he pressed forward. "I will, there's no denying that."

Bannon tried to summon his ice magic but his own strength began to fail. Blood trickled from the corner of his mouth and his body began to ache. He quickly found his own axe buried into his chest. He reached for Valdryn but the axe was ripped from his chest and exposed the frozen muscle beneath. He threw a haphazard punch but Valdryn blocked it with the axe, severing fingers. With the axe wedged into Bannon's hand, Valdryn was able to pull him close. A quick elbow strike to the jaw knocked Bannon on his back.

Valdryn knelt down with his blade slowly sinking into Bannon's chest. He took Bannon's hand in his and used his other hand to sink his blade deeper.

"Remember your oath," said Bannon.

The walls and floor began to crack and rumble. Ava and the hooded figure had disappeared and the cannon's blast grew unstable. Before Valdryn could react, a giant hand of shadow and metal broke through beneath him and pulled him down into the familiar darkness.

He awoke in a freefall but this time his mind was calm. He landed on his feet with his weapon readied for combat. Ahead of him was a slumped figure on their knees. Valdryn took one step forward but the ground beneath him melted away. He fell into a thick liquid and couldn't find his way out.

A hand breached through the surface. Valdryn reached out and pulled himself up. Whoever helped him was gone but the figure from earlier never moved a muscle. Torches faded in, revealing a circular platform. He looked down and noticed he was waist deep in demon's blood.

With every step he took, walls and pillars would rise from the darkness. He was caught in labyrinth flooded with blood. The walls were covered in scorch marks and the tapestries were faded with age. Wading through the murky halls,

Valdryn came to a walled off section bearing a familiar crest of a scroll centered on a shield.

"The academy's library," Valdryn muttered to himself.

Valdryn placed his hands on the library crest. He traced the scroll with one hand and the shield with the other. As his finger ran across the wall, the crest glowed along his tracing. His fingers trembled when he neared the end but he pressed on. When the crest fully glowed, the wall shimmered away like a reflection in a stream.

"Where we first met," he said, approaching the kneeling figure before him. His arms grew heavy and his heart was more broken than ever.

"And where we will say our final goodbye," said the young man.

<u>Chapter 23: Consumed</u>

"Master Valdryn," sighed the old man behind the counter, stacks of books and scrolls littering the top. "I expected the instructors to send someone more magically inclined."

"Like Sandra?" Valdryn mocked. "You know she views the library as something beneath her, right?"

"Impossible," he scoffed. Many of the elders preferred students like Sandra. The notion of swordsmanship was lost on those who devoted themselves to spells. His wrinkled face was barely hidden under his grey hood. He rang a small bell signaling a nearby acolyte. "Someone of her aptitude is a lover of all knowledge."

Valdryn rolled his eyes and laughed. "Someone of her aptitude believes she already knows everything. Now, I was told there was a problem with missing books."

The old man waved him off. "These are more than mere books you uncultured grunt. These are instructional manuals of all degrees of spells that—"

The old man droned on about the books. Valdryn looked around the library, pretending to pay him any mind. He and Tariv had grown accustomed to the elders looking down upon them. To some of the veterans of the academy, mixing arcane with martial skills devalued the knowledge available.

"Are you even listening?" asked the old man.

"Yes, something about you wasting everyone's time in a vain attempt at self-satisfaction," Valdryn eagerly replied.

"Follow the acolyte and remove yourself from my sight." The elder waved him off, not wishing to see him any longer. He quickly opened yet another book of arcane spells to occupy his mind.

Valdryn bowed his head, "Gladly."

The acolyte led Valdryn up the winding stairs to a never-ending wall of tomes. The Keepers were too busy organizing the shelves to notice their presence. Aspirants sat in their isolated corners with their faces buried in books detailing various spells. To even the most ambitious scholar, the wealth of information offered here would be intimidating.

"Please excuse the old man," said the acolyte. "They're all on edge when things are out of place."

"I learned quickly in my first year that thick skin is necessary," replied Valdryn.

The acolyte led him to a tall room with bookshelves spiraling up the walls. Blue spheres of light suspended in the air illuminated the books. A keeper was sitting at the desk, hastily scrawling in a journal. The nearby acolytes were searching through the shelves to find exactly what books were stolen. A few armed custodians were on patrol but Valdryn knew they were mostly for show.

"This is Keeper Carlin. She's overseeing the investigation," introduced the acolyte. "Keeper, this is—"

"Valdryn, the battlemage aspirant. I'd recognize those fierce eyes anywhere," she smiled. "How's your training coming?"

"Well-enough, Keeper," he smiled back. "So how does one steal from the brightest minds of the academy?"

"Mocking your elders? That's so unbecoming of you," she laughed.

"Perhaps them, but I'd never dare mock you," Valdryn said, stifling his own laughter. Carlin was one of the very few elder keepers who took interest in all of the academy's students. Anyone aspiring to be a better version of themselves was worthy of the academy in her eyes.

Carlin slid her journal towards him. "This is a list of the books stolen. Nothing exceptionally powerful or worth much in the market."

Valdryn read through the list, recognizing a few. The first one was a collection of stories from the Inquisitor Guild's earlier years. It was a second edition, donated for studying ancient beasts and mapping out locations strong with history related to magic. "Inquisitor Reports. Always a good read."

"I remember you being particularly interested in the Silverlight incident," Carlin said. "You wanted to be like Inquisitor Isaac, hunting monsters from the lost age."

His cheeks reddened, remembering the first time he read about Sir Isaac. "I don't recognize the second one. Guide to Dragon's Crown?"

"That mapped out the Dragon's Crown mountains but since they were destroyed in the war, it's not really important anymore," she said, sadly. "Some insist it could be used to follow the mines but none seem willing enough to try."

Valdryn continued down the list. Some were autobiographies of adventurers and treasure hunters. Some of the names he recognized from his father's stories. A few tourist guides to the different capital cities and outdated maps to once uninhabited regions were missing but didn't make much sense for a thief.

"Some of these could be in the hands of other acolytes or simply misplaced," said Valdryn. "But these last two were definitely stolen."

"General Spells and Tools of the Scout?" Carlin wondered.

"General Spells has utility magic, perfect for picking locks," explained Valdryn. "Belmont told me of the other book. I've never read it myself but it contains accounts of stealth magic and shadow manipulation."

"That's a bit advanced for a common thief. Perhaps they're trying to get better at the trade?" she wondered.

Valdryn thought on the missing books. Two useful books for a thief with a talent for spells, a few more for someone new to traveling and none of them were more than a few coins at the market. "Have you tried a tracking spell?"

"The library wards are active. We may have the knowledge of spells but we don't have the power to bypass the wards and the masters are far too busy to be bothered with this," said Carlin.

Valdryn came to a sudden realization. "A common thief, with little to no arcane knowledge, who was able to remain hidden during their time among the keepers and the acolytes. We're dealing with a child."

"A child?" she asked, uncertain.

"I might have been older than the standard student when I arrived here but I was still a child worth no mind, moving through unnoticed for a few months," he replied "I'll return your books shortly. It has been a pleasure, Carlin, as always."

The two bowed to one another before Valdryn took his leave. He returned to the entrance chamber and approached a series of shelves on the opposite side of the upper floor. There was a pathway among the shelves that led further back. He found a wall with the library's crest.

He had gone here during his initial years here. It was a quiet place, far from the judging eyes of the elders and their chosen elite students. Upon tracing the symbol, the wall faded away. A small child was sitting in the center reading through a book.

"So, you must be the thief the keepers are so concerned with," said Valdryn.

The child dropped the book and backed away but only to trip over his own feet. He pulled out a small knife though the dull edge and the quivering grip didn't allow for even the smallest threatening notion.

Valdryn put his hands forward and open, away from his weapon. "Hey, it's okay kid. I'm not going to hurt you." He slowly approached the book in the center. He noticed a bag full of the other books but made no remark. "I see you're also a fan of Isaac."

The child stopped shaking but kept his weapon up. "He was a hero. He killed that monster in the mines and saved everybody."

Valdryn nodded in agreement. "Is that what you want to be? A hero?"

The child nodded back.

"Heroes aren't known for stealing though," he said with a disappointed look on his face. Much like when his father did when he was younger.

"I don't want to. But the others make me," said the child. "But I'm running away tomorrow and one day, everyone will know of Jonas the Brave."

"Jonas the Brave? I like the sound of that," Valdryn said. "But you don't have to run away."

Jonas put his knife down and stood up. "What do you mean?"

Valdryn stepped closer, slowly, so as to not scare the boy. He knelt down and met him eye to eye. He saw something in the boy, something that reminded him of home. Jonas also seemed to have lost everything and now it fell to Valdryn to help see him through this chapter in his life.

"You can let go of your past," said Valdryn. "Become something more."

"I wonder now if you said that for me or for yourself," said Jonas. The stubble on his cheek still had splotches of dried blood.

Valdryn's mind returned to the present with a single tear in his eye. "Perhaps for both our sakes."

The two stared at one another but unlike the others interactions with his memories, there was no sense of violence. There was no instinct calling for combat, merely a hint of regret in their eyes. A father should never have to outlive his son. The voices had grown quiet and the room remained still.

Jonas looked just as he did when Valdryn left his body with the minotaurs. His face was pale and his eyes sunken with a hint of exhaustion hanging over him. The only difference was a bloody handprint over the damage in the armor.

"Do we have to fight as well?" asked Valdryn, hesitantly.

Jonas let out a light chuckle. "I'd prefer a little sparring, like my days in training."

"I'd like that," smiled Valdryn.

They approached one another. They bowed and drew their swords. As the initiator, Jonas made the first move. A simple strike from the left met with a standard block. They took turns alternating between attack and defense. Some strikes were swift and even came close to wounding but never decisive, never trying to do any real harm.

"Do you know why you're here, Master?" Jonas feigned an attack from the right. Catching his master off guard, he was able to hit his leg with the flat side of the blade.

"Because Barathel bested me," he replied. He locked blades and knocked his apprentice back. "And the dark spirit took control."

Jonas shook his head and increased his attack speed. "It's because you lost control. You became blinded by your promises to the dead."

Valdryn parried every attack and kicked Jonas's legs out from under him. He pointed his blade at him and tapped his chest with the tip. "But it's not too late. I can escape this place and beat them both... with your help."

Jonas accepted defeat but chose to lay there. "It's too late, Master. You lost when Barathel killed you. What remains of your body is under his control." Jonas pointed to the shadows in the back.

Valdryn looked up but saw no one. "What are you talking about?" He looked down but Jonas was gone. A bloody handprint stained the floor in place of his apprentice. "Not again."

"He was never really here, Valdryn," said a voice from the other side of the room.

Valdryn looked up a saw the hooded figure from before. "Who are you?" he cried out.

He stepped into the light and lowered his hood. Vibrant auburn hair flowed past his shoulders. He removed his mask and let it drop and skitter along the floor. Strange tattooed runes flowed up the right side of his jaw and looped over and around his right eye. "I am Zilendras."

"One of the traitors?" Valdryn readied his sword, preparing for the worst.

Zilendras gave off a half smile, reluctantly. "We were the ones who were betrayed. Just like you. We were caught up in our emotions and the demon took advantage."

"I've read about you. You betrayed the first king of the elves," he said, defiantly. "Why should I trust you?"

"High King Dra'Vallyn was my Barathel. He failed at his sworn duty and I acted." He drew his own sword but it was in a far more pristine condition than Valdryn knew possible. From behind Zilendras stepped forth two warriors.

Jonas was the first but his armor was now caked in blood and face gaunt. His eyes were bruised and bloodshot. Next was his father in the ceremonial armor he found in one of his treasure hunts. The green plating and golden filigree mirrored the sickly skin tone.

His father held out his hand called the blade to him. In an instant, the sword left Valdryn and nestled into his father's grip. "I am the scar that set you on this path."

"And I am the scar that sealed your fate," said Jonas. He wielded both halves of his broken sword. Gripping the top half of the edge, blood trickled down his wrist.

Zilendras threw his sword to Valdryn. He caught it with ease but saw his reflection in the polished blade. His right eye had become a smoky purple with black veins spreading down towards his neck along the pale flesh. His left eye maintained the fiery green burning bright.

"Kill your scars, Valdryn," said Zilendras. "And free your soul from its self-made chains."

Before Valdryn could speak, the two were upon him. They attacked like wild beasts with the pure intent to kill. Jonas was able to bypass Valdryn's guard and get in a shallow cut. The wound quickly healed but black veins spread out from the scar.

"Fail here and you will be consumed by the darkness. Succeed and we can see the demon destroyed forever," shouted Zilendras.

"If you and your allies couldn't beat him, what hope do I have?" Valdryn parried Jonas and hit him with a left hook. A quick pommel strike kept his father at bay but he was just out of reach from his slash.

"You get to learn from our mistakes," replied Zilendras.

Valdryn charged his father and locked blades. He was overwhelming the old elf and drove him to his knees. He had a chance at a killing blow but when he looked at his father, he felt like a child again. He remembered the days at the markets where they would look for more books. He remembered the dinners with his neighbors after working on the farm.

His father showed no hesitation in return. He pushed back and slashed upwards. The edge bit into Valdryn's armor and cut his side. Valdryn could feel his grip on the dreamworld slipping and he tried to be defensive once more.

"You cannot hesitate against the darkness," said Zilendras. "It preys on our hearts and destroys us from within."

Valdryn tried to listen but Jonas attacked from behind and drove his blade into his lower ribs. Valdryn yelled in pain and tried to strike back but his father caught the blade and threw him to the ground.

"If you can't fight back against your own shadows then the ones you claim to love died for nothing." Zilendras picked up his sword and turned his back to Valdryn.

Valdryn looked up at the two rotted warriors above him. He saw them for what they were before, the reasons he fought and strived. The man who raised him to protect all in need and the boy he raised to never stop improving on himself. He saw them for what they became, a haunting poison that drove him to the dark and festered the hate in his heart. The sensation of being powerless lingered in his father's eyes and the overwhelming failure in those of his apprentice.

"This is where we say our final goodbye," said Valdryn.

His father stood over him. As he raised his sword, Valdryn pulled the broken sword tip from his side and drove it into his father's thigh. Jonas tried to jump on top of him, but Valdryn used both his legs to kick him back. Valdryn disarmed his father and reclaimed his sword. Jonas tried to attack from behind again but Valdryn slid and slashed through his side.

"Yes, that's it!" shouted Zilendras. "Put these shadows to rest."

Valdryn thrusted his blade through his father's heart. As he turned to ash and dust, Valdryn could see the smile that always reassured him as a child. "Goodbye, father."

He walked over to Jonas who laid in his own blood. He gripped his side and held his hand out as though he was asking for aid, or for mercy. "Master, please."

Valdryn held his hand out and helped him to his feet. "I watched you grow from a thief to a battlemage in such a short span. I couldn't be any prouder of the man you became." Valdryn felt the tears well in his eyes. "Your death was the greatest defeat for me but it will not be the memory of you that defines me."

He plunged his sword through Jonas's heart for the last time. The look of failure in his apprentice's eyes turned to hope. "Rest now, Jonas the Brave. You saved far more than anyone will ever know."

The ashes of his loved ones fell away and the blood from the fight dissipated. Aside from the encroaching abyss beyond the pillars, the room had returned to a sense of normalcy. Valdryn stood in the center, staring at his arm wound with curiosity.

"Wondering why the black veins remain?" asked Zilendras.

Valdryn shook his hand, running his finger along the scar. "These aren't wounds from the fight. These are from allowing the darkness to take over."

"You have earned your second chance then," Zilendras smiled in approvement.

Valdryn met his eyes, confused. "How? He has my body."

Zilendras thrust his sword into the center of the room. The blade emitted a bright light and a small portal appeared above the pommel. "But he does not have your mind or your soul. Peer into the portal. You have one final lesson to learn before you begin your training."

Valdryn dwelled on his words for a moment before looking into the portal. His heart remained stalwart but his eyes bore regret.

<u>Chapter 24: A Lesson in Failure</u>

Zilendras dragged Barathel's mangled body up the cobblestone pathway leading to the Spire of Arcanum. The general was coughing up blood and losing consciousness but Zilendras wouldn't let him die just yet. He wanted Barathel to witness the full weight of his failure before taking his life.

"Come and save your dear General!" Zilendras held him before the guards on the outside of the tower.

"Is that the Blademaster?" wondered a guard.

"It can't be," said the other.

Zilendras left another cut on Barathel's cheek. He threw the general to the ground in front of the guards. "The longer you sit their asking questions, the longer Barathel will suffer. Remove the barrier and you will live."

More guards stepped forth from the tower entrance. Their attire was simple robes with standard vambraces to offer some form of protection. They wielded various weapons though the elite among them preferred staves. On the center of their chest was the blue flame crest of Ruvo.

"He's not the Blademaster," grunted Barathel. "But do not underestimate him."

"It's too late, Barathel," smiled Zilendras.

The first wave of guards moved to swarm him but Zilendras didn't offer them the chance. He charged the closest one and impaled him immediately. Two more summoned flames but he quickly reflected the magic with his sword and incinerated them. He was a threat unlike anything they've ever faced.

Zilendras halted his advance when he saw Barathel fading. He placed his hand on his chest and healed him enough the stop the bleeding but the pain remained. "You don't get to die just yet."

The tower guards had already swarmed him by the time he stood back up. The ones with staves beat him mercilessly while the others formed a magic barrier to contain him. A few guards grabbed Barathel and carried him into the tower. Without his hostage, he loses all leverage. Or so they thought.

Zilendras curled up and covered his head, letting his back take the brunt of the punishment. His body was bruised and on the verge of breaking but he couldn't help but laugh. "Your order has gone downhill drastically from the lack of a true enemy it seems." A quick pulse pushed the guards back. He was quick enough to grab one of them midair and drain his arcane energy, healing his new body almost to perfection.

The guards hesitated as they watched him snap the man's neck with ease. The fear and hesitation gave Zilendras what he wanted. With lighting speed, he swept within the barrier with broad and quick slashes. Blood sprayed and soaked the stone beneath his feet like a flood from a storm.

"The barrier will hold," said one of the elite guards. "Nothing can break through."

"Nothing except true power," said Zilendras. He thrusted his blade through and pierced the elite's heart. "You have all forgotten the old ways. You cannot not hope for victory without knowing your enemy." The barrier fell and the guards' screams washed over the tower, diminishing the hearts of the ones inside.

Barathel leaned against the wall, barely holding himself up. Every part of him was in excruciating pain. He peered out of the window and caught a glimpse of the massacre down below. He hobbled towards the tower's core crystal, a vibrant blue gem the size of a dwarf, resting on an altar.

"How are your wounds, General?" asked a guardian.

The General sat on the floor and rested his back on the altar. "He stopped the bleeding but the pain still lingers."

"If he's not Valdryn than who is he?"

"A parasite," Barathel replied. Another guardian brought him a flask of water. He drank quick and deep, if only slightly disappointed. "I forgot of the Guardian's sobriety."

The guard waited for his answer. The screams and shouts outside were wearing him down and not knowing the one responsible would haunt him in the world beyond. "Sir?" persisted the guardian.

"Zilendras. Traitor to the High King. Fourth member of the Knights of Numra. Master of dark magic." Barathel looked down at the blood stains across his armor. A sad look crept down his face. "My failures cost Valdryn and allowed Zilendras to possess him, destroying his mind."

The screams outside stopped. The guardians prepared their defense as Zilendras began breaking the door. The world was silent. The only thing they could hear were their own heartbeats mirroring the slams against the door. The wood gave way and splintered as the mangled corpse of a guardian busted through.

"Make your final moments good ones," said Barathel. "The memories are all we have when we pass to the realm beyond."

Zilendras impaled a guardian with his own staff, snapping ribs upon entry. Before the guardians could react, he was on another with his blade through his throat. He turned the bottom floor into a butcher's room. Two stairwells wound up the height of the tower on either side with guardians blocking the paths, but nothing would stand in his way now.

"None are safe from the shadow's reach."
Zilendras pointed his sword at the left stairs and
engulfed it in a black flame.

"We can't stop him," panicked some of the
guards on the opposite stairs.

"Nothing can," shouted down Barathel. "But
no need to make it any easier for him." He and the
guardians above rained down bolts and arrows but
to little promise. He was far too quick of a target
and they weren't even sure if they could hurt him.

Zilendras carved a path of destruction up the
stairs. With their resolve broken, the guardians
offered little effort in their defense. Some begged
for mercy but none would be offered. Zilendras
executed those who would not fight back and
slashed and stabbed his way through the others. He
grabbed one by the throat and used them as a
shield to block the incoming projectiles. He
reached the top with ease and came face to face
with last of the guardians.

"Such a sad sight when the fabled guardians
of legend have been reduced to this rabble," said
Zilendras. "Your predecessors fought me back
with such ferocity but you? You merely bought
yourselves a few more miserable minutes of
existence."

"Minutes you'll never get back. Minutes the
world will use to destroy you," said Barathel. He
fired an arrow with a small red flask at the end.
Zilendras used the dead guardian to shield himself
but the flask exploded upon impact. Bits of the

guardian scattered all over the room as Zilendras went flying back into the wall.

"Every second it takes for you to reach the core is another second for more guardians to train. You might succeed here but you will fail before the end." Barathel could feel the fire in his heart grow. His final moment would be valorous and defiant despite what the history books would say.

"We shall see," Zilendras replied, breathing deep. He let out a war cry and cut down the first guardian, splitting him in two. He parried another attack and reached for the guardian's throat. He easily crushed his windpipe and threw him to the side.

One of the elite guardians struck his cheek with his staff, breaking skin. Another elite slashed low with his halberd and sliced his thigh. Two more went for the killing blow but Zilendras impaled them with ice spikes, sending them over the ledge. An arrow from Barathel dug into his shoulder but he charged through the pain.

"Make him bleed, men!" shouted Barathel.

The halberd-wielding guardian went for the head but Zilendras dodged underneath. Zilendras slashed through his ankle and caught the oncoming staff attack. He sent a wave of flame through the staff, reducing most of it to ash but exploding the back half into shrapnel. The guardian's hand turned into a bloody mangled mess.

"Rejoice in the pain, guardian," mocked Zilendras.

The guardian threw himself on Zilendras's blade and wrapped his arms around him. Another staff broke his nose in a quick strike followed by a disorienting swing to the head. Zilendras twisted his blade and enlarged the wound. The guardian quickly dropped from blood loss. Zilendras stomped on his neck with a sickening crunch.

Zilendras heard footsteps from behind and grabbed the attacking guardian's wrist, holding his axe in place. He didn't anticipate the knife in his side. He gritted his teeth in pain and sliced the guardian's arm off and buried his own axe in his skull, killing him instantly.

"You only delay the inevitable," said Zilendras. He pulled the blade free and healed the wound. "You deny the simplest of truths." He disarmed one of the remaining guardians and threw him to the ground, bringing his blade down upon him.

Barathel rushed in and blocked with a guardian's staff. He spun the blade to the side and struck Zilendras in the gut to push him away. "What truth is that?"

Zilendras sliced his hand on his sword and used the blood to coat it. A shadowy flame birthed forth from the blood and conformed to the shape of the blade. "The darkness comes for all. It is inescapable and undeniable. Darkness is death, death brings new life."

Barathel's eyes widened," Don't do it."

Zilendras unleashed the dark flame in an arc. Barathel and the handful of guardians who kept their distance were able to duck underneath but those closer were instantly devoured by the flame and reduced to ash. The tower core was able to absorb the magic but then reflected it in a forceful blast that obliterated the roof and separated the remaining defenders.

Barathel was slow to recover and Zilendras went for the advantage. Two guardians stepped between them but Zilendras quickly sent their heads rolling. Another guardian threw his spear but was easily dodged. Zilendras retaliated swiftly with a shard of ice through his skull.

Only three remained between him and his target. One used a giant maul and summoned all of his strength. He brought the full force of his weapon down, barely missing and smashing through the floor boards. Zilendras hit him with a palm strike to the chest. He grabbed him by his hood and dragged him through the pommel and haft of his own weapon.

The next, though injured from the blast, wielded a scimitar with speed and grace. Just a second too late to save his comrade, he rushed in with furious cuts. His attacks barely made contact but were enough to slow Zilendras, if only briefly. He allowed the guardian to cover his body in small and shallow cuts before severing his arms. He thrust his blade through the guardian's gut and wretched the blade upwards.

He threw the body to the side to deflect the oncoming energy from the final guardian's staff. The blue glow from her weapon grew to a near blinding intensity. Zilendras merely laughed at her futile efforts and reflected her spell back at her, leaving behind a smoking corpse.

Barathel readied his staff, aiming for strikes to the chest. Zilendras moved without hesitation. Barathel jerked back, tricking Zilendras to go for the guard. Before he could react, Barathel swung his staff and cracked him across the cheek. He got in a few more quick jabs before Zilendras cut his staff in half and kicked him back.

"Such needless death, General," said Zilendras. "You and the rest of the fools could have lived to fight another day had you only cooperated."

"Helping you and your masters is its own death," Barathel replied. He used each halves of the staff like batons. He stayed on the offensive with a flurry of swings, though Zilendras barely reacted.

"You mistake survival for cowardice. You cannot kill the darkness for it is a natural part of the world." Zilendras threw a left hook with full force, pushing Barathel back. "Your gods thought themselves beyond the natural order. Their so called 'victory' resulted in the mere banishment of both sides at the cost of their lives."

Barathel continued his attack. "One doesn't need to know death to know defeat."

"Today you will know both." Zilendras gripped the edge of his blade with one hand and parried both of Barathel's strikes. With the General exposed, he drove half of the hilt into his side. Barathel gasped for air as Zilendras grabbed him by the throat and threw him onto the tower core. He thrusted his blade at Barathel's chest but the weary general, with some fight left in him, grabbed the blade with both hands. "Why won't you just stop?"

Barathel looked up at him, with sorrow and failure. Blood trickled down his arm and dripped along the floor. He struggled to find the words but then caught a glimpse of something in his eyes. A flicker of green light shone from underneath the purple shadows. "You think it's just me? I'm just one part of a larger whole."

Zilendras pressed harder. The tip of the blade pierced his skin but Barathel kept his grip strong. "You can send an army against us. We invite the conflict."

Barathel laughed, feeling the blade slip deeper. "It won't just be an army. The world will rally against you and your masters. A new pantheon will rise while you and your ilk will fall to fading memories." The General smiled, loosened his grip and embraced the end.

Epilogue

Two men walked the littered and ruined streets of Ruvo. They stared at the small groups of huddled citizens who had tents to replace their destroyed homes. Soldiers kept the peace while members of the Caladus Academy and the Inquisitor's Guild lent what aid they could. The quiet in the streets was a stark contrast to the battle waged just a few days ago.

"It's hard to believe the Blademaster is responsible for all of this," said the younger man.

"The chaos of our world was kept under lock and key and endless watchful eyes," replied the older man in a grizzled voice. The plague mask he wore muffled his voice only slightly. He tugged on the straps holding something wrapped in cloth on his back. "Then three days ago it all came crashing down and our world is weaker and exposed after the loss of Ruvast's relic."

The mages were rebuilding minor damages to housing so the carpenters and masons would have an easier time reinforcing the structure. The guild was handling the undead and insect corpses, studying the effects of the black blood. Some were helping citizens with their temporary housing while asking them about what happened.

"What do you mean 'exposed'?" asked you young man.

The other man laughed. "I often forget the surge in new recruits. Look at the sky. Any bit of that seem natural to you?" The sky above the isle had turned black, as though someone ripped a hole clean through. Lightning froze along the black, like cracks in a window. "There's more to this world than even high-ranking inquisitors know."

"My apologies, sir," said the young man, sheepishly.

"You don't need to apologize for not knowing, initiate," the older man reassured him. "Simply pursue knowledge every chance you get."

The two nodded to one another and turned down an alleyway. The warehouse area had been quarantined for the guild to perform their studies so the nearby tavern and surrounding buildings were utilized for treating the injured. A few fighters sat outside waiting to get their new set of bandages. Guards were posted to ensure no one got too greedy and tried to steal extra medical supplies.

"Sirs," saluted one of the guards. "How can we help you?"

"At ease, soldier," said the older man. "We've been told there was a young woman volunteering here. A young elf, burn mark on her face."

"Yes, sir. She's been very helpful these past few days I believe her name is Eve," replied the guard. "If she's not on the first floor helping the healers then she'll be upstairs tending to her friend."

The older man nodded in thanks, "As you were."

The interior of the tavern was crowded from wall to wall. Most of the space was taken up by beds for the injured. Some were having their broken bones mended while others were in a deep rest from their amputations. The bandages and poultices were kept behind the bar where a mage was put in charge of keeping track of the stock.

The inquisitors looked at the injured and their healers. Some had clear signs of being soldiers but others were simple civilians. When the battle grew darkest, all stepped in. From farmer to dock worker, all joined in defending their home.

"I don't see her, sir," whispered the young man. "She must be upstairs."

"You stay down here and offer what aid you can," ordered the older man. "Learn a few things of healing, perhaps, and I'll go talk to this 'Eve'."

A few citizens with lesser injuries were also lending a hand in caring for the more severe patients. Though they couldn't offer much in the way of healing, they could run supplies to those most in need. A few were sitting beside the stairs, sharing a dirty bottle of spirits. The innkeeper shared his secret stash for once.

A young girl was at the top of the stairs, throwing bloodied bandages into a bucket. Each room had a candle resting outside the door but only four of the six were lit. The young girl put out the flame of the closest candle and closed the door.

"How did they die?" asked the inquisitor.

Slightly startled, the young girl turned around, "His wounds just wouldn't heal. The strange creatures must've got him."

"Strange creatures?"

"The bugs," she replied. "Anyone they wound rarely survives."

"Antivenom, then, could at least ease their suffering," he said.

The girl's eyes widened in realization and quickly ran off to fetch off more supplies. With the hall clear, he opened the door and spied into the darkness. He sensed not only the pain the young man went through but he could even sense his fated moment on the battlefield. He clutched his own chest in the very spot the young man was bit.

He quickly closed the door and left the spirit to rest. He ignored the other rooms and approached the last door on the left, as though he knew precisely where he needed to be. He could sense the bittersweet emotion from beyond the door. The woman, this 'Eve', was worried about her friend.

"You'll wake up and we'll fix this," she muttered under her breath.

"How is your friend?" asked the inquisitor.

She immediately stood and grabbed her knife, prepared to defend herself. "Who are you? You're not one of the healers, that's for sure."

He put one hand up while pointing at the crest on his shoulder. Though not the same as the standard symbol, it still bore the seeking eye the guild had adopted as its standard. He then slowly removed the sword from his belt and rested it against the wall.

"That's not the usual guild symbol. Where's the flame and crossed swords?" she quizzed.

"I'm of an elite group within the guild. The book wrapped in chains represents our mission to protect forbidden knowledge," the man said. "Knowledge that your friend unwittingly uncovered."

"My friend?" she stared confused. "Tariv isn't much of a knowledge seeker. I'm afraid you have the wrong person."

The inquisitor smirked, "Your other friend, Yvette."

She dropped her guard, momentarily, at the realization that she isn't unknown to him the way she is to the citizens. She couldn't sense any ill intent from him, no matter how hard she pulled on her instincts. He knowns more than most, had the drop on her, and more than likely had combat experience.

"Valdryn isn't gone yet," he said, interrupting her thought. "We can still save him, and in turn, save our world."

"What? How?" she asked, almost frantic.

He grabbed the item in cloth he carried and laid it on the floor before her. He removed the leather straps and slowly unraveled the cloth, leaving her on the edge of curiosity. She was confused but only briefly. It was missing its vibrant sapphire but her eyes widened nonetheless in awe when she realized what she was looking at.

"His sword," her voice trailed off. A trickle of tears fell on the blade. "We can use this? To save him and undo what I started?"

"Dear child, what occurred that day was set in motion long before you were even born." He took the weapon and rolled it up once more, securing it tightly to his person. "But the sword is a strong symbol of his past. It represents everything that steered him through life. The bond he forged with his weapon allowed him to imprint a shard of his own soul. It is the only thing that can save him."

"And you want my help?" she wondered.

He nodded. "But you and I will not be alone. The mage, Ava, and the minotaur tribe will be aiding us. They'll be preparing a boat for us to leave as soon Tariv is well enough to travel." He removed a satchel of herbs and potions and placed it by the bed. The inquisitor prepared to take his leave when Yvette reached out for his arm.

"How do you know all of this?" she asked, almost demanded.

He chuckled to himself and removed her grip to loosen his mask. Underneath he revealed himself to be more than just the average human. A row of sharp teeth shown through his charismatic smile. A claw mark scar ran down his left cheek. But what startled Yvette most of all was his eyes. Thick rings of black with golden pearls at the center that burned brighter than the sun peered at her.

"There is far more to this world than a few books could ever teach you. You need only an open mind and a willingness to peer into the unknown."

www.ingramcontent.com/pod-product-compliance
Lightning Source LLC
Chambersburg PA
CBHW032140190626
46814CB00005BA/1778